HART OF DARKNESS

THE HART SERIES

S.B. ALEXANDER

RAVEN WING PUBLISHING

DEDICATION

Albert Einstein once said, "Life is like riding a bicycle - in order to keep your balance, you must keep moving. Throughout the writing of this book, I had one person to help me keep my balance. She kept me moving and motivating me. So this book is dedicated to you, Heather Carver for not letting me fall off the bike.

1

DILLON

Tearing my gaze away from my banking program, I rubbed my eyes before I checked the time—almost midnight. I threw my head back, blowing out a long breath.

The couch across from me was calling my name. I'd been sleeping in my office on and off for the last two months since I'd opened a shelter for girls—runaways, girls who needed to get off the streets, or girls who needed to get away from abusive partners. Actually, I'd been exhausted since I purchased the three-story home eight months ago. I'd scoured estate auctions, yard sales, and thrift stores like the Salvation Army and Goodwill for beds, linens, and any type of furniture. I'd been lucky to find couches, desks, kitchen appliances, beds, a ping-pong table and other necessities at a low cost.

I considered myself frugal. I didn't need fancy stuff. I wanted to make sure the girls who landed at the shelter had at least a decent bed with linens and a cozy environment so they would feel protected.

My attention drifted to the small framed photo of my sister, Grace, that sat next to my computer. Her picture was a reminder of why I'd opened the shelter, and I hoped that one day she might walk through the front door.

Her tawny-brown eyes had flecks of gold, much like mine. If any of my siblings resembled me, it was Grace. My brother Denim was the blond in the family, with striking blue eyes. He took after our father's side. Duke had a lighter shade of brown hair than Grace and me, and his eyes were reddish-brown, or chestnut-colored as I remembered my mother saying

"Where are you, sister?" I mumbled to no one. "I'm sorry I left you with that monster we called Dad." I traced my finger over her small nose. "I'll never give up looking for you."

My stomach knotted as I dipped back in time to that day.

"Dillon, please don't leave me," Grace cried. "I can't handle Dad alone anymore."

I moved a strand of wavy hair behind her ear. "Duke and Denim will watch over you."

She threw her arms around me. "They're not you. You take care of me. You protect me from Dad."

"I promise, our brothers will make sure Dad doesn't beat you." I held back tears, thinking about how I'd caught my old man slapping the shit out of Grace on more than one occasion. "You remember what I taught you? Don't walk away. Run."

Pain zipped up my arm, and I blinked, realizing I was trying to crush the frame with my tight grip. Grace had taken my advice and ran. I hadn't meant for her to run away or disappear off the face of the earth. I'd only wanted her to get the fuck out of the same room as our alcoholic father.

Regardless, the shelter was dedicated to her and every girl who needed a place of refuge. Sadly, though, I could only take in ten girls max. It was a start. Shelter or not, I wasn't giving up hope that Grace was alive, although after four years of scouring the Boston streets, it was hard to stay positive. I hadn't found one damn sign of Grace, not even a dead body.

If I hadn't gone into the merchant marines, she would have been here. But I had trusted my brothers to watch over her. I'd trusted that they wouldn't let anything happen to her. Instead, when I'd returned home, my family was a mess. Grace had left home. My younger brother, Denim, was in jail for murder. My older brother, Duke, was into some bad shit as a loan shark and probably other illegal crap I didn't care to know about. And my old man was still a drunk, oblivious to his sons and daughter.

I didn't talk to Duke much. I couldn't. Every time I saw him, I wanted to beat the crap out of him. I blamed him more than I blamed Denim for not taking care of Grace. He was the older brother. The one who was supposed to watch over all of us. The one who I'd looked up to. The one who'd broken my old man's nose the night he wouldn't stop kicking me in the gut, all because I'd smarted off to him over something as stupid as dinner. I didn't like waxy green beans, so I'd thrown them in the trash. My old man had caught me, removed every one of them from the trash, and shoved them down my throat until I was gagging and throwing up. Then he'd proceeded to use me as his punching bag, only he'd used his steel-toed boots, ramming them into my gut over and over again.

"I work hard to put food on the table for you," he'd yelled then kicked. "How dare you throw my money away!"

The door to my office groaned before my best bud and right-hand man, Rafe, waltzed in, sporting his usual buzz cut. Since we'd met in the merchant marines, he'd never wavered from his hairstyle. I, on the other hand, grew out my hair the moment I'd stepped foot onto dry land.

He flicked his chin at me. "It looks like a hurricane hit your desk."

I arched a brow, more at Rafe than at the pile of receipts and bills littering the desktop. It looked like a game of Go Fish that Grace and I had played many times as kids. "What are you doing up?"

Rafe removed his gun from his lower back and set it down on the coffee table as he dropped his large body onto the couch across from me. "I let Josh have the night off. I was patrolling outside and saw your light on."

I tapped a key. My screen flashed into camera view. "It seems quiet out there. Unlike last night."

"If that fucker returns tonight, I'll tear off his head." Rafe's deep voice could scare a brown bear.

Leaning back in my chair, I locked my hands behind my head. "Norton is going to be a problem. I need to talk to the Guardian. They have some badass motherfuckers on the security staff. We could use more help." The Guardian was owned by Jeremy Pitt, Russian mob boss. He stacked his team with mostly ex-military dudes who knew how to defend and protect anyone and anything. But I was going to request Hunter Thompson, who was non-military. I knew him. I trusted him, and he was as much of a badass as his colleagues.

Rafe propped his big-booted feet up on the coffee table. "Are you good on the budget for this place? If not, I could float you some. I have a ton saved from our days at sea."

I tapped another button on the keyboard. "I'm good. Just making sure the checkbook balances, that's all." I had a lot of money invested in stocks and bonds. During my time at sea, I'd learned everything about the stock market, thanks to the captain of the ship. He'd been into investing, and on many nights, he and I would talk stocks. I'd made a nice nest egg. I also had a kick-ass financial advisor, who'd helped my nest egg grow.

My cell phone vibrated and bounced across my metal desk. A call at this time of night was never good. I suspected it was the cops, calling to tell me that my old man was in jail again for drunken and disorderly conduct. I wasn't sure why they called me. I'd always told my father he could rot in jail. Maybe he was hoping that his persistence would pay off. *Not in this lifetime.*

Eddie's name brightened the screen on my phone. My heart skipped a beat. "It's Eddie at the morgue," I told Rafe. Then I pressed the phone to my ear. "What's up?"

Clang. Clang.

"Shit," Eddie said. "Hold on."

I heard another *clang,* followed by what sounded like an explosion.

"Eddie?" I asked.

"Sorry. My tray fell. Look, we had a young girl come in tonight. We haven't been able to identify her."

The blood drained from me. I hadn't heard from Eddie in several months. His last call had brought me down to the morgue to identify a Jane Doe who he'd thought matched Grace's description. The girl hadn't been Grace.

"So you think she could be Grace?"

"Maybe," he said.

"On my way." I disconnected before he could say anything else. It was best to see the body.

Rafe rested his elbows on his knees. "Still trolling the morgues? Man, you need to stop. I'm not saying give up hope, but it's got to be gut-wrenching to see dead people, let alone a young dead girl who could be your sister."

He was spot-on, although I could count on one hand how many times Eddie had called me down to the morgue. Still, the five times Eddie had lifted the sheet or opened the body bag, I'd lost my dinner. Each girl had either died from a drug overdose or had been murdered.

I was still wrestling with my feelings on how my own brother could murder someone. As teenagers, my brothers and I had been in a gang. We weren't innocent in the least. We'd drawn blood on many occasions during our gang fights, especially when our rivals had hurt Grace to get back at Duke for slashing the tires on one of their cars. That had been a bad night for Mike Santos, the boy who had taken his fists to my sister. I would've liked to say that I'd gotten satisfaction out of beating him until he couldn't see, but it had only served to give me a wake-up call, especially after both of us had ended up in the emergency room.

Rafe snapped his fingers. "You've been spacing out a lot lately." He loomed over my desk. "You look like shit too. Seriously, man, you need to let your quest to find Grace go." Casually, he backed away, maybe because of the scowl I was sporting. "I'm only saying consider your health and yourself."

I ground my back teeth together as I snagged my phone, wallet, and keys off my desk. "I know you're looking out for me, but I'll decide when I'm ready to give up on looking for my baby sister."

He scrubbed a hand over his head. "I've always been straight with you. I'm not going to change now. So put yourself first. Find an outlet, or better yet, find a woman. When was the last time you were with anyone?"

I chuckled. Rafe was worried about my love life, which was nonexistent. I didn't have time for a steady relationship. I didn't want one either. I had sexual needs, of course, but I took care of those with an occasional hookup now and again.

I skirted around my desk. "The talk of my sex life is off-limits." I didn't fear much in life, but I cringed at the idea of settling down or even meeting someone who would steal my heart. I'd never been in love, so I couldn't say what the feeling was all about. With my luck, the woman would learn of my fucked-up family and run like a gazelle. "Grace is my life." I waved a hand around. "The Hart of Hope shelter is now my life." At least I was doing something good.

Maybe that would negate all the bad shit I'd done as a rebellious kid. Maybe that would erase all those memories of driving a knife into someone or getting kicked and punched by my drunken old man from the age of six until I reached puberty. Then I'd gotten up the balls to punch my father right back, and he'd let me until he unleashed his strength, sending me to the hospital with a broken nose.

Fucker.

"Hold down the fort. Camera is live on my screen."

Rafe nodded as I walked out.

The first floor of the shelter had an open floor plan, which consisted of a living area that melted into the kitchen toward the back of the house. I wanted women to feel warm and protected and give them space to relax as if they were home.

Aside from the bare walls that needed some artwork, the place was coming together. I'd gotten the idea for a safe haven after seeing young girls walking the streets at night, being beaten by their pimps, getting high on drugs, or even sleeping on the streets. The idea had cemented itself even more when I helped Bee and Allie, two girls I'd found one night. Allie had been her pimp's punching bag, and Bee had been eating out of the trash. I'd taken them into my home and given them a chance to rebuild their lives. Recently, they had saved up enough money to move out and into an apartment together. I was so darn proud of them.

I hoped like hell that maybe Grace had found someone like me or a refuge somewhere in the country.

I fingered my keys as I approached Norma's desk, which had a direct view of the open floor plan and sat adjacent to the entryway that led out to the front door.

My eyes landed on a sticky note on her computer. *Remind Dillon to pay the electrical bill.* I snagged a pen from the cup and scribbled on her note, *I paid the bill this evening.*

My mouth curled on one side. I'd met Norma through Kross Maxwell's wife, Ruby. Both of them had lived on the streets, which was one of the reasons I'd asked Norma if she wanted a job working at the shelter. She knew how to relate to the girls we brought in.

After I punched in the key code to lock the door, I heard a muffled voice. I reached for the gun I usually carried at my back but came up empty.

Fuck. I'd left my weapon in my desk drawer.

The shelter was situated on a corner lot in a half-decent neighborhood in Boston. The street was usually quiet. The neighbors kept to themselves, and two houses around me were for sale and vacant.

I didn't advertise or have a sign out front. I didn't want to risk an abusive pimp or partner showing up and wreaking havoc. Sure, news about the shelter could spread to the wrong people, but that was the reason we had security.

I climbed down the steps of the wooden porch, scanning the area. The tall and dense oak tree in the yard kept the home semi-private from the neighbors across the street.

Instead of heading to my car in the driveway, I walked down the brick path from the house to the sidewalk. I spied Norton staggering toward me with what looked to be a gun in his hands.

My pulse picked up speed. A drunk with a gun wasn't a good sign.

I could have darted back in the house, but then Norton would have made a scene and woken the neighbors, who weren't all that thrilled about having a shelter nearby. It was best if I attacked the situation head-on.

The good news was the gun was at his side.

I backtracked until I was in my driveway. If he came onto my property, then I had a leg to stand on if I had to use force.

He stopped at my mailbox.

I raised my hands in the air as if in surrender.

The one streetlight stood tall between the shelter and the vacant house next door, giving me the light I needed to see that Norton's eyes were glossy.

"I want to see Angel." He slurred his words.

My pulse rarely ticked higher than sixty-five beats per minute unless I had a lead on Grace. But a skinny, gaunt drunk with a gun was rather terrifying. The liquor oozed off him in waves.

"What makes you think she's here?" I asked, even though I had an idea.

He cocked his scruffy head, stumbling closer. "I followed her this morning."

Against my wishes, Angel, one of my guests, had gone back to her house to get some clothes. I'd counseled her that it wasn't a good idea, but I couldn't stop her. She'd said Norton always left for work at dawn so he wouldn't be home.

I lowered one arm and stretched out the other as I inched two steps closer. "Hand me the gun, Norton. You're not a killer." I didn't know that for sure. I knew he'd beaten Angel until she was black and blue.

His hand began to shake more as he swayed before he lost his footing on the curb. I lunged at him, more to catch the gun than him. Once the twenty-two was safely in my hands, I tucked it in the back of my jeans, quietly blowing out a breath, relieved that neither one of us had gotten shot.

Sweat trickled down Norton's temple as he stared at me with glossy eyes, reminding me of my old man and how he'd done wild things when the liquor overpowered his senses. One time, he'd stumbled into the kitchen with a steak knife pointed at me. Luckily, a chair had saved me that night during dinner.

"Man, get clean," I said. "Take a shower. Get off the alcohol. If you want, I can give you an address where you could get help." Manny, a guy I'd met from checking shelters around the city for Grace, would take Norton in. He had a sore spot for alcoholics since he had been one himself. Now he gave his time, effort, and money to helping men like Norton.

Norton pivoted on his heel, staggered, then darted down the street.

Rafe cleared his throat behind me.

I handed the gun to Rafe. "I would like to say he's harmless, but I'm not sure."

"Never assume, dude," Rafe said.

I marched up to my car, my pulse slowing. "I'll be back as soon as I can. I suggest you call in Josh. Norton will be back." I was certain about that. He'd been a pain in the butt the last two nights, and if he showed up with a gun again, we were in for some trouble.

2

———

MAGGIE

I stretched my arms over my head, yawning. The newsroom was as dead as it should be at midnight. I'd been burning the candle late every day for the last month, trying to verify my sources and chase down leads on a local gang, the Black Knights, who were known for their stronghold on the sex-trafficking market in Boston. But I'd come up empty on every lead I'd chased. I even checked the morgue regularly for women who had died because they'd been abused or violated, and still no cigar.

The gang task force had no leads either, according to my contact within the gang unit.

Then three nights ago, as if the planets had aligned, my source on the street had found out that some guy named Cory had messed up one of the girls working a street corner. I'd asked Misty, a nightwalker, if she had heard Cory's name.

Her response had been, "Yeah. Rumor is he's with the Black Knights."

Elation, rage, nervousness, and so many other emotions, like the need to kill Cory Calderon, had bloomed strongly. If I could prove he was part of a sex-trafficking ring or anything illegal, then I could exact my revenge on the man who had beaten, raped, and left me for dead when I was fourteen.

I was striking out, though. Cory didn't have a police record according to Rick, one of my sources at the police department.

I flipped through web pages on Harold Calderon, CEO of one of the largest investment firms in the country. The picture on my screen showed the gray-haired Harold at a benefit for one of the local children's hospitals in the city. At his side was his son Cory.

I gritted my teeth. Cory stood with his barreled chest puffed out, his thinning black hair styled back with lots of gel, and an innocent grin on his chubby face. The man was anything but innocent. Sure, he could've grown out of raping girls. He could've gotten his act together. But I didn't think so. I believed once a rapist, always a rapist. I shifted my gaze to the elder Calderon, wondering if the man beat his wife, wondering if Cory took after his father. Cory had to have learned how to prey on women from someone.

I kicked myself in the butt each time I replayed that night. I'd run from my seventh foster dad when he'd hobbled into my room, slobbering all over himself and me. At first, I thought he'd been too drunk to find his own room until he whispered my name and put his hands all over me. I'd shoved him off me, which wasn't hard, considering the alcohol had made him wobbly, and I'd run as though my life depended on it.

And I'd run right into another monster.

The city street was dark, barely a light anywhere around. I jumped over bushes, tripping in the process. My knees connected with cement, pebbles, and rocks. I looked over my shoulder through watery eyes, pushing to my feet as fast as I could. I didn't think my foster dad would follow me, but I couldn't take the chance.

Once on my feet, I ran, my breath labored, my lungs burning. I had no idea where I was going.

The sound of a car engine filled the air.

Run. Run. Run, *my inner voice supplied.*

I pounded the pavement, grunting, crying, and dizzy. I mopped tears from my eyes as the car drew closer.

Please let it be a policeman.

I braved a look as my legs kept going only to plow into a trash bin. I wobbled, my heart sprinting like a horse racing to the finish line.

The car slowed. A boy's voice, deep and commanding, said, "Hey, sweetheart."

The hairs on the back of my neck shot up.

The boy whistled. "Want to have some fun?"

I had no business taunting him, but I wasn't thinking clearly. I started to run again but not before throwing him the finger.

He wolf-whistled. "Seems to me you want to fight." He banged on the car door. "Stop, Jerry."

Fear, strong and powerful, gripped me. I searched for life in any of the houses on the street, but every home was dark.

My legs burned. My chest hurt. My vision was compromised.

When I got to the next block, which was as dark as the one before it, footsteps slapped on the sidewalk behind me, and the only light was from the car that was still on my heels.

My legs were giving out.

Hands went around my waist.

"Put me down," I screamed. I wailed. I kicked. I even threw my head back, and it collided with the boy's forehead and nose. A bone cracked.

Chills ran down my spine as pain exploded in my head.

The boy yanked my hair then dragged me to the car and threw me in the back seat.

I tried to plead with Jerry, who had wild blue eyes. But he only focused out the windshield and gripped the steering wheel, while his friend climbed in next to me.

"Drive, Jerry. Get the fuck out of here."

Blackness seeped into the sides of my vision as houses sped by outside the window. The boy and car were saturated with booze and cigars.

He somehow got me on my back as he straddled me.

I squirmed. I kicked. I screamed at the top of my lungs to no avail. He was so much stronger.

He pulled out a switchblade from his pocket. "Shut the fuck up." Then he dug the point of the blade into my neck.

I saw my own death. At that moment, I realized no one would miss me. No one would even care that I'd run, not even the foster home I'd run from.

"Cory, man, put the knife away. Your old man won't get you out of a murder charge."

I whispered his name, repeated it in my head, promising myself that if I lived, I would hunt this boy down and kill him.

Cory ignored his friend as the car moved at high speeds.

My body bounced as the car sped over the uneven streets, but that didn't stop Cory from ripping my clothes off and violating me over and over again.

My vision blurred. Tears poured out. But I was a fighter, always had been. So I turned my head slightly, and my lips came into contact with his ear. In one quick move, I bit down on his earlobe as if I were the animal and not him. I bit so hard that I was tasting his blood.

"Bitch." He spat in my face before he shoved the knife into my neck.

Pain, hot and burning, flew through my body. My vision was on the verge of going dark.

His friend shouted, "Calderon, what have you done?"

Then I lost consciousness.

The police scanner crackled, bringing me out of my morbid memory, one that plagued me night after night.

I adjusted the volume.

"We have a robbery in progress," the lady on the scanner said.

My desk phone rang. I jumped a mile out of my rolling chair. "Marx here," I answered.

"Mags, I tried your cell phone several times. You okay?" Ted asked.

I moved file folders, looking for my cell. "Um… I think it's dead."

"Glad your phone is and not you," he said in a relieved tone.

I warmed, knowing someone cared about me. "I know how to protect myself. How many times do I have to tell you that?"

I'd learned how to physically fight from my former gang leader, who had saved my life. Lou Ruiz had found me crumpled against a dumpster, on my deathbed, after Cory had thrown me out with the trash. Sadly, Lou's life was taken from him in a drive-by shooting not long after he'd rescued me.

"Just because you've been in jail and in a gang doesn't mean you're immortal." Ted chuckled, his cigarette-laden voice coming through loudly.

"Don't remind me." I'd been in jail for petty crimes several times. My police record had raised a red flag with the paper, but Ted had given me a good reference. "Anything going down tonight?" He occasionally threw me a bone for a story, but his bones were stories about robberies or something vanilla where I wouldn't get hurt or into trouble with the wrong people, like a gang or drug lords.

"Nothing you need to worry about." He sounded as though he were hiding something.

I cracked my neck, clenching my teeth. "Does it have something to do with the Black Knights? Have you connected Cory to them?"

Ted knew about what Cory had done to me. He'd asked me why I hadn't called the cops that night. I had a couple of reasons. I'd been too afraid of going back to my foster parents, which would've happened since the cops were mandated to return runaways to their foster families. Even Ted had confirmed that. If I hadn't been put back in the foster home I'd run from, then I would've been sent to another one, and I couldn't, nor wouldn't, go back into the foster system. I'd also been frightened out of my mind that if I ratted out Cory, he would find me and kill me.

Despite that, Ted knew I wanted revenge. He also knew what Misty had relayed to me about Cory and the Black Knights.

Silence reigned over the line.

"Ted?" I snapped like a rabid dog. "Where?"

"Go home and get some rest. We'll talk in the morning." He hung up.

I snarled loudly.

I punched in Rick's number on my desk phone. Rick worked for Ted, and on one or two occasions, he had given me a small opening behind Ted's back. I didn't know if he felt sorry for me or wanted to get in my pants. His line rang three times before he picked up. "I can't talk, Maggie."

"Come on, Rick. Ted won't share."

"Sorry, Mags, Ted's orders."

I liked Rick and didn't want to put his job in jeopardy.

The scanner lit up with chatter, blaring in the empty room. "We got possible gang activity at Bleven and Third."

Bingo! I hung up faster than the speed of light and tore out of the building.

3

DILLON

I rang the buzzer on the door behind the hospital. A cat meowed somewhere nearby, and the stench of piss drifted up my nose as I rang the buzzer again. The late August weather was hot and humid, and with it came all kinds of odors that made my stomach churn, especially in the alleys of Boston.

Eddie answered with his white lab coat draped over his small shoulders. He peered out as though he didn't want anyone to see him letting me in. Then again, he would get into trouble if his boss found out I was there. I had no official business with the morgue, especially not after hours. I'd met Eddie at some point during my search for Grace when I started visiting morgues. At first, he'd been reluctant, but he had a distant family member that had gone missing years ago so he had a soft spot for me. Although I did slip him some cash when he called.

Once inside, the sound of the clicking lock echoed. Eddie flicked his head toward the double doors before he hurried his short legs into a dimly lit hall then into the glaring lights of the morgue.

A chill curled up my spine as I followed him in. No matter how many times I'd been around dead people, I always got queasy, and not just from seeing dead people, but from the stainless-steel compartments on the side wall. I might have been crazy to think that those drawers would shoot out and a dead person would sit up and scare the fuck out of me. A psychiatrist would have told me that my fear stemmed from finding Grace in a similar position.

I sucked in lots of air when my gaze landed on the body laid out on the table in the middle of the room, covered by a sheet. I wanted to find Grace, but not in a morgue.

Sweat began to bead on my forehead as I got closer. *Please don't let her be Grace.* As I took one step toward her body, acid swished in the pit of my stomach.

Eddie slipped on latex gloves. "I called you down because the girl has a birthmark underneath her ear." He ponied up to the table across from me and pulled down the sheet.

My knees wobbled as I scanned her body with fine precision. Her brown hair was caked with blood. She was wearing jeans with holes up and down the legs, blood-coated tennis shoes, and a ragged T-shirt.

When I'd left for the merchant marines, Grace had been twelve years old with porcelain skin, silky brown hair, and a look of pure innocence. I'd sworn I would know her the minute I saw her, but eight years and puberty certainly could change a person's appearance. I guessed this girl's age to be about twenty, the same age as Grace.

Eddie turned her head. "Here's the mark." He moved her earlobe out of the way.

The light-brown spot was definitely a birthmark, but it was small and not the shape of Grace's. My heart rate slowed. "Grace's birthmark is lower on her neck and on the right side not left, and its shape resembles a broken star. Where's the picture I gave you of Grace?"

"Sorry, someone cleaned out the desk," Eddie said. "I can't seem to find it now."

I took a deep breath then let it out. "How did she die?"

Eddie lifted her T-shirt. "I would guess from this. I suspect she was a mule. I'm sure my examination will find traces of drugs in her stomach."

I pressed a fist to my mouth to stave off the nausea that was a minute away from gushing out at the sight of how the girl's stomach was sliced open.

Eddie ripped off his gloves. "I need to get to work on her. I'll let you know if any other girls matching your sister's description show up in here."

The problem was that by then it was too late. I didn't want to find Grace in a morgue or learn she'd been a drug mule. "Do you know who within the police department is working this case?" It had been over a year since I probed the cops, and with other morgues in the city, maybe they'd seen someone who resembled Grace.

Eddie shoved his hands in the pockets of his lab coat. "A Detective Hughes. He's head of the gang force. He called earlier. He wants us to alert him when the autopsies are done. I doubt he'll tell you anything." He got a faraway look in his gray eyes. "We've also had a reporter snooping around. She's working on a story about sex trafficking."

Holy hell. I certainly didn't want to think that Grace had been sold to some fat fuck.

Eddie loped over to a small desk in the far corner. "Who knows? This reporter might have seen or even talked to a few girls along the way." He picked up a card. "She works for the *Boston Eagle*. A Maggie Marx."

The name Maggie conjured up a memory of a girl I'd known in my gang days—wild blond curls, pretty, shamrock-green eyes that sucked a person in. She'd been the only girl in one of our rival gangs. Despite her beauty, she was a hard girl to forget with the six-inch scar on her neck. Ogling her from across enemy lines was as far as I'd gotten. Her leader, Lou, would've shot me dead if I'd gone anywhere near her, and I'd been tempted a time or two.

"You look like you know her?"

I lifted a shoulder. "I knew a girl by that name once." There was probably a ton of Maggies in the city. "What does she look like?"

"Curly blond hair, dark-green eyes, and a scar on her neck that she tries to hide with a scarf."

I traced a line at the base of my throat down the center of my chest. "Here."

Surprise swept over his face. "Yeah."

Wow! Small world. "I know her." I was curious if she would remember me.

Eddie wolf-whistled as he handed me her card. "Man, she is sexy as hell."

If it was the same girl, and the scar was a dead giveaway, I would bet she was even more beautiful now.

I pulled out my phone, tapped in her cell phone number, then handed the card back to him.

"You're calling her now?" Eddie sounded horrified. "She's probably sleeping."

He should have known that finding my sister took priority over anyone or anything.

The line rang four times before Maggie's voice mail picked up. "Hi, Maggie. I don't know if you remember me. Dillon Hart?" I proceeded to give her my number and the address of the shelter, where she could find me. "I would like to talk to you when you get a moment."

Eddie motioned to the door. "I'll walk you out. Hopefully Maggie will return your call."

I wasn't worried. If she worked for the paper, I knew where to find her.

I handed Eddie a Benjamin as I always did when he called me down to the morgue.

He slapped me on the back. "Oh, and I wouldn't contact Detective Hughes this time of night. He's kind of a prick."

I had kind of forgotten about the detective when Eddie mentioned Maggie anyway.

"Thanks for the advice," I said before trekking to my car.

Maggie Marx. I didn't know if she could help me, but I had a butterfly feeling in my stomach. I didn't get the chance to determine whether it was my gut trying to tell me something or not because my phone rang. For a brief second, my pulse sped up until I saw Rafe's name on the screen. Then my pulse really took flight. "Did something happen?"

"Norton is back. No gun this time. He was trying to break in through the basement door in the backyard. He's drunker than a skunk. I had to knock him out. He's sleeping on the lawn chair. When you get back, I'll drop him in front of the police station. Are you on your way?"

"I'm getting in my car. The cops won't do anything with a drunk. Take him to Manny's." If Manny couldn't help him, then I might have to involve the cops.

Rafe chuckled. "Manny isn't going to be happy. He likes those who want to get help themselves."

"True, but Manny can handle Norton. Besides, Norton likes to beat women not men."

"He pulled a gun on you, man."

I started the engine. "Not really." Norton had the gun at his side. "My gut tells me he was scared."

"You do come off kind of scary," Rafe teased.

"And you don't." I laughed. "I'll be there in about twenty minutes." I hung up.

As I drove back through the empty city streets, save for a car here and there, I tried to shed the image of the dead girl. I honestly didn't know if I could look at any more dead girls.

Maybe Rafe was right. I should let Grace go. I had to consider that maybe she was dead. But until I laid eyes on her body, I wasn't going down that road, especially not after questioning a handful of prostitutes over a year ago. I'd had a mini breakthrough when a girl named Daisy recognized Grace from the picture I'd shown her. In particular, she'd recognized Grace's birthmark. According to Daisy, she had seen Grace at a soup kitchen on Asher Street. Even though I'd come up empty after weeks of staking out the joint, I wasn't ready to give up on finding my sister.

4

MAGGIE

I parked two blocks from a sea of red and blue flashing lights. I grabbed my bag, hopped out of my car, and ran up to the crowd that had gathered around.

I sidled up to an older lady. "What's going on?"

She didn't even look my way. Instead, she lifted up on her tiptoes to see over others' heads. "Word is the cops are in a standoff with some gang."

My internal radar was firing on all cylinders. "What gang?"

She clutched the robe she was wearing. "Not sure."

I plowed through the throng to get a better view. Some protested as I wiggled my way up to a man in blue, whose name read Miladin on his uniform shirt. I knew some cops but not him.

Police cruisers and unmarked cars littered the street on the other side of the police barricade.

I flashed my reporter credentials. "I'm here to see Detective Ted Hughes." I scanned the men in blue and some in plain clothes. Ted was tall, lanky, and sometimes hard to miss with his thick mustache that was similar to the actor Tom Selleck's. I did another once-over and spotted Rick. He wasn't as tall as Ted, but he was husky, compliments of the gym he lived at during his off-duty hours.

Officer Miladin narrowed his dark eyes. "Civilians are not allowed past this barrier."

"I work for the paper, so let me through." I knew working as a reporter held no clout to get me into an active police scene, but most cops knew I was close to Ted.

Officer Miladin stabbed a finger at another police barrier along the sidewalk in front of the brick homes that lined the street. "The media is over there."

I didn't budge from my spot. "You're new. Aren't you?"

Miladin's voice dropped an octave. "I said over there."

I huffed and decided it wasn't worth arguing. Ted would only kick me out anyway.

I spotted Deidre, a news reporter for CBNT, a local station in the city. If anyone had a lead, it would be Deidre. She was relentless in her hunt to get the big story. I was about to make my way over to her, when a shot rang out through the humid night.

People screamed and scattered.

The cops took cover behind their vehicles.

I managed to duck behind one of many cars parked along the curb. The lady in the robe joined me, breathing heavily, while the crowd scattered to take cover.

Then silence ensued.

I slowly peeked through the car window, when the lady in the robe nudged me.

She pointed a red-painted nail toward the driveway of the house across from us. "Look."

A girl with bold red hair darted from the back of the house, setting off the motion sensor.

Miladin, who had abandoned his position, edged along the base of the house and down the driveway. He said something into his radio, when the redhead climbed the chain-link fence.

Considering the girl was running, I suspected the cops didn't have the house completely surrounded. Or if they did, then their attention wasn't on the girl.

The crowd seemed to be holding its breath. A helicopter whirred above, cutting through the soupy silence.

Officer Miladin reached out to grab the girl when she flipped over the fence. Then a rotund man came out of nowhere and tackled Miladin to the ground. They fought, rolled, and punched each other until Miladin won, securing the man's arms behind him.

The light from the helicopter shone down, lighting up the yards of the modest houses in the neighborhood.

Officer Miladin walked his perp back toward the crowd in handcuffs. Then he said into his radio, "She has red hair."

I fumbled for my camera then snapped several pictures. I used the car as my anchor to steady my arms and aimed my lens at the houses across and away from the scene. At the moment, no one was chasing the red-haired girl.

A radio crackled. "All clear inside."

I focused my lens back on the scene, watching the cops scatter in and around the house. I debated what my next move would be. I didn't know if I should walk up to the media group and get the scoop or go in search of the redhead, who could probably give me details of what had happened, rather than waiting around for the canned speech the police would give reporters.

After I stowed my camera, I watched Miladin shove the rotund perp into a police cruiser. It wasn't Cory, and I didn't recognize the guy.

The lady in the robe hurried away as did the rest of the onlookers. I stayed put to examine more of the scene, hoping that I would see cops escorting other gang members, like Cory, out of the house. Instead, I spotted Ted, and he did a double take when he saw me.

He crooked his finger at me but didn't appear happy, probably because he'd all but ordered me to go home when I'd spoken to him on the phone.

If I ignored him, I would only irritate him, and then he would send the cavalry for me. I wandered his way.

His mustache twitched, his gaze never wavering from me until his radio crackled. "Go."

"Sir, you need to come inside," a voice said through the radio.

"Be right there," Ted responded.

I fidgeted with my thin scarf then put on my reporter's hat. "Detective Hughes, was this standoff tonight with the Black Knights?"

"Cut the crap, Mags. I told you to go home." His words were laden with frustration.

I rolled my eyes, catching a glimpse of Rick standing near the house and talking on his phone. "I'm a reporter. As much as you don't like me getting involved in stories that could be dangerous, too bad. That's my job. Why would you think I would listen to you anyway?"

His tense shoulders lowered. "You got a point. I don't want to see you get hurt."

I pouted. "I love you too, Dad," I said with equal parts snark and affection. "So, are the Black Knights involved? You caught one gang member. Any others inside?"

He pursed his lips. "The only story you should uncover is who your parents are. Have you given more thought to what we talked about the other day?"

Hell to the no. I wasn't looking for my parents. They'd had the nerve to abandon me when I was a baby, so screw them. Although a tiny part of me wanted to know why more than anything. Ted had offered several times to help me since he had the resources to do so.

"You'll regret not knowing where you came from, Mags. Family is important. Maybe your parents did what they did to save you."

Whatever. That wasn't the topic at the moment. "Looking for my parents isn't going to keep my editor happy." That was the truth. "Besides, you're my family. You cared for me. You took me off the streets."

He grinned like a proud father, when his radio sparked to life. "Ted," Rick said.

I flicked my gaze to where Rick was standing, but he wasn't there. Too bad. I would've liked to have tried to coax him into giving me something.

"I'm on my way," Ted said into his radio. "Oh, Mags, I've instructed Rick not to give you any more intel. So don't ask." Then he crossed the pavement to the two-story brick home.

I could have argued until the sun came up, but I wouldn't have gotten anywhere. Ted was a hardened individual and staunch in his decisions, especially when it came to protecting those he loved. Not to mention, he couldn't and wouldn't divulge facts of any investigation. Otherwise cases could be ruined and thrown out of court.

The news reporters were finishing up their late-night segments. I thought about saying hi to Deidre, but she was busy talking into the camera.

The crowd had scattered.

The helicopter was gone.

I was speed walking toward my car, looking down driveways and over fences, in the off chance I would spot the redhead. When I reached an intersection, I glanced in both directions. A streetlight illuminated the roadway, but not all that well. In the blink of an eye, I spied someone in the shadows at the edge of a house across the street.

I jogged in that direction, looking around me, making sure I didn't have any creepers on my tail. I always carried a knife, which was in my messenger bag. When I made it to the driveway, a cat screeched as though someone had kicked the poor thing.

I stopped. "I know you're back there." I kept my voice soft in the off chance it was the redhead. "I'm not a cop. I promise. I saw you run from the house, and I just want to make sure you're okay."

The petite form came into view, scared, bruised, bleeding, and frightened.

I sucked in a sharp breath. "What happened to you?"

Fear lived deep in the girl's blue eyes. Her red hair was covered in leaves. Her lip was split, her white frilly blouse was ripped, her shorts torn, and cuts marred her long legs as though someone had decided to use her as a sculpture. Surely, hopping fences couldn't have given her the bruises so quickly.

Her gaze darted up and down the street. "I need to hide."

She needed first aid. "The cops can help you." She definitely wasn't a suspect but a victim, for sure.

Her head moved back and forth at a rapid rate. "No cops." Her voice squeaked like a dog's chew toy. "Please help me."

Her plea sent a chill down my spine. My horrible night all those years ago flashed before me. "Come on. My car is one block down."

She hesitated, licking her bloody lip.

"I promise, no cops. But if you don't come with me now, they will find you." That much, I was certain of. I was surprised Ted didn't have a man canvassing every nook and cranny in the near vicinity for her. Whatever was in that house had to be bad to divert the cops' attention away from a potential suspect or victim.

I had so many questions skipping through my mind. First, I needed to help the girl, and not by turning her in. I trusted Ted. But at the moment, the girl needed a friend and not an interrogator. I carefully grasped her hand. "We need to move."

She came with me willingly. When we were safely in my car and on the road, she sighed then started crying.

I rubbed her arm lightly with the back of my fingers, careful not to put any pressure on her bruises. "Let it out." Crying was a great release. I always felt as though tears held all the bottled-up pain, and when tears fell, the pain inside eased.

She cried as I sifted through my brain, trying to think of where to take her. I could take her to my dingy apartment. I had a bed, a second-hand couch, a coffee table, and no air conditioner. I nixed the idea since the possibility existed that Ted could stop by.

When I was several blocks away from the crime scene, I pulled off to the side of the road, in front of a closed convenience store.

The girl looked around. "What are you doing?"

"I need to think." I didn't want to drive around since my little VW Bug was low on gas. "There's a homeless shelter a mile from here."

"No. I'm a mess. I don't want to call attention to myself. They might call the police. If Miguel knows I went to the cops, he'll kill me. Also, no hospital. They would definitely alert the police."

"Do you have a name?"

She sniffled. "Nadine."

"I'm Maggie. I want to help you, but I'm coming up empty on where to lay low for tonight. And who is Miguel? Your pimp?"

Ted would be angry if he found out about Nadine. I didn't think I was breaking the law.

"Miguel is a very bad man, but yeah, he's my pimp."

"Is Miguel part of a gang called the Black Knights?"

She hiked a small shoulder. "Never heard of them. Look, if Miguel finds out that the cops have me, he'll kill me."

I pulled out my phone. "Is Miguel the one that hurt you?"

Her cold, clammy hand covered mine. "It doesn't matter who hurt me. Please. I need one night to regroup."

I wanted to ask *then what,* but I knew she would go back to Miguel. All nightwalkers returned to their pimps.

"The guy the cops caught—was that Miguel?"

"No. I don't know his name. He's a new guy who works for Miguel."

"What were you doing at that house?"

Her hand was on the door. "You're sounding like a cop now, and I've said enough."

I swung out my arm to stop her. "Nadine, I said I would help, and I will." *Even if it's for one night.* She needed first aid. Maybe the next morning, I could convince her to speak to Ted.

She diverted her attention to my phone.

"I need to check this message." I didn't recognize the number of the voice mail. Sometimes Ted had one of his colleagues check on me if he was busy. "It might be my dad." That wasn't a total lie since Ted was kind of a father figure.

I didn't want Nadine walking the streets. If she did end up dead, then I wouldn't have been able to live with myself. She sat back as I listened to my voice mail.

"Hi, Maggie. This is Dillon Hart. I don't know if you remember me. Anyway, can you call me or stop by when you get a chance." He proceeded to spit out his number and the address of a shelter. "I would like to talk to you."

My eyebrows drew together. Dillon Hart, as in the Hart brothers of the Silent Seven gang, was calling me. I'd wondered what had happened to him after all these years. He'd been the cutest of the Hart brothers. I knew his brother Denim was in jail for murder. That had been headline news about four years ago. Regardless, Dillon owned a shelter.

Talk about odds.

5

DILLON

I parked in the driveway alongside Rafe's souped-up truck then absorbed the quietness for a few minutes. Pinching my nose, I closed my eyes. Sleep was starting to take over. Rafe was right. I needed to find an outlet or a woman. Too many sleepless nights at the shelter plus bills, spreadsheets, and a dead girl in a morgue were all starting to take a toll on me.

The small gym in the basement sounded like a great way to unwind, and so did getting laid. The problem with the latter was that I didn't have anyone I could call. My past hookups had been with women I'd met at clubs. Since I'd bought the shelter, I hadn't even been out to eat, let alone to a nightclub.

I couldn't help but remember how I'd almost opened my heart to someone. Man, she was still beautiful, with black hair and blue-gray eyes, not like the usual blondes I had a thing for. I grinned when I thought of how she'd been trying to avoid a guy at Rumors nightclub and how I'd decided to make out with her so he wouldn't notice her. I'd been waiting for her to slap me. Instead, her body had molded to mine, soft and perfect. And then there was the kiss. *Whoa!* Her lips had been like silk. Her tongue had tasted of mint, and the way it had played with mine had made me hard in an instant.

I shucked the images of Lizzie Reardon. I couldn't have a girl who'd been saving her heart for her childhood sweetheart, Kelton Maxwell. Besides, love didn't have a home in my world, not only because I was afraid any woman would run like my mother had, but also because until I found Grace dead or alive, I couldn't give my entire self to someone.

Then you might not ever get married, fall in love, or have a family.

At some point, I would have to call it quits. My problem was that I couldn't. My blood began to boil at how I wanted to turn back time and change my decision to go into the merchant marines. I'd trusted my brothers, though.

"I did watch after her when you joined the merchant marines," Duke had said. "I couldn't babysit her twenty-four hours a day."

Grace had never believed that Denim or Duke would protect her from our father. I banged a hand on the steering wheel. It was my fault that she was missing. She'd trusted me. I was such a fucking asshole. I'd wanted to get away from my old man so badly. I'd wanted to find a better life rather than get abused by my father or even die from some gang fight. More than that, I'd wanted to make money so I could return home and take my sister out of the caustic environment she had been living in.

I growled, recalling a conversation between Duke and me in his penthouse about eight months ago, right before I'd signed the mortgage papers for the shelter.

"She's probably dead," Duke had said.

"How can you stand there, dressed in your fancy suit, and tell me Grace is dead?" I'd shouted at the top of my lungs. "How can you believe that? No one has found her body."

"I've seen what the streets can do to people. Come on, Dillon. Use that smart head of yours. It's been four years since Grace left home. Don't think for a minute I didn't go looking for her. I did. If she's still alive, maybe she doesn't want to be found."

"Or maybe, brother, someone kidnapped her." That was the last thing I'd said to Duke. Since then, we hadn't spoken, even though he lived in the city.

I rubbed my eyes, shook off my ire and every other emotion burning through my body, and went into the shelter.

As soon as I was inside, I heard a car's engine. Rafe was monitoring the cameras on Norma's computer screen. "VW. They're parking in front of the house."

I stalled in the doorway that connected the entry to the common room. "Where's Norton?"

"I did what you said and called Josh in. He's got his eye on Norton."

The doorbell rang.

Not taking his attention away from the screen, Rafe said, "Two girls. One looks in bad shape."

I hurried the short distance to the front door, with Rafe not far behind.

When I opened it, my eyes landed on the redhead first. Her hair was disheveled, her body was black and blue, and it appeared she'd been rolling around in a pile of leaves. Then my gaze flicked to the blonde, and my jaw came unhinged.

"Dillon? I'm Maggie. You called." Her voice slid along my tattooed arms, smooth, silky, and downright ball-squeezingly sexy.

I opened the door wider.

The redhead immediately padded in, appearing a little agitated. She craned her neck up at Rafe then pivoted on her heel and went back to the door. "I'm out of here."

Rafe and I swapped confused shrugs.

Maggie blocked the girl. "Nadine, they're not going to call the cops." Maggie gave me a pointed look. "Right, Dillon?" Her voice was soothing, like a mom's.

That all depended on what we were up against. My goal in taking in women was not to interrogate them, but to give them refuge. However, I had a couple of questions, or one important one. First,

Nadine needed some medical attention, as in Band-Aids and antiseptic. I didn't see any cuts that required stitches.

"Rafe, can you get the first-aid kit?" I asked.

Nadine hugged herself. "That dude reminds me of a gang member." She tipped her head at Rafe's retreating form.

I could understand her trepidation. Rafe was a big dude and wore a *don't fuck with me* expression most of the time.

"Nadine, I can assure you no one will hurt you here. Both Rafe and me, no matter how scary we might seem, we'll protect you with our lives." That was no lie. Rafe would cut off any man's head who preyed on women, as would I.

Nadine reminded me of Allie and Bee and how uneasy they'd been when I offered them a place to stay. They hadn't budged at first. Bee had come before Allie, but Bee had been homeless and desperately needed food, a shower, and a warm bed. I'd given Bee full reign of my house all by herself for a few nights to prove to her I wasn't a rapist or anything of the sort and that she could trust me. Even the two women who were asleep in their beds at the moment had been apprehensive when they'd first arrived, but Norma had helped to ease their tension, the conviction in her voice much like that in Maggie's.

"See," Maggie added. "You're safe."

Nadine's tense shoulders loosened as she stepped into the common room. Maggie sashayed her very curvy hips in behind Nadine, while I locked us in. Then I joined the women, who sat down on the U-shaped couch.

After a beat of silence, Maggie jumped to her feet and threw her arms around my neck. "It's so good to see you and to know you didn't die in a gang fight."

I wracked my brain at where her sudden affection was coming from. She was acting as if we had been good friends at one time, when all we had been were enemies. Despite that, my body suddenly reacted in ways that weren't appropriate at the moment. For sure, Rafe was right. I needed a woman to relieve some of my stress.

I backed away. If I didn't, I would be escorting her down the hall and into my office so I could throw her on the couch. "You look great." Boy, did she ever. Maggie was sexier than Eddie had mentioned. The curly hair she'd had as a teenager had turned into soft, wavy locks as a woman, and her large hips were making me all warm inside. Not only was I into blondes, but I liked my women with meat on them. "And you too are not dead."

Most of the members from my gang were either in jail, dead, or into some bad shit, like my brother Duke. I knew that the men who had been in Maggie's gang had followed the same path.

She tucked hair behind her ear then adjusted the scarf around her neck. "I could've been if it weren't for a cop who helped me turn my life around."

"Cop," Nadine muttered. "You know a cop?"

Maggie returned to her spot next to Nadine. "Please relax. I brought you here and not the police station."

As though that was all she needed to hear, Nadine slumped against the couch.

Maggie unleashed her bag from across her body. "I can't believe you own a shelter. Why?" She took inventory of the first floor. When she glanced up, awe was written all over her face. The high ceilings with wood beams gave the room a spacious feeling.

That answer would have to wait. I was more concerned with Nadine.

I parked myself on the arm of the couch. "Nadine, what happened to you?" Debbie and Angel, the two women asleep on the third floor, had come to the shelter looking much like Nadine. Seeing a woman fucked up by a man made me want to use the guy as a punching bag.

"She was a victim in a standoff between a gang and the cops earlier tonight," Maggie said. "She was lucky to get away. Can she stay here?"

The red flag waved in my head. My one question before anyone could stay here was, "Are you running from the cops?" I didn't expect anyone to say yes even if they were. But I had to ask because I didn't want to get entangled with the law. I could be charged with harboring or aiding and abetting.

Rafe waltzed over, carrying the metal container with all the necessities to bandage up someone. "Standoff with the cops?" He set the first-aid kit on the large square coffee table then took a seat on the edge of the couch opposite me.

"Won't the cops be looking for her?" I asked.

Maggie began cleaning the blood off Nadine's face with astringent wipes. "I'm sure they will or are. But Nadine feels like she would be in danger if she goes to the cops."

Nadine winced but let Maggie tend to her wounds anyway.

Rafe and I exchanged a silent look that asked *what do we do?*

"Can I stay here?" Nadine's distressed tone pierced my heart.

I rubbed my beard. In my time searching for Grace, I'd come into contact with girls who didn't want to involve the law. Hell, Allie and Bee were two of the girls. But at that time, I hadn't been running a shelter that was also a business. Now I had to toe the line.

On the flip side, I couldn't throw Nadine to the wolves. I wasn't saying the cops were corrupt, but I'd known a few to side with the bad guys. Jeremy Pitt came to mind. Not only that, but if something did happen to Nadine after I said no, then I would feel like a piece of shit for shoving her out the door.

"As long as you need to." The words fell easily from my lips despite the consequences.

Rafe gave me a cursory glance before he said, "Maggie, you realize you can get into trouble for interfering with an investigation."

She set down the first-aid kit. "Nadine's a victim. So I don't see how. But I'll handle the cops." Her tone was confident as sure as it was dark outside.

Man, her voice was like warm butter, jolting me in all the right places.

Nadine yawned.

"Rafe, can you show Nadine to a room on the second floor?" I didn't want her waking up Angel and Debbie.

Rafe unfolded his large body. "Come on, Nadine. The rooms are upstairs through that hallway." He pointed to an archway on the side wall midway, down from where we were sitting.

Maggie caught Nadine's arm. "Please don't go back to Miguel."

She gave Maggie a sad look. "Thanks for helping me."

Then she and Rafe vanished upstairs.

Maggie leaned forward, elbows on her knees. "She's going to go back to her pimp. I know it."

"They usually do," I mumbled.

Runaways were scared and easily swayed, especially by pimps who had money and offered them a bed, clothes, and food. I wasn't sure if Nadine was a runaway, though, and as much as I could talk to her about not returning to her pimp, I got the feeling she wouldn't listen.

Maggie fiddled with her scarf. "I was hoping that the standoff tonight was with a gang called the Black Knights for a story I'm doing for the *Boston Eagle.*"

I'd heard of them. They were into drugs and guns.

"Reporter, huh?" She didn't need to answer that. I said it more out of envy that she had gotten off the streets and out of a gang. "Are they part of the sex-trafficking story you're working on?" Maybe the gang had graduated to bigger and more disgusting opportunities.

She pursed her full pink lips. "How do you know that?"

"We have a mutual acquaintance. Eddie at the city morgue."

"That's why you called me?" Her tone led me to believe she was more intrigued than anything.

"Eddie had a young dead girl come in tonight. A drug mule, it seems. And he thought she might have been my missing sister, Grace."

She flinched. "Your baby sister? Whoa!"

Then out of nowhere, it dawned on me. Maybe Nadine knew Grace or had seen her. Nadine definitely wasn't going anywhere until I showed her Grace's picture.

6

MAGGIE

I should have been leaving since Nadine was safe for now, but the couch was too comfy, and I wanted to learn more about Dillon.

He stared at me with so many different emotions dancing in his golden-brown eyes. I was sure I had several going on in mine too. I couldn't believe, after all these years, that I was in the same room as Dillon Hart. The Hart brothers had been my enemies, but Dillon had been my favorite. He had a brooding outer appearance, but underneath all that toughness was a teddy bear. I'd picked up on that when he'd defended his sister, much like Lou had protected and defended me. Back then, though, boys and dating weren't on my list of things to do, not after what Cory had done to me. Moreover, if I'd had any notions about approaching Dillon, Lou would've cut off his manly parts, or those of any boy, for that matter, including the ones in my own gang if they'd breathed on me the wrong way.

My gang days were long gone. I didn't have Lou to fight off the men, and I'd gotten past my fear of a boy touching me. It had been hard when I'd first had sex at the age of twenty. The man I'd been with had been gentle and kind. I'd soon realized that the more sex I had, the more fun it could be, especially when two people wanted the same thing.

My phone rang, breaking the silence between Dillon and me. I shifted in my seat, wanting to ignore Ted's call. The quietness in the room was soothing, and Dillon's gaze bouncing over me had my lady parts singing. Maybe it was the lip ring and the diamond stud in his nose that got me all heated. Or maybe it was how his beard hugged his strong jaw or how his tousled brown hair fell to his shoulders. I came to the conclusion that it was all of the above, the whole darn package, at least above his neck. I didn't venture lower or examine his tatted arms. Otherwise, I would have been beet red.

I heaved a sigh as my phone continued to blare. I had to pick up, or else Ted would keep calling.

"Are you going to answer that?" Dillon asked in a husky tone.

I puffed out my cheeks as I set my sights on the ping-pong table behind Dillon for no other reason than to not look at the boy who made the butterflies take flight in my stomach.

The ringing stopped… then started again.

I lifted the phone to my ear, my thoughts taking a downturn to Nadine. I felt as if she'd punched me in the gut harder than anyone had in the past, and I'd taken some fists in my stomach. A small amount of guilt plagued me. I'd been praying she would tell me her pimp was Cory, not Miguel. That name didn't ring a bell to me.

"I wanted to make sure you got home safe," Ted said.

"Did you consider that I could be sleeping?"

"I know you, Mags." Ted's voice was like sandpaper. "When you're trying to find dirt for a story, you'll go to great lengths to get the facts."

He spoke the truth. I considered myself relentless when I wanted something.

"Can you confirm that the gang you were up against tonight is in fact the Black Knights? What about the guy you arrested? Can you tell me his name?" Nadine had said the guy the cops caught wasn't Miguel, but she didn't know his name.

Dillon watched me intently.

Ted let out a low laugh. "My case is not for the media. When I have something that I can share, you'll be one of the first ones to know."

I believed that last statement was a lie. If his investigation uncovered the Black Knights, Ted wouldn't want me anywhere near that case, especially if Cory Calderon was involved. Like Rick, Ted had also told me Cory was clean. When Ted learned what the boy had done to me, he did some digging. At first, I didn't believe him, which was why I'd asked Rick to confirm things. But Cory didn't even have a parking ticket. I would guess his rich daddy was paying someone off within law enforcement to conceal Cory's records.

"You know I'll do my own digging."

Ted harrumphed. "I'm well aware of that. Remember, Mags, if you intrude on a police investigation, there will be consequences. Family or not."

I rolled my eyes, even though he couldn't see me. "I want to see Cory pay for what he did to me." Ted wouldn't throw me in jail.

Yeah, but you could lose your job. Better yet, you could lose the opportunity to exact your revenge on Cory Calderon. Then again, it was becoming increasingly difficult to get anything on a guy who frequented charity events and was considered a good boy.

Dillon grinned, and when he did, tingles peppered my body.

Since when did I get tingles from a guy who smiled at me?

Since the hottest guy you've seen in quite some time is sitting across from you.

Suddenly, I realized the last time I had sex with a guy was more than a year ago, maybe two. At least I had my trusty vibrator. Still, a woman had needs, and the image of two bodies sliding together, making glorious music jolted me right between the legs.

Dillon had a blank expression as his gaze roamed all over me, making those butterflies flutter endlessly. He was certainly better to look at than the ping-pong table. His chiseled biceps were yummy. The tats on his arms told a story, at least I assumed they did since he had the name Grace inked on his arm.

"You've got to let Cory go. Now get some rest." Ted disconnected, killing the butterflies in my stomach.

I would get Cory if it took me forever.

I barely lowered the phone, when Dillon started in. "That was your cop friend?"

I yawned. The long day was hitting me all of a sudden, or more like my adrenaline was nonexistent now. "Ted Hughes."

"As in Detective?" Dillon asked.

"You know him?" That would be weird… or cool… Actually, I didn't know what I thought about that, although Ted was well-known in the city as the commander of the gang force.

"Eddie mentioned him. So are you saying that the guy who gave you your scar is the leader of the Black Knights?"

"I can't prove it yet. I have a source who heard a rumor about Cory Calderon being connected to the Black Knights."

Dillon threaded long fingers through his hair. In the soft light coming from the lamp next to him, I could see the exhaustion evident in his face. "As in Calderon Investments?"

I wanted to be those fingers. "You know Cory?" My heart sped from zero to a hundred in a flash. If he said he was good friends with the man, I might punch him.

"My financial advisor works for the company."

Suddenly, I wasn't tired anymore. "Who? Harold, the owner?" My mind was spinning like an out-of-control tornado. Maybe Dillon could introduce me to his contact, then I could pose as a client and do some investigative work. On second thought, that wouldn't work. I didn't have money to invest.

"Your mind is going crazy." Dillon's voice lowered my pulse a little.

Dillon was my age at twenty-six. I only knew that because I'd asked Lou about the Hart brothers. He'd given me the basics—ages, where they lived, and to stay away from them since they were rivals. We weren't enemies anymore, and I wondered where Dillon had gotten enough money that he needed a financial advisor. Only old people had those, unless he was into drugs or another illegal business. My mind was diving into the deep, dark abyss with thoughts of sex trafficking and the idea of him opening a shelter. He'd asked me about my story earlier.

I shuddered a breath, playing with my scarf, a habit I had when I was nervous or thinking.

He gave me the same wolfish grin he had earlier. "I know what you're thinking. The shelter is legit. I'm not into anything illegal like sex trafficking. I truly have made wise investments. And no, I don't know Cory. I've never met his old man either."

He spoke with sincerity and passion, erasing my morbid thoughts. I did believe him.

He wormed his way closer to me until we were almost thigh to thigh. "No need to be nervous." He proceeded to remove my scarf, exposing my cleavage. I would've slapped his hand away, but his ocean-scented cologne was gluing me to him, and the gentle way he was untying my scarf gave me reason to pause. Probably because I was excited he was so close, whether I wanted to admit it or not.

I should've worn a high-neck shirt like I usually did. But I didn't have any clean ones. The only shirts left in my wardrobe were V-necks.

He dragged a rough finger down the length of my scar, eliciting an array of tingles that chugged their way south as if they had a mind of their own. "This right here is part of who you are. Don't hide it."

My breathing ramped up. A man had never said a word about my scar except Ted, but he'd said something in a fatherly sort of way, not raspy and breathy like Dillon had. Then again, I didn't like to show off my disfigurement. It prompted too many questions that only brought up the past.

Slowly, Dillon's long lashes swept down across his strong cheek-bones as his gaze fell to my lips. His hand was still on my scar, which meant it was very close to my cleavage.

Damn.

"Battle scars are beautiful," he rasped.

I jumped up, my pulse off the charts. This time, my excitement was vastly different than it was when I was thinking about sticking Cory in a jail cell. I'd come to the shelter to help someone in need, not have sex with the owner, although that wasn't such a bad idea. What worried me, though, was my heart. I could fall for Dillon in a flash, and I wasn't ready to go steady with anyone. Frankly, I didn't know if I would ever settle down, at least not until I accomplished my mission of exacting my revenge on Cory.

Dillon chuckled, his deep timbre licking across my skin. "I'm sorry. I couldn't help myself. You're more beautiful than I remembered."

Yikes! My throat was as dry as the Sahara Desert.

I moved to the ping-pong table. "Do you play?" *Nothing like deflecting.*

He stalked toward me with a sense of purpose as if he were planning to lay me out on top of the smooth green surface.

I might have let him.

His mouth curled on one side. His hair was untamed and silky around his shoulders, and his swagger screamed that he knew how to handle a woman in bed.

Kill me now.

I was tempted to hop up on the table and open my legs, but that wouldn't be ladylike.

Dillon's arm went around my side, and I froze as if I'd never been kissed by a boy before. Now that I thought about it, I'd never had a mind-blowing kiss that made my toes curl. Nevertheless, just when I thought he was going to pull me to him, he snagged a paddle off the table instead.

Images of him using that paddle on me only made me cross one leg over the other.

He edged back, examining the paddle as though he were looking for cracks. "My brothers and I played as kids."

I let out a quiet sigh, thankful he didn't kiss me or that our bodies didn't touch. I wasn't sure what I would've done. Scratch that, I was ready to rip my clothes off for him.

Vibrator, here I come.

His biceps bunched as he rubbed a hand over the surface of the paddle.

Say something. "I heard your brother Denim is in jail."

In a flash, Dillon was on the other side of the enormous table, not showing me his cards, so to speak. "I really don't want to talk about my brother. I was hoping I could ask you about the sex-trafficking story."

I was hoping I could ask you for one night of unadulterated passion.

He traded the paddle for his wallet. "My sister, Grace, went missing four years ago at the age of sixteen, but it's been much longer than that since I've seen her." He swaggered back and handed me her picture.

I studied the young girl but didn't recognize her. When I'd been in a gang, I'd only heard of Grace but had never seen her.

"It's a shot in the dark, but I thought that with the stories you work on, that maybe Grace Hart was one of those stories."

If she had been, I would've remembered the name. Yet sometimes faces didn't come with names other than Jane Doe.

His hand brushed mine. When it did, I freaking whimpered.

He cocked his head.

Busted.

"She's young." My voice cracked as I studied the girl who resembled Dillon. She had warm brown eyes like he did, and her hair was a smidge lighter than his dark brown. I dipped back to some of the stories I'd done on girls of the night or even dead girls who'd had a sad story to tell. I couldn't recall anyone resembling Grace.

Craning my neck to look up at him, I handed Dillon her photo as my heart severed at the misery that lived deep in his eyes.

"I haven't done any stories on a Grace Hart, nor have I seen anyone like her. She's young in this picture."

"She's fourteen in that photo," he said. "I don't have a more recent one. I was gone so much for the merchant marines that I hardly came home much. Anyway, she's twenty now."

"I hate to be blunt, but—"

He held up his hand, sadness oozing from him in buckets. "Don't say it. I've heard a million times that she's probably dead." He touched his heart. "In here, I don't believe she is."

I admired him for having hope. "Why not?"

His long fingers disappeared in his unruly locks as he began pacing. "Over a year ago, I talked to a woman on the street who claimed she saw Grace at a soup kitchen down on Asher Street. I watched the joint for days but never got anywhere." Desperation weaved through his words.

I couldn't fault him for that. I was itching to find Cory, of course for different reasons. I studied Grace a little more closely. "Is that a birthmark on her neck?" Of all the stories I'd done, I couldn't recall a female with a birthmark that resembled a broken star.

Dillon stopped dead in his tracks, drawing in an audible breath. "Have you seen her?"

I rested my butt lightly against the ping-pong table, holding on to the edge. "Again, I haven't. I can check my files, though, and I'll talk to Ted. He's seen a lot on the streets." That was the least I could do.

Dillon came up to me, and again my pulse became erratic, even more so when he settled next to me, his leg grazing mine. "Thank you. You can keep the picture. I have a few."

As much as I wanted him to touch me again, I couldn't get involved with him. I was afraid he would take me on a journey I would never recover from, one that had love somewhere in there along the way, and that scared me to no end. I was afraid I would end up in a strained or nonexistent relationship in which the husband and wife argued constantly, much like the foster families I'd been in.

I had a long day at work tomorrow anyway. I grabbed my scarf and secured it around my neck.

Dillon made some sort of low noise.

I didn't know if he was trying to tell me not to put on the scarf, but I said, "Habit. I'll be back tomorrow to check on Nadine."

As Dillon walked me out, an idea bloomed.

"I want to find dirt on the guy who gave me this scar. You want to find your sister." I shrugged. "Maybe we can help each other out." Personally, I wanted to get to know the real Dillon Hart and not the rival gang member I knew long ago.

Professionally, as a reporter, I wanted stories, good, bad, or indifferent. And Dillon had a story to tell, particularly because he'd started a refuge for battered women. *Former Gang Member Turned Entrepreneur Gives His Heart To Helping Women In Dire Straits.* Now that was a headline, although not one that would put Cory behind bars.

Intrigue flashed in his eyes. "What do you have in mind?"

Aside from the thought of him running those rough, calloused hands all over me, kissing me, and giving me a night to remember, I had another idea. "Can you introduce me to your financial advisor?"

We lingered on the porch, the heat of the night hotter than a bonfire.

"I'm not sure you'll learn much about Cory by talking to my financial advisor. But I can do something better."

I held my breath, my mind blank on what he could offer me other than his hot bod.

"Denim might be able to give us some dirt on the Black Knights. Prisons are notorious with gangs. I know the cops won't tell you jack, but does your detective friend know who's running the show?"

"Ted says whoever is at the helm of the Black Knights is a ghost. If gang members are caught, they don't talk. They'd rather rot in jail."

"All the more reason for me to reach out to Denim," Dillon added. "Give me a few days."

I lifted up on my toes and kissed him on the cheek. "Thank you." I didn't know much about gangs in prison, but if they were anything like the ones on the streets—closed mouth and protective of their people—then Denim might not be able to learn anything.

I waved as I hurried to my car.

He watched me until I got to the driver's side door.

"Dillon, again, I'm sorry about your sister." I truly was.

His heated gaze caressed my face, slowly and oh-so-sensually, before I ducked into my VW and sped away. A block down, a giddy feeling tickled me. I'd reunited with a man who made my stomach do somersaults and backflips. More importantly, I was blanketed by a renewed sense of hope that I might get some info on the Black Knights.

7

———

DILLON

I sat at a table in the visitor's room, waiting for the guard to get Denim, as I replayed the night before, or hours before, in my head. I hadn't been able to sleep a wink, not with Maggie on my brain. I'd snapped about twenty imaginary shots of her from the time she'd sashayed into the shelter until the time she'd driven away. I'd bitten my tongue when she walked to her car. I'd been a second away from asking her to stay the night. All those visions of her I'd had as a teenager paled in comparison to my thoughts of her now and what I itched to do. We were no longer enemies. She no longer had Lou watching over her. We were adults and had free rein to do as we pleased.

My lack of sleep, however, was from more than a blonde with long wavy hair and a body that made me harder than stone. My gut was signaling to me that something big was about to happen. I couldn't pinpoint what yet. I believed that every person I came into contact with played a role in my life somehow.

Maggie was going to play a role, maybe to test my resolve not to get serious with anyone. Or maybe she would be essential in leading me to Grace. Or maybe I was in her life to help her slay her demon named Cory Calderon. I certainly wanted to cut the fucker's head off for what he'd done to her, and the same went for the asshole who had taken his hands to Nadine, who had still been tucked into a bed when I'd left at the crack of dawn that morning. I'd made a point to check. Maggie and I both knew she would go back to her pimp, but I was praying she wouldn't.

Aside from all that, those snapshots in my head had Maggie and me beneath the sheets, her soft skin against mine. Man, I didn't know what had come over me when I decided to touch her scar. I hadn't been prepared for the jolt of electricity that fired through me either. The heat was unbearable and in a good fucking way.

All I knew was that I had to get close to her. I hated that she was self-conscious about her scar. The more my finger had traveled down the length of her scar, the more my groin had pulsed. I'd been ready to explode when my eyes landed on her large, round breasts. I wanted to suck, lick, and play with them as well as her wide hips, her toes, and everywhere in between.

Focus, man. You're at a prison to talk to your brother, not to get a boner over a woman who all but ran from you. I did like how she'd squirmed and her breathing had ramped up and how goose bumps had popped up on her arms the more my finger danced along her skin. She wasn't running from me, but herself. I had no doubt she wanted me as much as I wanted her.

Sadly, thoughts of Maggie vanished when the door to the room squeaked open. My brother sauntered in, wearing his normal cocky grin. Nothing seemed to bother him. Even as a kid, Denim used to laugh at our old man when the bastard had lashed out at him.

"Give it your best shot," Denim would say to dear old dad before he broke out in a fit of laughter. Our father would stumble toward Denim, waver, then swing his fists, at times missing his mark, which was Denim's face.

Duke and I had gotten pretty good at shielding ourselves after years of taking his beatings, but we hadn't been laughing. We would seethe and spit fire at the man we couldn't believe was our kin. I made it my mission to never ever become the man he was.

I stood up to give my brother a hug. The last time I'd seen him was a week after I'd spoken to Duke, which was eight months ago. I tried to see Denim on occasion, but once I'd purchased the shelter, my time had been limited.

Denim and I went in for a manly hug until the guard piped up. "No touching."

My brother rolled his eyes before he dropped his big body into the chair across from me.

The guard said, "You got fifteen minutes, Hart." Then he took up a position at the door he and Denim had emerged from.

I slid back into my seat.

A beat of silence stretched around the empty room that was filled with other tables and chairs.

I swept my gaze over my brother, who was wearing a white T-shirt and an orange jumpsuit folded down to the waist. His blond hair was tied back in a low ponytail, his blue eyes were bright, and his jaw was littered with stubble. He seemed happy. "You look well."

"You look like shit. What brings you here? Did you find a crack in my case to get me out of this fucked-up hell?"

I'd never believed my brother would murder anyone intentionally. Self-defense was a different story, and the potential of dying came with being in a gang. But Denim had been accused of murdering a notorious member of the Southside Creepers. It had shocked the hell out of me when I learned he'd been arrested for killing someone.

"How many times do I have to tell you, a lawyer won't touch your case?" I'd spoken to an attorney right after I returned home from the merchant marines. The high-priced lawyer wouldn't touch Denim's case for all the money in the world. The man was into winning, not losing.

Fucker.

"Didn't you tell me you're friends with a lawyer? A Maxwell or some name like that?"

I laughed at the notion that I would bring Kelton Maxwell into the picture to retry Denim's case. Not that I was laughing at Kelton. He was sharp as a whip and was studying criminal law. "Kelton is in law school."

"So? He can take a look at my file. It would be a good learning experience for him. Maybe he knows a good lawyer. Look, the public defender I had was worthless."

We were getting off track, yet I couldn't help but feel my brother's pain and frustration. "Bro, I'm here because I need your help."

He smirked. "I can't imagine how I can help you. Remember, I'm in prison."

"Do you remember Maggie Marx from the Bloodhounds?"

He let out a low whistle. "How can I forget her? You had a major boner for that chick. Have you finally got her in the sack?"

I had no reason to turn red. I was talking to my brother, the same one who had asked about sex nonstop when he was going through puberty. Hell, most of us in the house had had to take cold showers and not because we'd been jacking off. But Denim had been.

"Aw, my brother is blushing."

I flipped him off. "She's a crime reporter for the *Boston Eagle,* and she's working on a story. She believes that the Black Knights have a stronghold on sex trafficking."

The light in his eyes snuffed out in a matter of seconds. He gave the guard a cursory glance before he leaned over the scratched table. "That gang is badass motherfuckers that you don't want to get involved with. I mean, they wouldn't think twice about ripping your insides out if you even breathe in their direction."

The word gang held fear for most of the general population, but not anyone who had been in one, or so I'd thought. Denim was visibly shaken at the mere mention of the gang's name.

"Did you have a run-in with them?" I couldn't help but ask. Normally, he wasn't fearful of much, at least he hadn't been when we were causing all kinds of trouble as kids.

"I would love to get my hands on one of them and tear off his head, but I suggest you stay away from them. You've got things in your life where you want them. So don't go poking the bear."

I slapped a hand over my heart. "You care." I seriously was touched. As brothers, we'd grown apart after I left for the merchant marines. "I'm trying to help Maggie out. She believes the dude who gave her that scar on her neck is with the Black Knights."

He shook his head, his expression still cautionary. "Revenge will get her killed, and maybe you too."

"I only want to find Grace or find out what happened to her, and Maggie might be able to help me. Aside from that, think for a minute if Grace ended up in a sex-trafficking ring and was sold to some fat fuck."

He winced as he clenched his fist. "Are you saying the Black Knights could be responsible for Grace's disappearance?"

I shrugged. "Not at all." I prayed not. I didn't know much about what the Black Knights were into or if what Maggie believed about them held any truth. "Look, you told me the last time I was here that the Black Knights ruled E block. So can you put feelers out and find out what the gang is up to and who runs the show?"

His lips formed a thin line. "I'm not in E block, but for Grace, I'll see what I can dig up."

He loved our sister as much as me. I knew Duke did too, though Duke had a funny way of showing it.

"You blame yourself for Grace taking off, don't you?" Denim asked. "I do too, brother. I do too. I'm really sorry that I didn't pay more attention before I got busted."

All of us had had our own way of dealing with our father. Duke had never been home, and when he was, he'd hidden in his room in the basement. Denim and I had hidden in the treehouse in the backyard. As drunk as our old man had gotten, he couldn't climb up the ladder without falling, and he'd tried several times.

I swallowed the lump in my throat. That was the first time I'd heard Denim apologize. "I do blame myself."

"Bro, I need to get out of here. I may look like I'm happy-go-lucky, but this place is killing me inside." He pounded his chest with his fist. "I want to help you find Grace. More importantly, I want to find the fucker who set me up."

It was possible that someone had set up Denim to take the fall. If so, the million-dollar question was who? The other elephant in the room was why? He had to have royally pissed off someone who had the skill and smarts to do that. "The cops found the gun used to kill that gang member in your backpack."

"It wasn't mine," he said despondently.

I blew out a breath. "Denim, look. I'll talk to Kelton. He does work for a law firm that has lawyers who can take a look at your case."

He opened his mouth.

I held up my hand. "I'm not promising anything. Now, how long will it take you to do some detective work?"

"Bro," Denim said. "Maybe you should check with Duke. Our brother knows the streets and has connections. He might have more insight about the Black Knights."

"I plan to when I know I won't send him through a wall. Of all people, he should've been turning over every stone to find Grace. Lord knows he's had the men to do it." Why Duke wouldn't put his money and resources into searching for his sister still befuddled me.

The guard cleared his throat. "Time's up."

Denim sneered. "Give me a second, please."

The squat, bald man didn't move from the door.

"Duke did look for Grace. He even beat the shit out of our old man to see what he did to send Grace over the edge. Which, as you know, was his drunken ass and verbal abuse."

That might have been true, but Duke had led me to believe that he didn't care about Grace anymore, nor had he shown any signs of remorse or sadness.

Denim pushed back his chair. "Give me until Friday to see what I can find out."

Friday was three days away. "Why that long?"

"My block and E block are in the yard together on Thursday." Worry flashed in his eyes.

I got the feeling that what he was about to do was dangerous, but he was a big, tough boy who could handle himself.

In the meantime, I needed to talk to Nadine, call Kelton, talk to Manny over at the men's shelter to see how Norton was doing, and see if Maggie had had any luck finding something useful in her files.

8

MAGGIE

ap. Ring. Tap. Ring.

My colleagues pounded away on keyboards. Phones rang. Voices peppered the air. The newsroom sounded like a well-played orchestra without its conductor.

I sat in my cubicle, enjoying the hum in the room, which calmed me for some reason. I hated quiet. I hated to dive into my own thoughts and think about my past. But sometimes remembering my screwed-up childhood was the only thing that kept me dedicated to my revenge.

I slipped my hand underneath my chiffon scarf and felt along the raised ridge of my scar. I strived to shield my disfigurement as much as I could.

At times when I didn't wear a scarf because I forgot, people stared. I would have liked to think they were admiring my nice breasts. They weren't. Their horrified looks told me otherwise.

Sometimes I had to snap my fingers and say, "Up here." That usually ended with them getting red cheeks and saying, "Oh, I'm so sorry." The bold ones asked how I'd gotten the scar. My response was always, "Wrong place. Wrong time."

That wasn't a lie. If I hadn't gotten so pissed off at my foster dad for putting his hands on me, then my life might have been different. Then again, maybe not. I would've still been violated by a drunk person, just one who hadn't had a knife in his hand.

I traced the length of my scar up then down, counting to twenty-five—the number of stitches it had taken to sew me up.

That fuckwad Cory had cut me deep that night and shattered my confidence. He'd given me nightmares to last an eternity.

"I will get you. I will see you in hell," I whispered to myself.

Damn Dillon thought I was beautiful. I saw myself as deformed.

"Rise up," Lou had told me. *"Stand proud of who you are. Fight. Live. Breathe in air. And plan how you're going to get revenge."*

Revenge. That word held so much meaning to me. An eye for an eye. Retribution.

Lou had wanted to know who had carved me up like a piece of meat. He'd wanted to hunt Cory down not long after I'd healed. Doing so would have only put Lou behind bars for murder, because as outraged as Lou had been, he wouldn't have thought twice about putting a bullet into Cory, and I couldn't let him throw away his life for me. I'd also been too scared to even whisper Cory's name at the time.

He'd stolen my confidence. He'd made me weak and shy. *Thank God for Lou.* He had pulled me from the ashes.

And like a phoenix rising, I had emerged a new person. Renewed in my mission. Stronger than before.

Once I'd learned how to really fight, I was ready to face the world, because I wouldn't be handled by any man like that again.

Oh, I'd planned Cory's death a million times over as I lay awake at night when sleep escaped me. My nightmares were vivid scenes of how I would make him suffer. At first, I'd thought death would be simple, quick, and the best punishment for him.

But death was too easy. He needed to suffer like I had all these years, and losing his freedom was far more effective. As much as I wanted to see him dead, I wasn't excited to be surrounded by three walls and bars for my door. I'd seen the inside of a jail cell one too many times, and that was when I realized I had to devise another plan to exact my revenge.

I leaned back in my chair and caught myself before I tipped over.

Someone laughed behind me before Bruce showed me his ugly mug. Well, my editor wasn't ugly. He was rather handsome, in shape, and a great husband and father to his wife and two girls. I longed for a family like his. I didn't see marriage and children happening for me, though. Maybe because I'd been on my own since I was born, and the foster homes I'd lived in didn't have the loving families who doted on their little tikes or spouses. If I were lucky enough to marry and have babies, I would do my best to make sure they came first.

Bruce crossed his arms over his pink golf shirt as he leaned against my desk. "Are you working on that standoff you were at last night at Bleven and Third?"

I rubbed a hand down my face. "There isn't a story. Ted cut me off. I'm sure you don't want me to write about how a cop arrested one of the perps."

"Do you know who they arrested? Is he with the Black Knights?"

I pointed a broken nail at my computer screen. "All I have are those pics." It wasn't as if I could type "face piercing, balding head suspect" into a police database to see if he'd been arrested before. I also couldn't question Ted or Rick. Neither of them would give me info, not because I was cut off from intel, but because I was the media and had no business interfering in a police investigation.

But I kind of did interfere, and I kind of felt guilty that I hadn't told Ted about Nadine. I was hoping I could convince Nadine to talk to the cops later when I went to visit her. If she wouldn't budge, I might consider telling Ted the truth, if for no other reason than to help Nadine so she wouldn't go back to Miguel. Maybe Ted could get her to a safe house protected by cops. Sure, the shelter was considered a safe haven, especially with Dillon and Rafe guarding the home, but cops had secret hiding spots.

Bruce waved his hand. "Mags, are you in there?"

The images of the Latino suspect on my screen sharpened before I met Bruce's gaze.

He angled his head, a strand of his black hair falling out of place. "It's not like you to give up. What's going on? You're sitting here, staring off into space." He scanned my desk and picked up the picture of Grace. "Who's this? A new victim? She's young, like my daughter."

"Her name is Grace, and she's the sister of a friend of mine. That photo was taken when she was fourteen. She's twenty now."

"You think she's part of the sex-trafficking ring?" Bruce continued to stare at Grace's picture. "Boy, I would flip out if my girls were taken from me."

Dillon was kind of doing the same. "She went missing at sixteen."

"So why do you have her picture? Surely, she's long gone by now."

I couldn't argue with him on that. Statistics had shown that the crucial window for finding a missing person was forty-eight hours. However, there had been cases in which victims were found after years of being in captivity.

I yawned, making a whiny sound. "Sorry. I didn't get any sleep last night."

"We need a story for Sunday's crime section," Bruce said.

It was highly unlikely I would have a break in finding more dirt on the Black Knights before then. Investigative reporting took time. "I have an idea." *One that was stupid.* "What if I go undercover to get info on the gang or gangs. I could walk the streets as a call girl and see what I can drum up. Then I could get hardcore evidence on anything gang related, including sex trafficking if that's what they're doing." I'd pinpointed the Black Knights because of Cory. But a story was a story, no matter what gang it was about or what illegal activity they were into.

Bruce's angular jaw dropped. "Are you mad? No way. It's too dangerous. Leave that shit for the cops. They have people trained to go undercover." I opened my mouth to speak, but he pointed an ink-stained finger at me. "No. I get how you want to crack the story. But absolutely not. If you bring it up again, my next call is to Ted."

Well, shit.

Ted would lock me up until he and his team brought down not only the Black Knights but every gang in the city, which meant I would be a prisoner for the rest of my life.

I dropped my head back, grunted, and squinted at the LED lights above before focusing on Bruce.

"Promise me, Maggie, that you are not going to do something stupid." His kind voice had a razor-sharp edge to it.

I raised my hands as if Ted had a gun to my back. "I promise." *Maybe.*

"A story is one thing. Your revenge that you're dead set on is quite different, and that will get you killed."

"Yes, Dad," I teased.

Bruce mashed his lips together. "Sassing me will get you hand-cuffed to this desk."

Yes, Dad was on the tip of my tongue, but I couldn't be strapped to my desk. I had leads to follow through on. I had to find facts, and I had to find them fast.

First, I had to somehow get out of my funk. "I'm going down to the precinct."

"That's my girl," Bruce said.

He assumed I was going to grill Ted for info, and I would ask Ted again about the standoff, but I also wanted to ask him about Grace.

I scooped up the picture of Grace, collected my notebook, shoved it all into my bag, and started for the elevator.

"Oh, and Mags?" Bruce called.

I tossed a quick look over my shoulder.

He gave me a warm smile. "Be careful out there."

I saluted him as straight as a sailor would then hoofed down to the garage located underneath the building and got into my beat-up VW Bug. My little car was the perfect size for city life.

I sped up and out onto the busy city streets, where horns blared and buses screeched to a halt and the smell of car exhaust filtered in through my open window.

I zipped around corners and other cars until I was pulling into a space outside of Ted's precinct. I got out of my car and slung my bag over my body. As I crossed the street, I spotted Officer Miladin parking his cruiser in front of the precinct. Maybe I could get info out of him on the perp he'd arrested.

Lifting my chin, I dug deep for my flirty side and flipped my braid so it fell down my back as I waited at the curb.

Miladin eyed me as he climbed out of his cruiser. The man was quite different in the daylight. His dark eyes were a deep blue, like the ocean off the coast of the Bahamas. I'd seen pictures of the island and had immediately put it on my bucket list for a rainy day when I had money to take a vacation.

Miladin moved a piece of his amber-brown hair out of his eyes as he gave me an award-winning smile that could melt a girl where she stood.

I batted my eyelashes, mainly to appeal to him so he would give me information. "Do you remember me?"

He stepped up onto the sidewalk, undressing me with his eyes. He was definitely deciding if I was someone he would want to take to bed.

Standing out in the open with cops filtering in and out of the building, I began my own assessment of Miladin, who I guessed to be in his twenties. Some women went all gaga over a man in uniform—cops, military, and firefighters—but not me. I didn't see the draw. Still, Miladin was super easy on the eyes, with his broad chest, flat stomach, and muscular arms.

"The reporter, right?" He had one of those voices that would be good on the radio—distinct, clear, and sharp.

"*Boston Eagle*. The guy you arrested last night. You got a name? Is he associated with the Black Knights?"

He chuckled. "Nothing I can tell the press. Sorry, sweetheart."

My nose twitched. The word sweetheart always rubbed me the wrong way, thanks to Cory, and whenever I heard that word, I wanted to scrub my hands until the first layer of skin peeled off.

I clamped down on my tongue. Officer Miladin didn't need my wrath. But his good looks were downgraded to somewhat ugly.

He sauntered past me and went up the stairs and into the precinct.

I shook off my annoyance and took the steps two at a time. I went to open one of the double glass doors, when Ted strode toward me with a cigarette ready to light. The man was going to die from nicotine before he got shot on the streets.

I backed away to let him through. It was better to talk outside and not around his team. That way, I had his full attention.

As soon as he was outside, he lit up, took a drag, sighed, and blew out the disgusting smoke.

I choked.

He marched down the steps and over to a police cruiser. He used the hot metal car as his anchor. "You look tired."

"You look like shit too," I responded as I mimicked his move, resting my butt on the cruiser.

He puffed on his cigarette and blew out fancy circles.

Again, I wanted to gag. The smell reminded me of my foster days, drunken men, and bad memories. "Those things will kill you."

"So will chasing bad guys," he said. "What brings you down here?"

"Am I still cut off?"

He flicked ashes to the ground. "Next question."

The need to stomp my foot like a two-year-old was strong. "Come on. I want a story." I strapped on my sweet voice.

He dragged his index finger and thumb down over his graying mustache as he considered my statement, or maybe he was trying to find another way to tell me no. "What I can tell you is the guy we arrested isn't talking. So don't ask me if he's part of the Black Knights. What I can say is his name is Dan Silva."

His name didn't ring a bell. "What was he arrested for?"

Ted narrowed his eyes. "Not open for discussion."

No surprise there. Maybe Misty, my source, could shed some light on that name.

Onto my next task… I dug into the front pocket of my messenger bag and held up Grace's picture. "Have you seen this girl?"

He flashed his dark eyes at Grace. "I've seen a lot of girls, Mags. Faces are all running together these days. You know old age is setting in. Anyway, who is she?" His voice went up slightly. Ted was in his forties and had a hard look about him.

"Grace Hart. She went missing four years ago. I'm helping out her brother. He's been on the hunt for her since then."

He made a clucking sound as he chewed on his lip. "As in Denim Hart?"

I gave him a sidelong glance. "You know Denim?"

He dipped his chin. "I arrested his ass for murder."

I strained my brain, flipping through conversations I'd had with Ted. "How come I didn't know that?" Then again, he didn't talk about his work much with me.

"Who I arrest isn't your business. You should know by now I don't talk about work when I'm off duty. Anyway, this girl is probably dead."

"I'm helping Denim's brother, Dillon. He doesn't believe so. He says someone he talked to not that long ago saw Grace at a soup kitchen on Asher."

"Mmm," he mumbled.

"Does that mean you've seen her?" *Please say yes.*

"About a year ago, Rick and I were working on a case of a man we suspected had been involved in a bank heist. Our trail led to a tattoo shop not far from Asher called Skins and Needles. When we walked in, there was a girl getting a tattoo on her neck. Anyway, I thought one wrong move, and the artist could sever her carotid artery."

I stabbed my finger at the photo. "That's the girl?"

He lifted a plaid-covered shoulder. Ted liked to wear plaid shirts for some reason. "Don't know. But the mark on her neck made me think of that." His phone chimed. He unclipped it from his belt. "Yeah. Where? Are you sure it's the redhead? I'll be right there."

My heart stopped. My tongue wouldn't work either. *Oh my. How did he find Nadine? Now she's going to think I ran to the cops.*

"I got to run." He stubbed out his cigarette then darted into the precinct like the Flash.

A horn somewhere around me blew and kick-started my brain.

I fumbled for my phone. I had to warn Dillon for the sole purpose of making sure he was prepared, and I wanted him to warn Nadine. I didn't want Nadine to think I sent the cops to pick her up. She didn't want anything to do with them, so I didn't believe Nadine had called them. Dillon or Rafe might have. But they hadn't been all that happy about bringing the cops into the shelter, at least from what I could gather.

I dialed Dillon's number. The line rang and rang and rang.

Argh!

His voice mail kicked in. "Leave a message."

A delightful shiver cooled my heated skin as I heard his husky tone. "Seriously? I couldn't be excited from a voice on the phone," I whispered, waiting to hear the beep so I could leave a message. The beep never came.

Oh no. I hung my head.

"If you're satisfied with your message, press one," the nice lady on the other end said.

Instead, I hung up. It was better to hightail my big butt over to the shelter.

9

———

DILLON

Norma was typing away at her desk when I sauntered in after my drive back from the prison. Her lip ring shimmered as she ran her tongue over it, a habit she had when she was thinking and hard at work. She didn't even look up as I waltzed in, which wasn't normal. Her eyes always darted to the door.

Angel, Norton's spouse, glanced up from the couch. "Dillon," she cooed.

I pocketed my keys. "Your bruises are healing great."

She moved a strand of her sandy-blond hair from her face as she gently touched her left eye and cheekbone. "All thanks to you."

Angel, who had found the shelter through one of Norma's friends, had been my first guest. She had to know about Norton. I couldn't risk her getting hurt if she decided to return home. "Norton was here last night. You need to be careful, Angel. He was drunk but also carrying a gun."

Norma gasped.

Angel paled. "No one got hurt?"

"No. Rafe took him to a home for alcoholics this morning. Let's hope he wants the help."

Color returned to Angel's complexion.

Norma's shock over Norton morphed into irritation. "I called you."

I shifted my attention to the one person who had saved me when I was searching for an assistant I could trust. More importantly, I'd needed someone who could help the women as they came in, and Norma had been the perfect person for the job. She'd lived on the streets, pimped herself to put food in her belly, and she had a way of calming people down, me included.

I checked my phone and saw I had two voice mails and one missed call. "What happened?"

"That girl who came in last night took off. She doesn't happen to be the one that the cops are looking for? Dillon, we can't have any trouble here. You'll scare away our guests."

Motherfucker.

Norma rotated her computer screen before I could open my mouth. The headline blaring at me read, "Witnesses saw a redheaded girl flee the scene last night at a standoff on Bleven and Third."

I clutched the back of my neck and turned away from Angel so she couldn't see that I was seething as question after question surfaced. I should've had Rafe and Josh watching Nadine instead of Norton. Then again, women who came to the shelter were free to come and go.

Nadine's situation was different, though. She was running from a gang and from the law. She could end up like that girl I'd seen on the table in the morgue.

"I saw her sneaking out early this morning," Angel said.

I took in a breath before I pivoted on my heel, nice and slow and calm.

Fuck calm. I wanted to throw that stapler Norma had her hand on. I should've stayed instead of running out to see Denim. I could've talked Nadine out of leaving.

"Dillon." Norma used her sweet voice that I'd heard her use on Angel and Debbie, who was probably up in her room. "You can't save everyone."

Her last statement was like a blow from a sledgehammer, reminding me that I was a fuckup who couldn't save his own sister.

"Excuse me for a minute," I said for Angel's benefit more than Norma's.

Norma had seen me in a rage a time or two. Her patience was amazing. She'd watched me beat a punching bag I had in the basement until my knuckles were raw. I didn't use gloves like Kross Maxwell did. Bareback was my motto, along with *feel the pain,* and *see the blood.*

I glued on a fake smile as I crossed the room on my way to the basement.

Angel hopped off the couch and caught my arm. "Thank you for helping Norton, and I'm sorry I put you in jeopardy."

I was dumbfounded. She shouldn't be apologizing for him. "Norton's actions aren't your fault. Please don't ever believe that."

Up close, the thirty-year-old woman seemed to have new life injected into her. A soft pink hue pinched her cheeks beneath the fading bruises. Her blue eyes were crystal clear, and her short hair was shiny. She'd made a hundred-and-eighty-degree turnaround since she'd arrived on our doorstep a month ago.

"I'm working on it." She let go of my arm. "I tried to stop the redhead since she looked frightened out of her mind. She said something like 'I'm not safe here. And I don't want to put anyone in danger or get Dillon in trouble. Tell him thank you for me, though.'"

Man, I could have kicked myself in the ass over and over again. I should've done something more to convince her that she would be safe here.

Norma rolled back her chair. The sound clicked along the wood floor. "Angel, can you see how Debbie is doing?"

I whipped my head at Norma. "Did something happen to her?"

Debbie had shown up a couple of days after Angel. Like Angel, Debbie had come to the shelter on the advice of a friend of Norma's. Unlike Angel, Debbie hadn't been beaten, but she had been sleeping on the streets.

"I'll poke my head into her room." Angel regarded Norma then left.

When Angel's footsteps faded, I sat on the arm of the couch.

Norma took my hand. "Debbie isn't feeling well. We're not sure if it's the flu. Come on, you could use some coffee instead of the punching bag."

I followed Norma into the kitchen like a little boy following on his mom's heels. I barely remembered tailing my mom as she promised cookies and milk right before bed.

"The punching bag will take the edge off," I said.

She giggled. "I'm sure, but let's chat first."

Norma poured coffee. I set my phone down on the wood-block island then slid onto a barstool. We had a modest kitchen with second-hand appliances that didn't match, scratched-up stools, and a round metal table near the sliding glass door.

"Where's Rafe?" I'd spoken to him on my two-hour drive back from the prison earlier. He'd mentioned that he'd had no problem carting Norton over to Manny's. I'd raised an eyebrow at that, although as the booze had vanished from Norton's system, he was probably a different man. My father sure had worn a different persona the morning after he polished off a bottle of Jack Daniels—grumpy, quiet, and moving slowly.

Regardless, I would've suspected that Rafe would have been back by now.

Norma stirred sugar and milk into both cups, the spoon dinging the ceramic mugs.

She carried them over and took a seat to my right. "Rafe stopped at the store to pick up some cold medicine for Debbie."

As soon as the caffeine hit my tongue, I sighed. Maybe the caffeine would kick the frustration and anger out of me. I didn't think so, but I kept drinking as though the coffee was my bottle of Jack.

Norma eyed me over her cup. "Slow down. You might get a little tipsy," she teased.

"If I ever get drunk, please dunk my head in ice water and then lock me up." I wasn't kidding.

"You drink beer. Are you saying you've never been tipsy?" Her cute little eyebrows rose.

"I don't get drunk. I've only touched the hard stuff a couple of times, and I stopped. Drinking reminds me too much of my old man." As boys, Denim, Duke, and I would steal bottles of liquor from the cabinet. We'd wanted to see what the booze was all about since our father was addicted. After puking my guts out, I didn't go near liquor for a long time. "I'm worried about Nadine, the girl that came in last night."

"She's the one that fled the scene?"

"A girl I know brought her here. She ran into Nadine shortly after the standoff ended between the cops and a couple of gang members."

Norma lifted her chin. "Who's the girl you know?" Her tone was even.

We'd never dated—my choice, not hers. She was a pretty girl, blond hair, but not exactly my type. I liked women with meat on them. Maggie was a perfect example.

"Her name is Maggie Marx, and she's a girl I knew from my days in a gang."

She held her coffee cup close to her mouth. "I've never heard you talk about your gang days or a girl from your past."

My childhood wasn't something I reminisced about. "She's a reporter, and she's going to check her files for stories she's written on girls. Who knows? Grace might be one of those girls. Right now, though, Nadine isn't safe out on the streets. Anyway, you might see more of Maggie around here."

Norma's face blossomed into a cheeky smile.

I tapped in Rafe's number then hit the speaker button.

"What's up, boss?" Rafe asked.

"Nadine took off."

"Norma told me. Actually, I've been driving around the neighborhoods, looking for her. That's why I'm not back yet."

"I'll call Maggie. She might have some intel from her cop friend. Or maybe Nadine contacted Maggie."

When Rafe and I hung up, Norma grasped my hand. "Be careful. I mean with your heart. I don't want to see you get hurt."

"Where did that come from?" I felt as if I'd been hit from behind and had gotten whiplash.

She stood then set her coffee cup in the sink. "Your voice hitched when you said Maggie's name. Seems to me that you've had a thing for her since you were a kid." She wiped her hands on a dish towel. "I've got work to do."

When she passed me, I latched on to her arm. "Thank you for being a big sister."

She rested a hand on my scruffy face. "I would do anything for you, even beat anyone who had the nerve to break your heart." She kissed me on the cheek. "Now go release some steam. I don't want you to get an ulcer before you're thirty."

I already felt older than my twenty-six years.

"Kelton Maxwell is supposed to stop by, and I called the Guardian. They're sending Hunt Thompson over. He'll be working with us for a while. Oh, and you should have Hunt's contract in your email."

She gave me a cute smile. "It's on your desk." Then she sashayed through the living room and over to her computer.

I grabbed my phone and headed to the basement. Once at the bottom of the stairs, I flicked on the light. The entire basement was a workout room. Mats were scattered around on one side, and weights and a treadmill on the other side. I had big plans for the shelter, and one of those plans was to show women how to protect themselves, which was why I'd moved all my workout equipment from my house to the shelter. Plus, expending energy was a great stress reliever for the women as well.

I tore off my shirt and shoes then parked myself on the weight bench. I checked my messages before I called Maggie.

The first voice mail was from Norma, so I deleted that. The next voice mail was car horns and heavy breathing for about ten seconds until the honeyed voice I had embedded in my brain from last night said, "Seriously? I couldn't be excited from a voice on the phone." Then the message ended.

I listened to it again. I couldn't make out if Maggie was talking to herself and didn't realize the line had connected to my voice mail or if she was talking to someone else who had been with her.

Nevertheless, I smiled as if I'd gotten the biggest Christmas present in the family. *Talk about a voice to get me excited.* My fingers were primed to punch in her number, when heavy footsteps shook the ceiling above me. Voices droned, Norma's and Kelton's.

Then Kelton charged down the steps. "Hart, I hope I'm interrupting something with a woman down here."

I rolled my eyes.

The sharp-dressed Maxwell triplet emerged with his infamous cocky grin, while his blue eyes searched every nook and cranny. "No woman?"

"Why is your mind always on the opposite sex? Wait. Don't answer that." That was a dumb question on my part. Kelton Maxwell, former playboy, was now tied at the hip to Lizzie Reardon. She was beautiful and smart, the one girl who knew how to tame Kelton. She deserved an Academy Award for roping him in.

He tucked his hands in the pockets of his navy-blue pants. "You need to find a piece of ass or asses."

"Says the man who is almost married."

He scowled. "One, I'm not married. Two, I need to live vicariously through you now."

I snorted. "You'll be waiting a long time. So how goes the lawyer business?"

Kelton was working full time for a law firm in the city while law school was out for summer break.

He propped a shoulder against a support beam. "They got me working on simple cases when I'm not studying for the law exam. So what's up? You said something about your brother, Denim."

"He needs a good lawyer. I thought of you."

He slapped a hand over his heart. "I'm touched. You think I'm good. Aw."

"I know you're not out of law school yet. But can someone in your firm take a look at the case?"

He pinched his chin with his fingers. "Didn't you tell me no one would touch Denim's case?"

I leaned forward, elbows on my knees. "I only talked to one lawyer. Maybe he didn't look hard enough. Maybe the public defender didn't either."

"Why now, man?" Kelton asked. "If I recall, you and your brothers aren't tight."

A growl sat heavy in my throat. If I could have two wishes, one of course would have been to see Grace walk through my door, but the second one would have been to have a relationship with my brothers like the Maxwells had.

When I'd first seen the family together, the four brothers in particular, I'd gotten so envious of how close they were. How they would die for each other. How they put each other first. How protective they were of those they loved. How their parents were sickly sweet and doted on each other.

I wanted all that with my brothers and my family. But I would never have what they had, not with a brother in jail, a brother working illegal businesses, a sister who was nowhere to be found, and a father who thought booze was the love of his life. Oh, and a mother who had decided to leave her children behind.

"If I'm being honest, I want a relationship with my brother. Plus, I've never believed Denim purposely set out to murder anyone." I'd been so consumed with finding Grace that I hadn't paid attention to Denim, and after seeing him earlier, I missed the relationship we'd had as kids.

"For you, man, I'll look at the case. I'm not promising anything."

"Thanks." I could check another item off my to-do list. I'd accomplished a great deal before the clock struck noon. But the day wasn't over in the least. Nadine weighed on me.

Light footfalls prodded down the steps.

Kelton pushed off the beam and slid over to stand next to a cabinet so he could see who was coming down.

I glanced up, thinking it was Norma, but found Maggie with shock cascading off her as she fixated on Kelton.

My first instinct was to shove Kelton out of the room. The man was a female magnet.

Maggie's green gaze bounced from Kelton to me then back to Kelton. "Maxwell?" Her throat bobbed as she played with her scarf.

I wanted to vault off the bench and rip that flowery fabric from her neck. *No, you don't. You want to use Cory as a punching bag.*

One corner of Kelton's mouth tipped upward.

As I watched the silent exchange between Kelton and Maggie, it dawned on me. "You two slept together?"

Maggie's mouth fell open.

Kelton ran one of his large paws through his styled black hair. "I swear on my sister's grave that we didn't sleep together. The question is how do you two know each other?" He wagged a finger at us.

Kelton and I had been friends a long time, and I knew he was telling the truth. But the tension between him and Maggie felt like a fist to my gut.

Great way of deflecting, man. "Gang life." My gaze slid to the woman who was doing things to my body that I couldn't control. But the idea of Kelton and her, whether they'd slept together or not, tempered my libido.

Fucking Maxwell.

I would never forget the first time he'd shown up on my doorstep, looking for Lizzie. She and I had met through a cousin of mine because she'd wanted to purchase a gun. I'd offered her a place to stay and nothing more. Regardless, Kelton had had this bravado, which he still harbored, but that snowy day on my porch, Lizzie had all but brought him to his knees.

Allie and Bee had watched their exchange from behind a curtain. I couldn't help but watch too. I swore Lizzie had held a magic wand in her hand that day and waved it over Kelton, who had melted into a pile of mush in freezing temperatures. That was some power to have over a Maxwell brother.

Still, I couldn't help but feel a pang of jealousy, even though I knew the man was madly in love with Lizzie.

"I got to run," Kelton piped up, shredding my trip down memory lane. "We'll be in touch, Dillon." He swaggered up to Maggie.

I clenched my teeth hard. *If you touch her, I will coldcock you.*

He nodded at her. "Nice to see you again."

She stood statue-still. "Maxwell." She stole a glance at me with her lips slightly parted and her cheeks flushed.

Whether she was embarrassed or shocked or both, she didn't need to be. Her past was none of my business. Yet the idea of Maggie with any man, past or present, made my stomach knot in ways I'd never felt before.

10

MAGGIE

I didn't move from my spot at the bottom of the stairs. I didn't even open my mouth to speak, which was so unlike me. But Dillon's statement that Maxwell and I had slept together rendered me speechless. The tone in his voice screamed of jealousy, and that gave me mixed emotions. In one breath, I was all toasty inside, knowing that Dillon would fight for me. In another, his jealousy gave me reason to pause. Sometimes when men were fighting over a woman, that meant feelings were involved. Dillon couldn't possibly have feelings for me. After all, we didn't know each other well enough to develop any sort of feelings except for lust. Maybe I was reading too much into the situation.

The silence between us grew as I fiddled with my scarf. I wanted to speak, to say anything to break the tension, but I had no words. Not to mention, Dillon was shirtless. Tattoos not only decorated both arms, but his chest had the Latin phrase *alis grave nil* inscribed across a red bird wing. Latin had kicked my butt in college. I'd only taken the course because I thought it would be cool to learn a language from ancient times. The only word that had made sense to me was grave, which meant serious in both Latin and English.

Dillon dragged his gaze from my head down to my toes, which curled when he settled his eyes on my face. His hooded golden-brown eyes made me hold my breath as though we were standing toe to toe and his lips were a hair from mine.

I got the feeling he wanted to throw me on the mat and devour me. Yet my intuition was telling me he was trying to understand my relationship with Kelton.

"Kelton and I danced and drank, nothing more," I said, feeling compelled to give an explanation. I didn't have any lingering attraction to the Maxwell either. Sure, he was handsome, but not like the man in front of me.

Dillon gave me a cheeky grin. "I heard your voice message."

The topic of Kelton became a faded memory as my cheeks turned tomato red upon realizing Dillon had heard my admission about his sexy voice.

"Th-that." My knees finally unlocked at the mere thought that I'd just stuttered. I never stuttered. I dropped down on the bottom step. "Busted."

He finally chuckled and stood up. His jeans rode low, showing that thin line of hair, or what I liked to call the happy trail. "Nadine is gone."

And just like that, any tension, sexual or otherwise, was history. "Wait. So the cops didn't find her here?"

He tilted his head, and his hair flopped to one side. "Why would they find her here? Did you say something to your cop friend?"

I narrowed my eyes. "I promised her I wouldn't, and I didn't. Anyway, I was talking to Ted when he got the call that they'd found the redhead. Honestly, I thought you might have called them or that someone in the shelter did." I might as well lay my cards on the table too. After all, we both assumed the other had blabbed on Nadine.

He puffed out his cheeks. "No one here alerted the police. She took off early this morning. Nadine told one of my guests that she wasn't safe here and that she didn't want to put anyone in danger."

I gulped down a ball of fear as I clutched my stomach.

A muscle ticked in Dillon's jaw. "Is she alive?"

I squeezed my eyes closed for a second. God, I prayed she was. "When Ted got the call, he took off so fast, I didn't get a chance to ask him anything." It hadn't helped that my tongue wouldn't work.

Dillon brought his rough hands up to his mouth in prayer formation then began wearing a hole in the cement floor in a narrow spot off the matted area near me. "I shouldn't have left the shelter early this morning."

I pushed to my feet and grabbed his arm. "Stop. You're making me dizzy, and you can't blame yourself." I should've stayed at the shelter last night and kept Nadine company. She'd been alone and scared.

He looked at my hand then met my eyes. All thoughts of Nadine were slowly dissipating as my heart fluttered. Then Dillon's large palm was on my face.

Pitter-patter, pitter-patter went my heart.

I swore if his hungry gaze weren't preoccupied with my lips, he probably would have seen my heart pumping out of my chest.

I dragged a hand up the arm that had Grace inked on it.

He didn't flinch. Instead, he traced my bottom lip with the pad of his thumb. I'd never had anyone treat me so tenderly, as if I were a rare gem. The heat in the room rose and continued to rise the more his whiskey gaze roamed over my face, wild and free.

Oh, what I wouldn't give to run through fields of daisies with Dillon chasing me. Not to have a care in the world. Not to have revenge simmering in my blood. And not to have any memories of my childhood. I could stop my crusade to put Cory away. I could lose my memories by thinking of the future. But I had one problem.

I slid my hand under my scarf and fingered my scar. I would always have the memory of what Cory had done to me.

I choked back tears, when I wanted nothing more at that moment than for Dillon to kiss me and take away the memory of what I'd been through.

Touch me. Tempt me. Kiss me. Feel me. Those statements played like soft lyrics in my head.

Dillon lowered his hand until he was untying my scarf. "Maggie." My name on his lips was like discovering chocolate for the first time— sweet and addicting. He had rendered me powerless to do anything but bat my eyelashes.

His pinky finger danced over the sliver of scar that was poking out from the collar of the dirty shirt I'd pulled out of the laundry that day. Luckily, the shirt had only been worn once.

While he continued to feel along the scar, causing goose bumps to erupt along my arms, I mentally took pictures of his body. I wanted to remember every rugged edge. The man was an art specimen, with the Chinese symbol below Grace's name, the red wing on his chest, and a host of other symbols and Latin sayings. I swore he should be on display in some art studio where guests could admire him.

I scrubbed a hand over his pecs. "I think I might have a lead on Grace."

He jumped back as if I'd set him on fire. Turmoil, shock, and excitement washed over him. He found the cabinet that Kelton had been leaning against and used it to support himself as he shoved a hand through his tousled hair.

Stupid me had to go and talk.

He gave me flutters, sweaty palms, and tingles, weird feelings I'd never experienced with another man before. I wanted more of those wistful, steal-the-moment feelings that caused heat to blanket my body and made me feel as if I were the only woman in his world.

Sadly, I wasn't. His sister took that spot, and rightfully so, which was why my mouth was slightly ajar at how he wasn't probing me more for information on the bomb I'd dropped at his nice, bare feet. They were big, but clean and manicured.

I clapped my hands. "Dillon? Did you hear what I said?"

He flinched. "Loud and clear."

I ambled closer to him until I could reach out and touch him, but I didn't dare. We had business to take care of, and if I did touch him again, I wouldn't stop until we were tangled together.

I held on to the strap of my messenger bag. "Talk to me."

He stretched out one muscled arm and hooked a finger around the belt loop of my cotton slacks. "Why are you making me crazy?"

I giggled. I would like to have known that answer too. Not even twenty-four hours had passed since we'd reconnected after all these years, yet it felt like yesterday that we'd faced off in a fight that had ended in bloodshed. Not my bloodshed, but that of the boy who had dared to touch his sister.

I wanted to stay rooted to Dillon, but my musical ringtone, indicating that Bruce was calling, made me step back and dig into my bag. Dillon pushed off the wall and grabbed his shirt.

"What's up, boss?" I asked.

"Are you still down at the precinct?" Bruce sounded as if the story of the century was about to break.

"No. I'm following another lead." *One that has nothing to do with the Black Knights.* Or maybe it did. A girl could hope.

"The news is reporting that the cops found the body of a girl who they suspected was part of the standoff last night."

"Who? What does she look like? Do they have a name?" My entire being knew it was Nadine. Ted had even asked his caller if it was the redhead. Granted, I hadn't heard if it was or not.

When Dillon finished putting on his shirt, he angled his head at me.

"Sorry," Bruce said. "Don't know more than that. See what you can find out. This could be the opening you need for a story, maybe one on the Black Knights." Then he hung up.

I could rush down to the scene, wherever that was, or contact Ted. But since the news was just breaking, the information and evidence wouldn't be available yet. Tears burned my eyes as I tapped on my phone and searched the Internet for the news that Bruce had mentioned.

Dillon closed the distance between us then tipped up my chin with the touch of his finger. "It's Nadine. She's dead. Isn't she?"

I couldn't help but bawl my eyes out. "I think so. I should've stayed with her last night."

Dillon wrapped me into his hard, warm body, rubbing my back.

"It's not your fault. She was under my protection. I should've done everything I could to prevent her from leaving the shelter."

We stood in each other's arms. The only sound was me sniffling into his T-shirt. I wanted to stay glued to him, but he eased away then kissed me on the forehead. "Let's find out for sure if the body they found is in fact Nadine's."

I wiped tears away as I resumed searching the Internet. The headline came up, so I read it out loud in between sniffles. "Police found the dead body of a young girl they suspect to be part of a standoff last night." Deidre was the author on the story. She had to have someone in the police department feeding her information. That alone made me want to scream. "Sounds like Nadine. She was the only girl that I knew was there, although Ted's team was itching to show him something inside the house. Nadine didn't mention any other girls." Of course, I hadn't asked. I'd been so determined to find out if her captors were part of the Black Knights.

Revenge will blind you. Ted's words blared in my head.

I fired off a text to Ted, asking him about the headline and what the girl looked like. When I finished, I focused on Dillon. His eyes were somewhat glossy. He seemed to be somewhere far away.

It was my turn to wrap my arms around him. He didn't stiffen, nor did he back away. He let me hold him, and whether it was because of Nadine, Grace, or our past, the man was stealing my damn heart.

At that moment, I grew a little closer to Dillon.

He cleared his throat. "So, you said you had a lead on Grace?"

We untangled from each other.

"When I showed Ted Grace's picture, he was reminded of a girl he'd seen in a tattoo shop last year. We should check it out." I was there more about Nadine, and I did have a story to write, although Grace could be a story too.

"Don't you have work to do?" Dillon asked.

"I am working. I'm following a lead."

"Then I'll drive," Dillon said with renewed excitement.

I couldn't help but feed off him.

11

—————

DILLON

The woman sitting next to me in the passenger's seat was driving me batshit crazy, both emotionally and physically. Sure, my sister was front and center, and my heart broke for Nadine. But Maggie seemed to be overpowering what was most important to me—Grace. When Maggie had unloaded that she had a lead on Grace, my knees had locked as if she'd put a spell on me.

I'd never been so drawn to a woman before in my life. Her light, soapy scent fogged my brain, even more so when she'd been in my arms. Man, the way her cotton slacks hugged her curves sent waves of heat straight to my groin. And her hair—her hair was braided, the tail falling down to the middle of her back, and all I wanted to do was wrap my hand around it while I did things to her I never thought I would do to any woman. Maggie gave me the vibe that she liked her men raw and rough, and that made my dick hard.

When I'd run my finger over her bottom lip, I'd stopped the shudder that was primed to rack my body. More than that, I'd been close to throwing her to the mat in the weight room. I would've done it if she hadn't broken down in tears.

Flicking the blinker, I made a right onto Harrison Avenue. When I did, my blood gelled.

My foot hovered over the brake, tapping it now and again to slow the car. Familiar storefronts with apartments above them, graffitied walls, and run-down buildings decorated the street. My head swiveled sluggishly before the boarded-up apartment building on the corner sent me back to the past.

A horn blared behind me.

Maggie slapped my arm. "Snap to."

The only thing I was about to snap was my steering wheel. It couldn't have been a coincidence that Detective Hughes had seen a female who resembled Grace in a tattoo shop on Harrison Avenue. I didn't believe in coincidences.

My heart beat like the little drummer boy.

If the girl Ted had seen was Grace, that meant Grace was alive a year ago.

My heart was ramming against my ribs. *But why hadn't she contacted my brothers or me? You left her. Maybe she doesn't want to see you.* I refused to believe that my own sister would disown me as though I were someone she hated. Maybe she thought I was still at sea with the merchant marines. It had been hard to communicate with anyone back home when I was on a ship in the middle of the ocean.

My gut twisted.

My head hurt.

My heart was on a collision course with a sharp object. At least I felt as though the dull pain in my heart was intensifying, particularly if Grace didn't want anything to do with me.

"Did you hear what I said? Skins and Needles is one block up, on the right." Maggie pointed out the windshield.

I grunted for no other reason than not to scream at the top of my lungs. Confusion, anger, and excitement had a way of tangling together to the point that I was almost seeing stars.

I pulled into a spot in front of a cigar shop.

Maggie gripped my arm. "You're pale."

I released an audible sigh. "I've walked this street up and down for hours, watching that apartment." I stabbed a finger at a run-down building next to the one that had graffiti painted on the foundation. "When she first left home—ran away, disappeared, who the fuck knows—a friend of hers told me she hung out with a boy who lived there."

Maggie's green eyes glistened as she opened them wide.

"It was a dead end. The last time the boy saw Grace was a week before I knocked on his door when she first went missing." It was more than a dead end now that the building was abandoned.

I climbed out, careful not to swing open my door too wide with the oncoming traffic. The hot August sun was sliding down behind the row of buildings across the street. A handful of pedestrians walked in and out of stores.

I joined Maggie on the sidewalk outside the cigar shop.

She hooked her arm in mine. "You're still pale. I think you need my help."

What she deemed help differed from my definition. I might have been in shock at the moment, but I wasn't immune to her female scents or charms. The woman had some magic juice in her that made me want to fall on my knees and kiss her feet.

Fuck, man. Get your head out of your ass and stop thinking about your dick.

I chuckled at myself.

"Something funny," she asked as we strolled like two lovers in a park.

"I'm not eighty."

She giggled. "It seems you've been off since I showed up at the shelter."

Maybe if I wasn't still processing you and Kelton dancing, which meant groping each other, then I might have a clear head. Or maybe I could think if I didn't feel responsible for Nadine, or you weren't driving me mad with the urge to fuck your brains out.

I gently unhooked her hand from my arm.

She frowned.

"Business before pleasure." I tipped my head at the Skins and Needles sign as I opened the door for her.

The bell dinged.

Shrugging, she sashayed in with a smile. "I like working with you."

And I want to see you writhing underneath me as we roll around on the matted floor, naked, sweaty, and enjoying the heck out of each other.

Following her inside to an empty shop, I mentally slapped myself and kept slapping myself as I ogled her ass.

The light aroma of cigars trickled up my nose, probably from the shop next door. The buzz of the tattoo machine filtered in from behind the curtained-off room directly ahead of us.

Maggie planted her hands on the glass-enclosed counter that had sketches of colorful artwork displayed inside, much like a jewelry case. She glanced down while I moseyed over to the loveseat near the curtain. Above the loveseat hung the business owner's license. Syd Wells was the name on the fancy paper.

"Hello," I said to no one.

"They're probably busy," Maggie added, checking out sketches as though she were deciding which tattoo she wanted. "I'm sure they heard the bell."

"I'll be right out," a male voice said.

I sauntered over to Maggie. "Which one do you want?" I wondered if she was sporting any tats underneath her clothes.

Her head came up. "Oh, hell no. I hate needles." She touched her neck.

I imagined that Cory was the reason she didn't like sharp objects. I didn't get a chance to ponder or speculate before a large man with scraggly blond hair emerged.

He wiped his hands on a towel. "How can I help?"

"Are you Syd?" I asked.

His beady hazel eyes shifted back and forth between us. "Who's asking? Are you two cops?"

"I get that a lot," Maggie said. "No."

I snatched my wallet and produced Grace's photo. "I'm looking for my sister, Grace Hart. We have reason to believe someone in this shop did some artwork on her. Have you seen her?"

Lowering his shoulders, Syd studied the photo while he scrubbed his dirty nails down his jaw. "That mark on her neck." His head bobbed. "Her name isn't Grace. She goes by Emily."

I swore an eighteen-wheeler came out of nowhere and smashed into me. I listed to one side.

Maggie's hands were on me. "Easy, big guy."

Syd threw his towel on the counter along with Grace's photo. "Take him to the couch."

Maggie guided me to the dilapidated couch, while Syd rummaged around in a cabinet near the curtain.

I sat down, staring at the dirty tiled floor. "You said her name was Emily."

Sitting down, Maggie wrapped one arm around my back and put her other hand on my bicep.

Syd handed me a bottle of water. "I would give you the hard stuff if I had any in the shop." He snatched Grace's picture and handed it to me. "That's the name she gave me. She's also self-conscious about her birthmark. So I tattooed and blended the mark into a colorful bird." He grinned as though he were remembering his art.

"Let me guess. A hummingbird?" Grace loved those birds and how they would frequent the flowery trees we had in our backyard.

Syd nodded several times. "I've done quite a few of her tats."

Whoa! "Has Grace been in here recently?" My stomach clenched.

"You mean Emily." He shook his head. "Not lately."

I shoved my fingers into my hair, grabbed a bunch, and yanked while I tried to get air in my lungs.

"Dillon, you stiffen when he says Emily." Maggie's tone held concern.

I shuddered. "Emily is my mother's name." I was stumped as to why Grace would change her name. The only thing I could think of was that she didn't want to be found, or maybe she just didn't like the name Grace.

Maggie gaped. "For real?"

I twisted the cap off the water. This one time, maybe a sip of alcohol would have calmed my nerves. Nevertheless, I chugged the warm liquid, which did nothing to soothe the fire in my throat.

Syd raised a finger. "You know, let me check my records to see the last time she was in." Syd's big body vanished behind the curtain.

I threw my head in my hands. My pulse bashed in my ears. *Boom. Boom. Boom.*

Maggie rubbed my back. Her efforts did nothing to douse the raging fire going on inside me.

Grace is alive. Grace is alive. Those three words blared in my head like a tornado siren.

I hurtled upright, grabbed the back of my neck, and walked over to the exit. Cars idled on the street, waiting for the light to turn green. Pedestrians went about their day as though they didn't have a care in the world. I would've given anything not to have lost sleep night after night, wondering if Grace was alive when, lo and behold, she was. I couldn't process the information. I didn't know how.

"Six months," Syd said at my back. "She was in six months ago."

I clenched my fists. I flared my nostrils. I tensed every muscle in my body.

She was at this tattoo shop six months ago. Six months ago. *Six months ago.*

I was never one to panic. I was never one to fly off the handle. I was never the person to punch first and ask questions later.

But I was on the verge of becoming someone I wasn't. I was on the verge of blowing a hole in the glass door with my fists. I was on the verge of losing my fucking mind. I should've been thrilled that my baby sister, the one I adored, the little girl who'd trusted me, was alive and had been for all these years.

I had scoured the streets, night after night. I'd practically lived at the morgues. I had put my heart and soul into finding her, and she was alive.

Maggie hovered close to me, but not that close. It was as though she were ready to catch me if I fell.

"If it's any consolation," Syd said in a somewhat tender voice, "Emily never appeared hurt or scared. She also didn't seem like she was running from anyone either."

The jagged jaws of a vise clamped down on my stomach, tighter than ever.

Duke's words flashed like a neon sign in my head. *"Maybe she doesn't want to be found."*

Why the fuck not? That was the burning question.

"So you never saw bruises on her?" Maggie asked. "Or any tats that indicated she's part of a gang? Say the Black Knights."

I could see Syd's reflection in the glass, and he shook his head. "No."

I should have taken comfort that she hadn't followed in my footsteps and joined a gang. Yet the word gang was becoming synonymous with sex trafficking, and the thought of Grace being involved in that felt as if someone had driven a dagger into my chest.

Crushing Grace's photo with my left hand, I pivoted on my heel and stifled every ounce of emotion I could. "Do you have any contact info on my sister? Or was she with anyone when she came in?"

Syd pressed his fat fingers on the counter. "I don't keep addresses and phone numbers on my clients, and she was alone each time she came in. Also no upcoming appointments either if that was your next question."

I got the feeling Syd was in tune to answering questions like this. After all, Detective Hughes had been in the shop once before to ask questions.

I stretched out my hand to Syd. "Thanks for your help."

He gave me a pitiful look as we shook. "I hope you find her." Then he grabbed a pen and paper from the counter. "Give me your name and number, and if she comes in, I'll give you a call."

After I scribbled down my info, which was barely legible, I stalked to the door, needing to rid my lungs of the cigar smell drifting around.

Syd cleared his throat. "Wait. I remembered something."

I gripped the doorknob and swore if he said something like *she was in here yesterday,* I would destroy everything in the shop.

"I overheard Emily talking on the phone the last time she was here about meeting someone at a bar called the Crow, if that helps."

I wanted to scream at him not to call her Emily. I didn't need a reminder of the woman who had left her children with the monster from hell. I did, however, wonder why Grace would use the name Emily. She hardly knew our mother. Grace had been two when our mother had walked out the door without even a goodbye or an "I'll be back for you kids soon."

I thanked Syd one last time and got the hell out into the fresh air before my lungs disintegrated into ash. I didn't even wait for Maggie. I walked up and down the street, stomping my feet into the uneven pavement and shaking my head as if I were a second away from seriously losing my mind.

Maggie leaned against my car, giving me the space I needed to cool down. I was going to need more than a bucket of ice to temper the madness taking hold of me.

After another round of pacing, I stopped near Maggie, bent over, and braced my hands on my thighs. The woman was seeing me lose my shit, but I didn't care.

I counted to ten slowly, breathing in the scents of the city, which were far better than the stench of cigars. Then I righted myself and focused on Maggie.

Her braid spilled down her chest. Sparkles glimmered around her eyes from the light-green eye shadow she was wearing that highlighted the dark green in her eyes. Her hands were tucked in her pockets, and she didn't give me any sense that she felt sorry for me.

"Are you ready to head to the Crow?" she asked.

12

MAGGIE

W e drove through the city streets in complete silence. I wanted to give Dillon some space to absorb what we had just learned. Several times, I itched to console him like he had me when we'd found out about the dead redhead. Ted hadn't returned my call yet, but right now my biggest concern was Dillon. I wasn't going to leave him in the state of mind he was in.

The traffic was the usual stop and go at red lights and roundabouts. Dillon's focus was on the road, while a muscle jumped along his jaw. Several times since we'd gotten in the car, I itched to rub his arm or take hold of his hand, but sometimes when I was thinking hard, I didn't want to be disturbed.

So I did a search on the Internet of the Crow and its location. The club's website indicated the address was located in an industrial zone of South Boston.

"If you want to check out the Crow, it's south of here," I said.

Dillon shook his head, his features still rock-solid with so many emotions.

I couldn't take it anymore. I grabbed his hand, which was fiddling with the cap of a water bottle.

He quickly jerked his head at me. Then as if some of the darkness was pulled from him, he gave me a half smile and squeezed the hell out of my hand. "I'm not ready to go to some bar right now. I need to regroup. I'm afraid I might tear someone's head off if they so much as tell me they've seen Grace recently."

"So where are we going?" We weren't headed in the direction of the shelter. Maybe he was taking me to his place. I wondered for a second if he lived at the shelter or had his own apartment. After all, the shelter was a nice home in an okay neighborhood.

He braked at a red light. "Do you need to return to work?"

I checked the time on the dashboard clock. Bruce would be wondering if I'd gotten a scoop on the dead redhead or if I had some meat for a story. But like any other day, I could work until the wee hours of the morning. As long as I had something for a story, Bruce didn't mind if I returned during normal work hours or not.

"I'm good." I couldn't leave Dillon in his state of mind. Well, I could, but I didn't want to. I'd been as shocked as him when Syd had shared all that information on Grace, or Emily as she was calling herself.

It was clear to me that Grace didn't want to be found. People changed their names for all kinds of reasons, but the most popular was either entering the witness protection program—which I didn't think was Grace's reason since she'd left home at sixteen, never to be seen again—or working as a call girl. My source, Misty, had changed her name. She'd revealed that fact when I asked her. She'd told me that all runaways or girls who didn't want even their pimps to know who they really were changed their names. I didn't need to add to Dillon's turmoil, so I decided not to share that tidbit.

Before long, we were pulling into Paul Revere Park, which was located next to Charlestown. The Zakim Bridge poked out in the distance, while pedestrians strolled along the myriad of paths surrounded by colorful perennials and ornamental grasses.

One of my colleagues had done a piece about the park and had described the area as multi-functional because its oval shape served as an amphitheater and concert stage for performances.

Dillon killed the engine. "Grace, my brothers, and I would come down here as kids. Parts of the park weren't completely done, and Duke liked to watch the construction. Grace loved the flowers. As for Denim and me, we liked to throw the baseball around. Come on."

The sun was still high in the sky for late afternoon. Inhaling the scent of fresh-cut grass, I couldn't help but feel all giddy inside. I was about to stroll through a park on a beautiful and hot summer day with a man who was making me want to give him my heart. I was beginning to think he had captured it when I'd first learned he owned a shelter.

As we wound our way down a path, Dillon's slipped his hand in mine.

Whoa! My belly was full of wild butterflies.

"You calm me, Maggie," he said.

I let out a soft chuckle, more out of nerves than anything. "Men have told me lots of things, but nothing like that."

"So they haven't told you how beautiful you are?"

We both kept our eyes on the path. I was afraid if I looked at him, I would get down on one knee and ask him to marry me. Okay, that was a little far reaching, considering I didn't want a serious relationship, or at least I hadn't until I met Dillon. Maybe marriage wasn't so far-fetched.

"Thank you," was all I could say. Only one other man had told me I was beautiful, and that was Lou, my former gang leader, when he was nursing me back to health. Actually, Lou had said I was pretty, even with the scar on my neck. I knew he'd been trying to lift my spirits and instill confidence in me. His compliment had drawn a smile out of me, but I'd had low self-esteem until I learned how to fight. Knowing I could protect myself made me stand up straighter, although I didn't want anyone to see my scar.

Dillon and I found an empty bench and sat down. He leaned his elbows on his knees. "What would you do if Cory was standing here right now?"

I did a double take. No one had ever asked me that question.

Dillon sat up and faced me. His golden-brown eyes were filled with so many questions.

I shrugged. "At first, I wanted to kill him. For so long, he's haunted my dreams. You know that Cory gave me the scar. What you might not know is that he raped me." I couldn't recall if Dillon knew that part or not, although word about my rape and stabbing had been whispered in gangs after Lou had rescued me. "Anyway, I couldn't repeat his name. I couldn't go to the cops. I couldn't even walk down a dark street anymore. But Lou showed me that I was a strong person. He taught me that as much as I feared something, that fear made me stronger. But after years of thinking about Cory and planning his death, I realized after Lou died that death wasn't the answer for Cory. He should suffer in jail with no option to ever get out. That and I didn't want to go to jail for murder. But if he were standing here right now, I would probably beat him until he was close to death but still breathing."

A crease formed in between Dillon's eyebrows. "Why didn't you go to the cops after he raped you?"

"I was scared of Cory retaliating. I was scared of returning to the foster care system. I couldn't go back to a home that was infested with hate and a drunk foster dad who was like Cory."

Dillon clenched his fists in his lap as he let out a low growl.

I rested my hand on his. "It's okay. I'm okay." It was evident he wanted to bash in some heads. "Why did you ask me about Cory?"

His chest lifted. "Because I'm not sure what I would do if Grace was standing in front of me. I'm mad at her. I'm hurt. I'm so many things right now."

Shock rifled through me at his admission of how he felt about his sister, although I could see how torn up he'd been at Syd's over learning that Grace could be alive.

"If that time ever comes, then I'm sure you will handle your reunion with the utmost love you have for her."

My phone beeped with a text. I didn't want to be rude and change the subject, but the text could be from Ted. I snatched my phone from the front pocket of my messenger bag. The text was from Bruce. *Did you get anywhere on the dead redhead?*

I sighed. I should get back to work.

As if he knew what I was thinking, Dillon said, "Let's go. I know you have to work."

We started for his car.

"I'm sorry," I said. "Maybe we can swing by the Crow later?"

"Maybe. Call me when you're done with work."

13

———

DILLON

After Maggie and I got back to the shelter, she took off immediately. She had work to do, and she was itching to talk to Ted since he'd never responded to her text. We still weren't sure if the girl they'd found dead was Nadine. I prayed it wasn't.

By the time I walked into the shelter, I'd lost some of my anger, thanks to Maggie. I'd been serious when I told her that she had a way of tranquilizing me. Her hand in mine was like a drug. On the flip side, listening to her tell me about Cory was both maddening and enlightening. In one breath, I wanted to do exactly what she'd said she would do if he'd been in the park with us. Yet she was so sure of herself, and I admired how she knew what she would do. I had no idea how I would react if I saw Grace.

Norma's laughter filled the room. Then a baritone voice echoed as a man chuckled. At first, I thought Norma had invited her boyfriend over until I sauntered into the kitchen and found Hunter Thompson, or Hunt as he liked to be called, standing at the island with a soda in his hand. I was a tall guy, but Hunt had three inches on me at six foot four, and he was built like a bear.

We exchanged a manly hug. The last time I'd seen Hunt was at

Kade and Lacey's wedding back in June when he was dressed in a tux and holding Kade's hand as his best man. Now he sported a golf shirt with the Guardian logo embroidered on the sleeve. He wore a holster around the waist of his jeans but didn't have a gun.

I dropped my keys on the island. "Thanks for coming on board."

His head dipped, and when it did, a stray blond curl fell over the scar he had above his left eyebrow. "It's a nice change from the crazies I usually protect."

He had no idea what he was in store for, particularly with men like Norton. But I would fill him in later. Right now, I needed a stiff drink. A laugh broke out in my head. A dormant part of me was my father's son. I did want to down something so strong, it would take away all the fucked-up emotions raging inside me. That calming effect Maggie had on me was wearing off.

Grace could be alive, and she'd never bothered to contact me.

She may not be able to. Someone may be holding her hostage.

Syd had led me to believe that Grace was happy and healthy and living her life without our father degrading her and swinging his fist at her face.

"You need to sign the contract before Hunt can start." Norma's soft voice cut through the hell that was waging a war in my head. When I blinked, she was hurrying out of the kitchen. "I'll get the documents."

Hunt straddled the stool. "You don't look so good."

I padded over to the fridge and grabbed a bottle of water then slid onto Norma's warm stool.

"Norma tells me you were chasing a lead on your sister. Is that why you look like someone pistol-whipped you?" Hunt brought the can up to his lips. "Do you need some help? The Guardian is a security firm, but they also have a couple of private investigators on staff."

I twisted the cap off the bottle. "I hired a PI about a year and a half ago, but he wasn't successful. Do you know of a bar called the Crow?"

Hunt worked many jobs at the Guardian, and one of them was a bouncer for clubs around the city. The only thing I knew about the

Crow was what Maggie had shared in the car, which wasn't much except that it was in South Boston.

Hunt shifted his brown eyes back and forth, studying me hard before the scar over his left brow crinkled. "It's a dive bar, or more like a biker hangout. Did someone see her there?"

I sucked my lip ring into my mouth. "Nah." I proceeded to tell him about the conversation I'd had with Syd.

When I finished my story, he said, "Anything could have happened in six months. I'll take some pressure off you around here. I'll work with your man, Rafe, and we'll keep things here buttoned up. Norma seems to have a handle on things too. So go fish out that lead." He glanced at his watch. "The bar should be getting busy in a few hours."

"Are you my knight in shining armor?" I teased.

He grinned, showing a set of perfect choppers. "I don't swing that way, dude."

I was about to ask him how his best bud, Kade, was doing after his honeymoon, when his phone rang. Fishing it out of his jeans, he headed outside to the small deck in the backyard, making himself right at home.

I played with my bottle cap, hoping someday I could have a relationship like Kade and Lacey had. I always knew the Maxwells loved hard. But seeing Kade say "I do" with enough love pouring off him to fill the lake behind their house shot shards of envy through me, almost tempting me to get married.

I laughed out loud.

Norma glided in. "Something funny?" She set the contract down in front of me then handed me a pen.

"I was thinking of Kade's wedding."

She sighed and gave me a funny look. "Oh my God. Why are you thinking about a wedding? I know you and Maggie are old rival gang buds, but jeepers, she didn't swoop you off your feet already, did she? And where is she, by the way?"

My cheeks heated. Before we'd gone to the tattoo shop earlier, Maggie and Norma had started chatting up a storm about scarves and shit. I took comfort knowing that Norma approved of Maggie. "She had work to do."

Norma's mouth was slightly ajar. "Are you blushing? Dillon Hart blushes for the first time since I've met him. This should be one of Maggie's headlines."

I laughed… and fucking blushed. *Since when do I get light-headed?*

Norma's small fingers grasped my hand.

I stopped fiddling with the pen.

"You need rest and a shower," she said. "Sign the contract and then head home. The shelter will be fine. Debbie is on cold meds, so she's asleep. Angel is curled up in her room, reading a thriller series. Rafe will be back shortly. He went home to shower. Hunt is here now. He'll start tonight."

I signed the contract. "Are you saying I stink?" I probably did with as hot as it was. I also needed a nap to take the edge off.

The slider whooshed open. "Sorry about that." Hunt stalked back in. "My brother, Wes, wanted to make sure you signed the contract."

I waved the document at him then gave it to Norma.

"I'll send it over to him right now." Her short legs carried her out of the room.

I trusted Norma. I trusted Rafe. And if Kade trusted Hunt with his life, then I had no worries about leaving the shelter with Hunt working security.

I got up and slapped Hunt on the back. "Thanks, man. I'll check in with you and Rafe later." I took the bottle of water and grabbed my keys.

"I'll walk out with you," Hunt said. "I need to get something out of my car."

I said goodbye to Norma then left. Once outside, Hunt strutted over to his truck that was parked at the curb, stuck his head inside, and emerged with a gun in his hand. He then proceeded to tuck the gun in his holster. "Be careful if you venture over to the Crow. Wes told me that place could get rowdy the later you go."

I was just coming down the last step on the porch, when a car screeched to a halt, blocking my driveway.

Hunt didn't move from the sidewalk.

A man with a thick mustache climbed out of the passenger's side with a gun in his holster. He regarded me then Hunt. "Is that you, Hunt?" the man asked.

The driver, stocky and somewhat bald, got out, rounded the vehicle, and sidled up to his partner.

Hunt met the two men halfway and stretched out his hand. "Detective Hughes, good to see you. Rick."

I darted over to my car, threw my water bottle on the driver's seat, then joined the men. So this was Hughes. I should thank him for turning Maggie onto Skins and Needles.

Rick took in the shelter before he set his gaze on me. "Are you the owner?"

"I'm Dillon Hart, and yes, I own this house. Is there a problem?" I hadn't done anything wrong, although maybe Maggie had told Hughes Nadine had been here, and he wanted to question me about the redhead.

Detective Hughes's head jerked my way. "You're Maggie's friend?" His tone hinted that he didn't care too much that Maggie was friends with me.

I nodded as Hunt regarded me with a confused expression.

"She's not here, is she?" Detective Hughes asked.

"Last I knew, she was at her office."

Rick rested his hand on the gun at his hip as though he were expecting trouble. "We have a lead that we're following up on."

Ted removed a photo from his back pocket and showed Hunt and me. "Have you seen this girl?"

I deadpanned at the picture of Nadine with a sheet covering her up to her neck. A sharp pain cinched my heart. If I said yes, they might raid the shelter. Then Debbie and Angel would panic for sure. And if word got out that the cops had searched the home, then that could ruin my business. In addition, I wasn't sure if Maggie would get into trouble with Hughes. A dark part of my brain wondered if Hughes knew Nadine had been there and wanted to see if I would lie.

My phone buzzed then rang. For the moment, I chose to let the call go to voice mail. It couldn't have been important anyway since I was at the shelter, unless Allie or Bee was in trouble. Or maybe Denim had found out something on the Black Knights. I threw out the last one since Denim had said he would be in the yard with cellblock E on Thursday, and it was only Tuesday night.

The ringing stopped.

"Can't say I have." Hunt's baritone voice pulled me back to the scorching night.

I shook my head once. "I haven't either." I couldn't answer truthfully without knowing if I would get Maggie into trouble.

The detectives glanced at one another as though they were speaking telepathically.

"Mmm," Hughes all but grunted. "We're canvasing the area since her body was found a mile from here."

My blood drained to my feet. *Did the men who held her captive follow her and Maggie here last night?*

Motherfucker.

Maggie could be in danger. The shelter could be too, and that alone caused me to squeeze the hell out of my keys.

Hunt nudged me. "What's wrong?" The man was a savant in reading people. I was sure the two detectives were as well, especially with the way Ted was giving the stink eye, as if to say *yeah, I know you're lying.*

My phone buzzed again.

This time I plucked it out of my pocket, not even looking to see who was calling. "Yeah." I said the word hard and abrupt, like *this better be good.*

"I've been trying to call you." Maggie's sultry voice calmed me for a second.

I covered the phone. "I have to take this." I walked down the street a ways, not bothering to wait for any acknowledgements from the detectives. If they wanted to haul me down to the station, then they were going to have to fight me.

When I was out of earshot, I said, "Ted is standing in my driveway at the shelter."

"That was why I was calling." Maggie's voice hitched. "The girl they found is Nadine. They found her not far from the shelter. Did you tell him that Nadine had been there?"

"No. Did you?"

"I haven't been able to. When I called him, the line went to voice mail."

"If they got to Nadine a mile from here, then you were followed last night. Ted needs to know."

"Let me tell him," Maggie said. "Besides, if you change your answer now, he'll just barrel into the shelter and start asking questions to your guests. They don't need that."

It touched me that she had Debbie and Angel's best interests at heart. "Fair enough. Oh, and Maggie, promise me you'll watch your back."

"Are you worried about me?" Her voice was sweet and silky, and the softness was sending a jolt of energy directly south.

I was worried about her. I was also a little concerned about a pimp or a gang that might be into sex trafficking knowing that I owned a shelter. Sure, they could find prostitutes and homeless women on the streets for their business, but the shelter might be an easy target to woo my guests or to kidnap them, especially if Nadine told her pimp where she'd been last night.

"Are we on to head to the Crow later?" she asked.

"Meet me at my house in two hours. I'll text you the address."

"Dillon," Hunt called.

"Got to run." I ended the call before I spilled my guts and said something I might regret, like I was developing feelings for her. The lust for her was messing with my head. That much, I was certain of. Or maybe I was falling for her.

I rolled back my shoulders and returned to the group.

A radio from the car crackled. Rick dipped his head inside.

Ted regarded me with cold, dark eyes. "You look nothing like your brother, Denim."

I did a double take. "You know my brother?"

"I arrested him," Ted said, as though he were proud of that day.

I couldn't recall who the arresting officer was in Denim's case. When I'd found out what my brother had done, he was already in jail. I had Grace to find anyway. She'd taken up my life more so than my brother.

"He's innocent," I volleyed back.

"Is that right?" Ted asked. "The evidence doesn't say so."

Rick popped his head out of the car. "Hey, boss. We got to run. Paul found something on our dead girl you're not going to like."

Ted considered me one more time before he and Rick got into the car and sped off.

"Asshole," I muttered.

Maggie had a soft spot for the cop, but fuck if I would. I had no doubt he had already formed his opinion of me before he met me.

"Easy, big guy," Hunt said. "That cop can make your life suck the big one."

Whatever.

"You knew the girl in that photo, didn't you?" Hunt said more than asked.

It was best I didn't involve him. I'd hired him to watch the shelter, nothing more. "I appreciate your help, but I'll handle the detectives."

Hunt caught my arm. "I'm here if you need me."

"Thanks. I'll call you later." I stormed over to my car, got in, and drove away.

I didn't need him. I needed Maggie.

14

───────

MAGGIE

I stood on Dillon's front porch in an upscale neighborhood with manicured lawns, nice, shiny cars parked in driveways, and two- and three-story homes that seemed cozy and lived-in by the looks of the curtains and soft lights in the windows. This was a major step up from where the shelter was located.

Damn, the man had done well for himself.

My knuckles were primed to knock, when my phone trilled. Ted's name came across the screen. I'd called him about twenty minutes after I'd spoken to Dillon. I'd wanted to give Ted enough time to wrap up his business with Dillon. Since then, Ted and I had been playing phone tag for one reason or another.

I'd never intended for Dillon to lie for me, and I hated that he had. Ted wasn't going to be happy when he found out either, which would strain any chance of him trusting Dillon, especially when Ted had arrested Denim.

Aside from that, when I'd learned from Deidre's news segment that Nadine's body had been found a mile from the shelter, I'd almost fallen off my desk chair. I wanted to believe that she and I weren't followed that night, but how else would anyone have known where to find Nadine unless she'd contacted someone before she left the shelter. I didn't remember if she'd had a phone on her, but the shelter had landlines.

"Hey," I said into the phone.

"I need you to come down to the precinct," Ted said coldly.

Icy chills zipped down my spine. "Why?" Usually when Ted wanted to chat, we always met at the coffee house down from the precinct. "Too many ears," Ted would say.

I had a feeling I was in trouble. Maybe Dillon had told Ted the truth after we'd hung up. Also if Ted wanted to share any information with the press, he would've said that.

"Just get down here. I have another call coming in." Then the line went dead.

I dropped my head back and sighed. If I didn't get my butt down to the police station, then Ted would put out a search party for me. But I was at Dillon's already. I had to at least tell him that I couldn't go with him to the Crow.

I was primed to knock again, when the door opened, and I lost my breath.

"I thought I heard something out here," Dillon said with a predatory grin as he casually held the edge of the doorjamb.

My stomach did a flip or two as I perused his tall body.

His hair was wet. Tattered jeans hugged his toned legs. His button-up shirt was open, showing parts of his winged tattoo. As if the god-like sight of him wasn't enough to send my body into a frenzy, I caught a whiff of his cologne, fresh and clean, on the light breeze, and I almost whimpered.

He opened his arm to wave me inside.

I shouldn't go in. Danger signals were flashing—seductive danger signals. *Tell him you have to leave.* The problem was my tongue was stuck to the roof of my mouth.

"You're letting out the cold air," he rasped.

His voice was igniting my body, and if that weren't enough to send me into overdrive, his gaze sure was as it did one of those roaming patterns, just like he'd done when I'd been standing in his basement. Then and now, my body quivered, and I swore I had a hundred and ten degree temperature.

I needed water desperately. I also needed to take a cold shower, but as the chilly air filtered out and over me, my legs moved until I was standing in his house, which felt like an icebox.

The door closed. The lock clicked.

I flinched.

Then Dillon's hands were on my shoulders as his breath tickled the back of my neck. He gently removed my heavy bag from my body. "Relax."

I giggled nervously. I considered myself a confident woman. I didn't mince words. I never melted into a pool of water when a handsome man touched me or was near me or even spoke. I was seeing a side of myself that was new territory—scary and amazing all at the same time.

As soon as I was free of the weight of the bag, I waltzed down the hall along the staircase, passing a living room and a bathroom before I entered the kitchen. Water, ice-cold, was on my mind, not how clean and nice his house was.

The sink was deep, and the faucet had one of those spray nozzles that would work to wash the sweat from my face and lower my body temperature.

Dillon's bare feet thudded until he was again near me at the sink.

"Water," I said.

He snatched a cup from the cabinet, added ice, then water from the built-in feature on the fridge.

When he handed me the cup, his fingers grazed mine ever so lightly, and tingles shot up along my scalp. Usually, I only felt that way when my hairdresser shampooed my hair.

My damn heartbeat was on a collision course with my ribs. I didn't waste any time gulping down the cool liquid, which didn't make a dent in quenching the fire burning a hole in my throat, nor did it calm the need that pulsed in my erect nipples.

Once the cup was empty, I set it down on the counter, looking at the floor rather than Dillon. I was afraid I would combust if I met his gaze.

Get a grip, woman. You're strong. You're confident, and no one rattles your cage. They haven't since Lou toughened you up.

I mentally slapped myself for being a nervous ninny. I'd slept with men before. Yet if I were being honest with myself, I was afraid that one night with Dillon Hart would ruin me. I wasn't completely sure I was ready to be ruined. I had a good life. I was working on getting my revenge on Cory. I got laid when I wanted. I didn't have to worry about someone breaking my heart or me breaking his.

Dillon, who hadn't left my personal space, placed a finger underneath my chin, gentle but firm. "Are you calm now? You seem nervous. Is it Ted? Did you tell him about Nadine?"

He'd said Ted's name as though he were ready to do a number on him, just as he'd done on that boy in my gang who had messed with Grace. Nevertheless, at the sound of Ted's name, my head came up and my eyes met his. My lust-filled bubble burst, and I felt a small amount of relief. For the moment, I didn't want to crawl up Dillon's hard body. I had to get down to the precinct.

"We've been playing phone tag." My voice sounded like Minnie Mouse.

Dillon's tongue snaked out like one of the bearded dragons I loved. And in the blink of an eye, that lust, primal and strong, came back with a vengeance. Ted's name was forgotten. The room dimmed. The hum of the fridge played like soft music, setting the mood. And boy, the mood was filled with tension, lust, anticipation, and heavy breathing, on my part anyway.

My chest rose, pushing out my big breasts that I sometimes wished were a tad smaller, only because they occasionally got in the way. But this was one time I wanted them to get in the way. I wanted to will

Dillon's hands to grab onto them, or at least relieve the pain throbbing in my nipples.

His gaze lowered the minute my chest lifted on an inhale. This time, he ran his tongue over his lip ring. His hooded eyes told me a story I would never write for the paper—maybe my journal or a filthy romance novel. Despite all that, I was dying to know how that shiny, smooth lip ring would feel against my clit.

As though we were slow dancing, he shaped my hips, turned me so my back was leaning against the counter, then caged me in as if I were an animal he was trying to tame.

I wanted to scream that I was a bad girl and needed to be taught a lesson. I wasn't into soft sex or making love. On the last word, I silently laughed. I wasn't sure what love was or how it felt. The word alone was foreign to me. I'd lived in foster care, where families fought, bickered, yelled, and hardly laughed. I'd never heard the word "love" uttered from one spouse to another. The closest anyone had come to showing me what love could be like was my boss, Bruce, and his family. The man got all sappy when he mentioned his wife. And while Ted was a widower, he'd treated me like a daughter, although he hadn't told me he loved me.

Despite all that, I liked sex rough, hard, and fast. I stared into Dillon's whiskey-colored eyes that dripped with trouble, the good kind, the kind that was sure to please me in every way, and I knew he was the right man for the job.

I itched to play with his tousled hair that had waves going in all directions—a look that suited him to a T. Then there were his lips. I took a breath. His full and perfectly shaped lips softened his rough, tatted, pierced, bad-boy appearance.

His hands went on each side of me. "If we're going to work together, then I think we need to come to an understanding." He untied my scarf before he dipped his head. As he did, a lock of hair fell forward, grazing my face as softly as a feather.

I shivered.

He chuckled as he kissed my scar—the part that was sticking out of my shirt. "I do want to murder Calderon for doing this to you."

Cory's name should've jolted me back to reality, but as Dillon lightly pressed his body against mine, all that made sense was to not think, just feel—feel his lips grazing my neck, his erection pressing against my abdomen, his breath tickling my skin.

My body became like warm saltwater taffy, pliable, bendable, soft, and gooey.

His lips traveled up to settle on my ear. "You're absolutely breath-taking." He grabbed hold of my braid then tugged, causing my head to fall back. Then he nibbled on my ear and my neck, almost biting me in some places, which was enough to make me push my hips into him.

He groaned.

I moaned.

"I want you, Dillon. From the moment I saw you the other night."

I could feel him grin against my jaw. "I'd like to say the same, but I think I've admired you since our gang days."

I tensed.

He let go of my braid, allowing me to right my head.

His hooded gaze was full of so much emotion. "Did I scare you?"

Words were on my tongue, but my jaw wouldn't work. I didn't scare so easily, not anymore. Oh, I'd been a timid soul after Cory did a number on me. But Lou had made damn certain that I would never be afraid to walk in the dark.

I wasn't afraid of what Dillon had said as much as I was afraid of myself—of feeling for someone. I studied him from head to toe, silently berating myself for what I was about to say. "You're right. We do need to come to an understanding, and as much as I want you, my *want* I think is different than yours. I'm not into relationships, short or long. I hook up with a man, and then I walk away. No strings." *Then why were you holding his hand in his car and then again at the park? Why do you feel this intense connection with him and feel like he gets you?*

He stepped away, far away. His jaw hardened. "No strings. Right.

So let's keep sex off the table. We work together. I help you with finding out more about the Black Knights, and you… well, you've already given me a great lead with the tattoo shop. I guess you held up your end of the bargain."

I liked his bluntness. What I didn't like was his tone, the finality that we would not have sex, and the pouty lips. Sure, he looked kind of hot with his bottom lip jutting out, but he couldn't possibly think that we were about to run off into the sunset and live happily ever after. In my world, there was no such thing as happily ever after.

As though he knew the war going on in my head, he said, "I'm not into anything steady either. I do like you. I do think you're beautiful. I am extremely attracted to you. But I'm not asking you to marry me. My sister comes first. Not you. Not me. Not anyone else in my life except the shelter." He held up his hand. "I'm sorry if I read you all wrong."

Whoa! My tongue was tied into a knot the size of the globe. I had to be a thousand shades of red, and my cheeks felt hotter than the sun.

He buttoned his shirt.

The air in the room thickened to the consistency of honey.

My stomach felt weird, as if someone was inside poking me with a sharp, pointy object.

I pushed off the counter. "Dillon, I'm sorry." I let out a huge breath. I really didn't know why I was sorry. I had to say something, though. "I agree too that we keep things platonic." I knew that would be difficult. I'd gotten to feel his hard body, his hand in mine, his arms around me. Hells bells, his scent was still clinging to my nostrils. "Despite the lead on the tattoo shop, I still want to help you find Grace." That was no lie.

Deep down, I believed her trail would open some doors for a good story, whether it was about the Black Knights or not. Plus, I had a huge soft spot for helping women. Dillon did too since he'd opened a shelter. I also didn't want to ruin building a friendship with him either, and sex would do that. Of course, my body was yelling at me that I was a doofus for not having a wild and crazy night with him in bed.

"Friends it is, then." He delivered the words evenly, with no emotion at all.

That sucked. I would've liked to have heard a little bit of disappointment. Then again, I was the one who'd backed off. He'd shown me a little bit of his so-called hand, but now he had his poker face painted on tightly.

His phone danced on top of the table near the window. He waltzed over and snatched it up. "Hello. Yeah. This is Dillon Hart."

I wasn't sure why I shivered when the color drained from his face. Maybe the cops had found Grace's body like they had Nadine's. The news was reporting that Nadine had been found with a bullet in her neck and that she'd bled out. I had yet to confirm that with Ted.

Oh crap, Ted! I needed to boogie out of there and fast. Otherwise, I wouldn't be surprised if Ted showed up at Dillon's door.

"I'll be right down." Dillon ended the call. "I need to go." The anger on his face said whatever news he'd gotten was bad.

"Can I help?"

A muscle ticked in his jaw. "It's family business."

The word family rubbed me the wrong way. It always did. I hated to see how mothers doted on their children or fathers played catch with their sons. I'd done a story on a family who had lost their son to a drunk driver, and they had given me pictures of him in a baseball uniform for my article. I'd stared at the picture for hours on end, crying at how tragic the story had been. But I'd also been envious of the dead boy who'd had parents that loved him dearly.

Jangling keys eroded my quandary.

"I know we were going to the Crow, but I have to postpone," Dillon said.

"Yeah, I forgot to mention before I walked in that Ted is waiting for me down at the precinct." I followed him out. "You didn't say anything about Nadine, did you?"

As he locked his house door, he said, "Not at all."

My nerves did a little jig. Guilt was setting in hard, particularly knowing that Dillon had lied to protect me. He'd sounded a bit irritated when he mentioned Ted's name earlier. I wondered if he was upset with me or if he'd had words with Ted.

I was about to ask him, when my phone beeped with a text from Ted. Not only that, Dillon was ushering me down the porch steps. So I made a mental note to visit the topic of Ted and Dillon later.

15

DILLON

I despised the bleach scents of a hospital. The aroma reminded me so much of all those nights my mom had cleaned up my old man's puke on the kitchen and bathroom floors. I'd found her several times on her knees with a bucket on one side, a bottle of bleach on the other, and a sponge in her hands.

Fucker.

I squinted at the invading fluorescent lights that rained down like a lightning storm on a summer night. An older lady sat behind the information desk, with her glasses perched on the tip of her nose, reading a book.

Anger cemented my jaw. I'd ground my teeth from my house to the hospital, mainly because of Maggie's presumptive nature that I'd wanted to whisk her off her feet. She was bold and so fucking sexy. My dick was still sporting a semi.

To say the woman was driving me to drink was an understatement. On top of that, my old man wasn't helping my mood either.

"I got a call from here telling me my father had been admitted," I said with so much scorn, the lady's gray eyes began swimming in fright. "Jerome Hart."

Her nails hit the keys, tapping at the speed of light. The sound ground on my every nerve. I didn't have time to coddle my father. What was I saying? I'd always left his ass in jail when he'd reached out for my help to bail him out. If he thought I was paying his hospital bill, the drunk had another thing coming.

"Room 242. Elevators are that way." She pointed an arthritic finger to her right.

"Stairs?" I asked. *Fuck the elevator.* I needed to keep my legs moving and collect my thoughts, one stair at a time.

The nice nurse who'd called me had been cryptic, only sharing with me that my father had been in and out of consciousness since he was admitted last night. She said she'd found my name in his wallet.

The old lady behind the desk said, "Stairs are next to the elevator."

I hotfooted down the deserted hall. At nine at night, the hospital had little activity from what I could see. I pushed in the door. Once I was inside the stairwell, the bleach odor wasn't as strong. In fact, I could smell cigarettes. Someone was disobeying the rules. I doubted smoking was allowed with all the chemicals in the hospital. But what did I know? I tried to stay away from hospitals since I'd been in and out of them when I was in a gang, yet here I was.

I blew out a breath, trying to figure out why I was coming to my father's rescue.

Grace, man. Grace.

In light of the news I'd gotten from Syd about Grace being alive six months ago, I wondered if my old man had seen her. I didn't think she would return home, but maybe she'd gone there looking for me, Duke, or Denim. I wasn't sure if she knew about Denim's predicament. He'd gotten arrested about the same time she'd left home.

The hospital was the perfect environment to corner my old man because at least he wouldn't be drunk.

I climbed one step, then two, thinking of dancing dogs and jumping ponies, any stupid thing to keep me from replaying the scene with Maggie. A platonic relationship was good, yet not so good. I didn't know how I would be able to keep my hands off the woman. I would've suggested a friends-with-benefits deal between us, but I was afraid that the more I touched her, the faster I would fall. Plus, with the breaking news on Grace, I needed my head clear. I also had to get my head clear to see my father.

I walked the second floor until I found room 242. I hesitated, or rather, I came to an abrupt halt.

A nurse came out of the room across from me. "Visiting hours are almost up," the short woman said as she glided down to the nurse's station at the end of the hall on the right, her white tennis shoes squeaking on the shiny floor. She was halfway there when she doubled back. Her brown eyes appraised me. "Are you Dillon Hart?"

I nodded.

She tucked a chart underneath her arm. "I'm Anita. I'm the one who called you. Your dad was found outside a bar last night, seizing and vomiting. He reeked of alcohol when the paramedics brought him in and was on the verge of being almost comatose. We've been giving him fluids. I'm sorry we didn't call you sooner. Apparently, his wallet fell out of his pocket in the ambulance. The paramedic brought it in earlier. Anyway, we found that he has alcohol poisoning."

No surprise there. "Thank you." She didn't need to know I hated my father or that I'd put up with enough of his drunken ways. Frankly, I was surprised he was alive. His liver had to be corroded.

"I'm down at the nurse's station if you need me." Anita bounced away.

I gritted my teeth and fisted my hands at my side. I hadn't seen my old man in a year or more. I'd gone home to find out if Grace had returned or if he'd seen her. But each time I saw him, he had a bottle of booze in one hand and a cigarette in the other.

I pulled out my phone. I should call Duke. He was the older brother. He should have been the one taking care of our father. On second thought, reaching out to Duke wasn't the best idea. He and I would get into a fight like we had the last time I'd spoken to him, although I did want to share the news that Grace could be alive and ask him if she had contacted him recently. Now that I was thinking of

Duke, I wondered if he might have some insight on the Black Knights since he operated in the world of illegal activity.

Someone inside my dad's hospital room coughed.

I rolled back my shoulders and walked in.

A light from the wall behind his bed glowed. Tubes were stuck into my father's arm as the IV dripped. His eyes were closed as the machine near him took his blood pressure.

The man had aged fifteen years since I'd seen him last. His blond hair was ninety percent grayish-white. His skin was wrinkled, leathery, and ashen. Dark circles stained his eyes as though someone had punched him. His lips were chapped, and booze permeated the air around him, burning my nostrils more than the bleach.

I gripped the rail at the bottom of his bed, trying to figure out how I could possibly be related to him. In the looks department, we didn't match. Denim was the only one who had the same features as our father. In morals, we sure didn't jive. My old man believed that abuse was the only way to run a household. I couldn't recall a time when he'd been a father who cared. Every day after work, he had sat in his chair, drank beer, and watched TV. Then beer had morphed into whiskey. Then he'd become a monster.

He stirred, his eyes fluttering open. When his blue gaze landed on me, the heart monitor came alive. I probably had a look that could kill as I towered over him.

He snarled like a rabid dog. "What are you doing here?"

I hate you too, old man.

I was holding on to the bedrail as if I were holding on to a ledge eighty floors off the ground. "Nice to see you too, Father."

He glanced around before he started pulling out the IV line. "I can't stay here. What happened?"

That was the thing with him. He drank to the point where he couldn't remember squat.

"You about killed yourself." I lifted a shoulder. "I'm surprised you're not dead."

"Leave me alone. I don't need you," he growled like an animal about to attack. He probably would have if those tubes he couldn't take out weren't taped to his hand.

"The feeling is mutual. But here I am."

Grace. Grace. Grace.

Her name was the only reason keeping me glued to the fucking tile floor.

"Get the fuck out."

I angled my head. "You can't possibly be embarrassed because you drank yourself into a coma."

He bared his nicotine-stained teeth. "Son."

"Don't call me that. You had a hand in making me, but that's as far as our relationship goes."

His throat bobbed. "I'll ask you again. Why are you here?" That tone of disgust that I'd been accustomed to while growing up dripped from each word.

"I learned today that Grace could be alive. Has she been home?" I knew it was a shot in the dark.

His face twisted into something far beyond anything I'd ever seen on him—regret, despair, and sadness. He averted his gaze to his lap.

"Has she?" My tone was hard.

"How's Denim doing?" he asked.

I moved from the bottom of his bed to the side and got in his face. "We're talking about Grace."

His puke-laden breath about knocked me backward. "If you boys would've stayed out of trouble, then maybe your sister wouldn't have run away."

If I hadn't left for the merchant marines, Grace would be with us. If Duke and Denim had kept an eye on her, Grace would be with us. If my old man weren't a drunk, a bastard, and an abuser, Grace would be with us. Hell, if the latter were true, then we wouldn't be a fucked-up dysfunctional family, our mother wouldn't have taken off as if she were being chased by the devil, and our family would have had a thread of hope of being like the one family I was envious of—the Maxwells. But I wasn't going down that road tonight.

I'd brooded many nights over how I longed for a family like the Maxwells—tough, solid, protective, loving, caring, and the list went on. My brothers should've had Grace's back.

Steam came out of my nose as I shuffled away two steps, letting out a laugh of all laughs—hard and evil. Rage pumped through me along with the need to ram my fist into my father's jaw. My gut hurt. My heart rammed against my chest, and I gritted my teeth to the point that I swore I heard one crack. "Says the father who deserves an award for worst father of the year."

"It's not my fault. If anyone's to blame, it's your mother. She left her children behind."

My nostrils flared, even though I agreed with him in part. "You drove her away. Therefore, you're at fault for everything that has happened to this family." My stubby nails poked holes into my palms. "Have. You. Seen. Grace?" I enunciated each word with a pause in between to prevent myself from going ballistic on his frail, old ass.

"Yes."

I cracked my neck, blinked about a hundred times, and winced. "Come again?"

He sighed as if he were shedding years of regret. "She came home about five months ago. Or maybe it was four. Or maybe it was the other night. I can't remember." His voice dripped with anguish.

Fuck his anguish. Hopefully, he was seeing the light, although I wouldn't wait up for him to get sober.

"Of course you can't," I mumbled. "You're a drunk."

He didn't look at me as he continued. "I got up off the couch to take a piss. I think it was two in the morning. I heard a noise like someone was shutting drawers. So I checked the rooms. When I opened Grace's bedroom door, I flicked on the light. She was standing there with a flashlight, rummaging in her dresser, stuffing things in a bag. She wasn't the innocent girl I knew. She had tattoos on her arms, her neck, and her hands. Her long hair was gone. That pretty hair she wore in pigtails is now shorter than yours."

I held back from spewing all kinds of barbs. I wanted to tell him she'd lost her innocence when he started slapping her around and telling her she was nothing but useless. Instead, I probed more. "Did you talk to her? Did she say anything like where she was living? Did she ask where I was? Or Duke or Denim?"

"The only thing she said to me was 'I was never here.'"

All signs so far were telling me she didn't want anyone to know she was alive, which was giving me one big fucking headache.

Silence, murky, cloudy, and stinky, hung over us.

My father's shaky fingers fussed with a thread on his blanket. "If I could take back what I did to her, I would."

I drilled daggers at him, waiting for more. What about me, Duke, and Denim? But I wasn't there to get an apology. And while every muscle in me had protested coming to the hospital, I was glad I had. The idea that Grace was alive six months ago, according to Syd, and four or five months ago if my old man was right, was perplexing, enlightening, exciting, and scary as fuck.

The idea that Grace was alive but hadn't bothered to reach out to me was unnerving. I was her brother. I was the one who had protected her from the man that stunk to high heaven.

You were the one who left her to fend for herself against a monster. And for that, I was angrier with myself.

I opened a drawer on the table beside the bed and found a pen. Then I scribbled Manny's address and phone number on a napkin that sat on top of the table. "When they discharge you, call this guy or stop by and see him." It wasn't a plea or a question, but a statement, and it was the only help I could give him. My father had shown more regret in the last fifteen minutes than he had my entire existence, and for that, my hatred for him diminished a tiny bit.

I didn't wait for his excuse of why he wasn't going to get help. I had a sister to hunt down.

16

MAGGIE

I played with my pesky hangnail as I waited for Ted. The gang unit was located on the second floor and tucked away behind a high security door. Using a rope, the police had also cordoned off the stairs with a sign that read, Police Personnel Only Beyond This Point.

Aside from the cop at the front desk, who had his head buried below the ledge of the counter, the station had minimal activity with only the occasional police officer walking by. I thought for a split second that the criminals had decided to take the night off.

I messed with my phone, clearing the apps hogging my battery life. Then I added Dillon to my contacts. I bounced my knee. I wasn't nervous about seeing Ted, but I was out of sorts over the exchange I'd had with Dillon. If I would've kept my mouth shut, I might have been coming down from an epic orgasm right about now.

Stupid me had to open my mouth.

A platonic relationship was for the best. I had to concentrate. I had to crack a nut in the story on the Black Knights, and if anything, I had to find some sort of news that would sell the Sunday paper.

I was flushing out a headline on what had happened to Nadine and how to tie her back to the standoff I'd witnessed. First, I had to get Ted to give me some facts I could print.

Footsteps clamored down the steps, and I was ready to hop up when I spotted Rick. He gave me a warm smile, his high forehead glistening as though he'd walked out of the gym.

"Mags," he said when he cleared the stairs.

I tucked my phone into my messenger bag and stood.

Rick gave me a hug, something he always did when he saw me. "Good luck with Ted."

I pulled away. "What's going on?"

"Rick," Ted warned as he came down, dressed in his usual attire of jeans, a short-sleeve plaid button-up shirt, and a gun on his hip—standard uniform for the gang unit. Well, not so much the plaid shirt, but the jeans and combat boots for sure.

Rick had the same style of clothing from the waist down, but he didn't do plaid.

"See ya, Mags," Rick said as he left the building.

The bald cop at the front desk acknowledged Ted with a dip of his head then went back to whatever he was reading.

Ted unhooked the rope, the light on his huge diver's watch illuminating. "We'll talk in my office." His brownish-black eyes didn't give away an ounce of emotion, which was typical of a cop, at least a good and seasoned one.

Nevertheless, I knew Ted. I knew when he was perturbed. His lips were pursed, and I could tell by the minuscule movement of his jaw that he was chewing on the inside of his cheek.

Clutching the strap of my messenger bag, I climbed up the steps as if I were scaling the stairs to the electric chair. "What's wrong?"

His mustache twitched. "If you don't want your ass arrested, you will do as I say." His tone permitted no argument.

Suddenly, my teeth knocked together. He knew about Nadine and me. I searched my brain as to how he could know. Dillon hadn't told him. More than that, I was scratching my head as to how I could get arrested.

"Up." His voice deepened to a growl.

I squared my shoulders and did as I was told.

At the top, Ted punched in a code.

Beep. Beep. Beep. Beep.

That was a familiar sound from when I'd been thrown in a cell a time or two as a teenager. Familiar or not, I shuddered.

A stream of cold air whooshed over me when the door opened.

Reluctantly, I stepped inside what the gang unit referred to as the pit.

We circled desks that were scattered around facing the huge, empty whiteboard. I imagined the board had been flipped over so I wouldn't see the evidence and pictures of suspects the team had on gang members. Regardless of why I was there, I had the urge to dash over to the board and see if Cory Calderon's picture was one of the gang members.

Ted had always said he didn't know who led the Black Knights. Part of me believed him. The other part of me didn't, only because he wouldn't want to ruin an investigation or put me in danger by telling me.

"You're mad about Dillon Hart. Aren't you?" I knew otherwise, although Ted always tried to give me fatherly advice on topics. Since I didn't date steadily, he hardly knew the men I'd slept with.

A large window separated Ted's office from the pit. A feeling of claustrophobia enveloped me, and I wasn't even afraid of small spaces.

Ted nudged me into his office, or more like blocked me from turning around and darting out of the building as if I were the Flash.

"Sit your ass in that chair." His deep, commanding voice made the hairs on my neck stand up.

I lowered my shaking body into the lone chair in front of his desk. A wall of honors and pictures stared back at me. Ted was a decorated police officer, having received awards for his valiant efforts on saving victims over the years.

Ted circled his desk, sat down, steepled his fingers, and glared at me. "I don't like that Dillon Hart. He's all wrong for you."

Inwardly, I sighed. I was there to get the third degree about Dillon. I could handle that. "I'll decide who's right or wrong for me." The shivers melted as confidence worked its way back into my bones.

"So I guess you'll decide if you sit in a jail cell or get to go home tonight," he deadpanned.

I clasped my hands together in my lap. "Instead of playing games, Ted, tell me why I'm here." If he wanted to play his cop game, then I could play my own.

He leaned back in his chair. "Tell me about Nadine."

There it was. And he didn't ask but commanded in his brusque tone.

How he knew wasn't even a question. After all, he was a detective.

I slumped my shoulders. "I ran into Nadine right after your standoff the other night." Although the other night was only last night, it felt as if months had passed. "She was scared. She didn't want to go to the cops. She said if she did, Miguel would kill her. I wanted to get her to safety before I called you. Anyway, when Dillon reached out to me about his sister, I learned he'd opened a shelter for women. So I brought Nadine there. I swear I was going to tell you, especially after I heard you found the redhead, but you took off so fast. I feel horrible that she's dead. All I wanted to do was help her."

I hung my head as tears sprang forth.

"Mags." His voice softened. "Did she tell you anything else about Miguel?"

I sniffled. "He was her pimp, and she never heard of the gang the Black Knights."

He rubbed a thumb over the corner of his mustache. "I should throw your ass in jail for nothing more than slowing down my case and not telling me."

"How did you know I was with Nadine?"

"A witness identified Nadine getting into a VW Bug. She didn't see you, and there are several yellow VW Bugs in the city, but you were at the scene. Look, I'm giving you a warning. Get in the middle of any of my cases, and I won't hesitate to lock you up. Are we understood?"

I nodded and nodded and nodded. "Yes."

He opened the top drawer and produced a white envelope. "I know, Mags, that you want to see Cory Calderon behind bars. But you can't shove your way into situations that are dangerous."

"I'm a reporter. We want the juicy stories. The paper wants stories that sell. I'm not in the market to get fired. Also, Cory needs to pay for what he did to me."

His expression grew somber. "Sadly, you don't have proof, and as much as I wouldn't mind throwing him in a cell, it would be hard for a judge to even take on a rape case from several years ago, and the statute of limitations on rape has passed. You've got to let go of your revenge for Cory."

Even if the statute of limitations hadn't run out, the rape would have been hard to prove in court. It would have been Cory's word against mine, which was why I hadn't pursued legal action.

I tugged on my braid, hard, as tears shot out. "You don't get it. You weren't the one raped. You weren't the one he carved up like a dead animal." With my hand, I hid my scar. I shouldn't have been so frightened of going to the cops after he raped me. "Sometimes I wake up in a cold sweat from dreaming about the asshole over me, smiling, like he'd just captured the winning prize." Tears were pouring out of my eyes. "I can't live until I get closure." All my strength that I wore on the outside crumbled.

Ted didn't move or speak. He didn't have to. His eyes became glossy. "Mags." Pain laced his tone. "I'm sorry. I don't have a solid thing on Cory. He's an upstanding citizen."

I refused to believe that. "My source tells me Cory roughed up a prostitute last week, and the rumor is he's with the Black Knights. He might not be the big boss, but he's part of that gang."

He scrubbed a hand over his face. "That may be true. But until you can prove that, we got nothing on the man."

Even though I knew that, I frowned anyway. "What do you have? Something I can print?"

"We've confirmed that the man we arrested, Dan Silva, is working for the Black Knights. He finally talked when we cut him a deal. I do have something you can't print yet. I will share with you only because I don't want you to start asking around about the Black Knights and get yourself into a dangerous situation." He pointed a stern finger at me. "I mean it, Maggie. No article until I give you the nod, and no asking your source on the street anything. You would only put your source in danger too. Are we clear?"

"Crystal," I said, salivating to hear the rest. I wouldn't betray Ted's confidence.

He rested back in his chair. "We now know Miguel Rivera is the pimp of all pimps and that he's the leader of the Black Knights. He finds runaway girls, homeless girls, and girls prostituting themselves, and cleans them up, takes care of them, promises them a life of riches, and then sells them to the highest bidder. I've got men out now looking for Miguel as we speak."

"Can you tie him to Nadine's murder?"

"Not yet. But that brings up another problem. She was found a mile from the shelter, which means you and her were followed last night, which is another reason I'm sharing some of the facts with you. I want you to stay at my house."

He wasn't ordering me, and even if he were, I could take care of myself. "Thanks, but I'll watch my back. I'm at the paper most of the time anyway, and I'm helping Dillon follow up on a hot lead about his sister. The one you gave me on Skins and Needles panned out. The girl you saw that day was Grace Hart."

He popped forward. "No shit?"

"We don't know much yet except she was at that tattoo shop six months ago. She might hang out at some bar called the Crow."

"It's closed for renovations right now," Ted said. "They had a small fire a few weeks back."

Dillon wasn't going to be happy about that.

Nevertheless, I sifted through my brain for other questions he might be able to answer or information he could give me for my story.

"What did you find in the house?" I remembered the urgency of his team wanting him to see something in the house.

He averted his gaze to the envelope on his desk. "A dead girl."

My blood became ice. I wanted revenge not only on Cory but on all those jerks like Cory.

Ted picked up the envelope. "We've contacted Nadine's family, but we haven't told them about her being the victim of a gang that is involved in sex trafficking yet. We will when we have all the facts. So you're clear to use her name in print, but nothing about the gangs."

So all I had for a story was her name, which wasn't much.

"And the other girl?"

"We haven't been able to contact her next of kin."

"She didn't resemble Grace Hart, by chance? Brown hair, tattoo on her neck of a hummingbird?" *Please say no.*

He pinched his chin. "Blond girl and no tats."

I release a quiet sigh. "I would like to talk to Nadine's family. I won't say anything about the gang or her pimp. I just want to learn more about her." A good story involved getting at the hearts of people.

"I'll send you their info. I want to talk to you about something else."

I eyed the envelope that he was guarding heavily. "Please don't start with Dillon. I'm not dating him. We're friends, nothing more."

Relief washed over his face. "Speaking of Dillon, he lied too. He was protecting you, wasn't he?"

I shrugged. "Please don't give him a hard time. I told him not to tell you. It was my job to do that."

I couldn't tell if admiration passed over him or something else. But Dillon became a memory when he lifted his chin. "I know you're adamant about not knowing who your parents are, but I've found your mother."

My head jerked back then bounced forward. I could've sworn someone had slapped me across the face. I could almost feel the sting.

He held up the envelope. "If you want to know, her address is in here."

I stood up and shook off the coldness running through my veins. "I don't."

He pushed to his feet and skirted his desk. "What are you afraid of?" His breath smelled like an ashtray.

Everything. "That I'll punch her and end up in jail." I swished the saliva around in my mouth. "She dumped me at a fire station when I was a baby."

Ted grasped the sides of my arms. "She wants to see you."

I jumped back like a kangaroo. "You've talked to her?" I choked on the words. "You're supposed to be my friend. You're not supposed to do something I said no to."

"Family is important, Mags. You've got a lot of pent-up hatred for not only Cory but for the way you were shuffled around the foster system. Maybe if you heard her side of the story, you could sleep a little better knowing why she did what she did."

"Do you know why?"

"If I did, it's not my place to tell you. You wouldn't believe me anyway. You need to hear it from the horse's mouth."

"How did you find her? Don't forget the firemen at the firehouse named me." According to one of my social workers, my file indicated that one of the firemen had been smitten with me. He'd wanted to adopt me, but he'd been single and didn't have the resources, but he'd given me the name Maggie, after his mom. The last name of Marx—well, the first family I'd lived with gave me their last name, which was Marx. That was the extent of my knowledge of my heritage.

Ted rested his body on the edge of his desk. "I talked to the people in the homes surrounding the firehouse. After many conversations, dead ends, leads, and trails, I found someone who remembered a pregnant young girl who had been dating a boy in the neighborhood. All I needed were the names of the girl and boy, and..." He extended the envelope. "Here's her info."

Curiosity was a fucking bitch. "I'm not ready."

He tucked the envelope in the front pocket of my messenger bag.

"Don't open it until you're ready." He prodded me with his dark-brown eyes.

Suddenly, I was wondering if I'd gotten my blond hair and green eyes from my mom. I wondered if she was on the heavy side like me. I didn't consider myself fat. I had wide hips, thick thighs, a small waist, and large breasts. I liked to call myself big-boned. My gynecologist referred to me as one of those ladies who had the structure for making lots of babies. I'd laughed at her comment. I didn't see myself having a ton of kids, or one for that matter. Which made me also wonder if my mom had had any more children. Boy, I wasn't sure it would sit well with me if she'd had a family yet given me up.

I started for the door, with the envelope burning a hole in my bag. I was tempted to dump it into the trash can on my way out.

"Mags," Ted called.

I tossed a look over my shoulder.

"Please watch your back."

"I'm too old to be sold to the highest bidder," I said. "They won't touch me." I wasn't certain about that.

As soon as I was outside in the open air, I clutched my stomach, willing the pain to go away, or maybe it was hunger pangs. I hadn't eaten since breakfast.

My phone chimed. Dillon's name blared on the screen. "Hey," I answered.

"What's wrong?" he asked. "Was Ted angry that you helped Nadine?"

I guessed I sounded as if the world was ending.

"Ted was pissed, but it's nothing." More than nothing. I'd gotten my ass chewed out by Ted over Nadine, then he'd launched a surprise attack I wasn't prepared for. "Ted told me the Crow is closed for renovations."

"I know. I had a bit of time after I took care of my family business. They open next week."

That news sucked the big one. I was about to spill everything Ted had told me about Miguel and the Black Knights then remembered it wasn't for the public, not even Dillon. I had to respect Ted's wishes. After all, he trusted me. "I have work to do anyway."

"I sense something other than Nadine is bothering you. You know you can talk to me," he said sweetly.

The problem was I wouldn't want to talk. At the moment, I wanted to screw someone's brains out. I wanted to feel something other than hatred, despair, and frustration. I wanted to feel as though my life had a purpose other than revenge.

"It's family business. Talk soon?"

"You know where to find me."

As soon as we hung up, I wanted to bawl my eyes out. The toughness I wore as a shield and a badge of honor cracked. Suddenly, I wasn't sure who I was.

If you know your past, then you can conquer your future. Those were my words and mine alone. As much as that statement made sense to me, I didn't think I could meet my mother, let alone forgive her.

17

———

DILLON

It had been two long days since I'd talked to Maggie, seen my father in the hospital, and learned that Grace could be alive. After I'd left my old man, I'd driven by the Crow. I'd even knocked on the club's door since the lights had been on, but no one answered.

The sign had read *Closed for renovations. Updates are posted on our website.* The grand reopening date, according to their sign, was next week. I was itching to talk with the owner or anyone in the club to see if they would recognize Grace. Now that my old man had given me a new description of my sister, I had a little bit more to go on, although I didn't need to know that her hair was short. The hummingbird tattoo on her neck was a clear identifier and hard to miss, as were the tats on her arms.

I lounged on the couch in my game room, with my laptop on my legs and my phone on the cushion next to me. The stereo was on low as I checked the Crow's website for any updates on whether they would open a little earlier than expected. I'd even called the number listed on the site, but the phone rang endlessly.

My next move was to see if Duke had seen Grace. I also wanted to ask him if he had any knowledge of the Black Knights. But my brother was out of town on business. I'd stopped by his penthouse and learned from the bellman that Duke wasn't due back in town until late the following week.

It seemed as if the stars weren't aligned for me to find out anything else on Grace, which was par for the course since I'd started searching for her. I would get a tiny ray of hope, only to find that the lead didn't go anywhere.

I was tempted to call Duke. After all, I didn't need to see him in person to ask questions. But I wanted to see his body language when I told him that our old man had seen Grace a few months ago. I wanted to read him when I asked if he'd seen her too. It was hard to think that Grace wanted nothing to do with me.

My phone rang, making me flinch a little.

"Dillon, it's Manny. I'm returning your call. Sorry, I've been busier than ever." I heard papers shuffling in the background. "Norton is still here. He's struggling through, but he seems to be a fighter."

"That's great. Any sign from my old man?"

"Sorry, I've been looking out for him, but no."

I wasn't surprised. I'd called Manny the day before to check on Norton and give him a heads-up that maybe, just maybe, Jerome Hart might walk his drunken ass into Manny's shelter.

"Thanks for the call. If Norton disappears or my old man shows up, can you give me a shout?"

"Sure thing. Got to run."

At least Norton had listened to me. I hoped that my father would take my advice since he'd gotten alcohol poisoning. I wished I cared as little about Grace as I did about my father. The notion that she could be alive was eating a hole in my stomach. One minute, I was smiling that she hadn't ended up like all those dead girls I'd seen in the morgue over the years, or like Nadine. Then the next, I was fuming.

I snagged the remote control for the stereo and turned up the song "Lullaby" by Nickelback instead of thinking about Grace. If I wasn't thinking about my sister, then Maggie occupied my thoughts constantly.

At the thought of her name, I shoved my fingers through my hair. I'd been dying to call her, but after our encounter in my kitchen on Tuesday, I'd wanted to give her some space. Something other than Ted was bothering her, and I didn't know if it was me or not. I'd been kind of cold to her during our discussion about a platonic relationship. I was also worried that she could be in danger. However, she'd mentioned that she had work to do, and I knew she had a deadline to get a story written for the Sunday paper.

The war going on in my head ended when a text from her lit up my screen.

Hey. Are you around?

I grinned and sighed heavily. *What's up?*

Are you free? Can I stop by?

I wasn't planning on heading over to the shelter. I'd spent the last two days in my office, doing paperwork, researching the Crow, trying to get a hold of Duke, and cleaning up the yard at the shelter. Angel and Debbie were doing well, and Rafe and Hunt had the security under control.

I'm at my house. Come on over.

The doorbell rang.

I arched an eyebrow as I ran upstairs.

The bell went off again. Surely, Maggie hadn't sped over here.

When I opened the door, my jaw dropped, not so much because she'd texted me while standing on my porch, but because the sadness in her eyes gutted me. I almost reached out to hug her, but we were doing the friend thing.

Friends hugged each other, but not me. One hug, and I would want to keep going. Hell, I had wanted to strip her bare when I was consoling her as she'd cried over Nadine. I wanted to throw her up against a tree at Paul Revere Park and kiss her lights out. But kissing equaled feelings that were too intimate for me. Plunging headfirst into a steady relationship wasn't what I was expecting, but I was on the verge of wanting that with and only with Maggie.

The woman was driving me insane. Platonic could go suck the big one. I could kick myself for suggesting we keep sex off the table.

She waved a hand in front of me as she glided in. "Hey. Now you're letting out the cool air."

My internal struggle waned for the moment as I closed the door. However, the need to pull her to me, taste her, and nibble on her was strong. So was the idea that I had a king-size bed upstairs that we could make use of.

I skirted around her before I gave in, whisked her off her feet, and took her to my room. "We can talk down in the game room." If she wanted more than friendship, then I had to let her make the first move.

Once she walked into the game room, she lingered near the entertainment center lining the wall adjacent to the door. She scanned the area, which was made up of a chaise lounge, a big-screen TV, a couch, a pinball machine, and a couple of other gaming tables. "I was wondering if we could talk." She lowered her gaze, seemingly embarrassed about something.

Shyness on her was a first, and I realized the look was sexier than her *I'm woman, hear me roar* exterior.

I eased down onto the couch that was facing the entertainment center, hoping she would come join me so I could make her feel comfortable.

"I don't have any girlfriends." Her eyes were darting everywhere but at me. "I work with women, but I don't tell them my secrets or hang out with them after work. I've always been a loner. If I did hang with anyone, it's been with guys. Since we're doing the friend thing, I need some advice."

We finally locked eyes, and I saw that pain etched her pretty face. Man, she was beautiful. Her lashes were long and soft, and the light color of brown brought out her shamrock-green eyes, sucking me in.

She slipped her hand into the front pocket of her messenger back and produced an envelope. "I spent my entire childhood in foster care. My parents left me at a firehouse when I was a newborn."

I couldn't help but open my mouth. What the hell? I thought I had a miserable childhood. I wanted to tell her I was sorry, but if she was like me, and I was beginning to realize she was, she didn't want pity.

"I'm not enamored with the idea of meeting my parents. But Ted went against my wishes and found my mom." She stared at the envelope as if she were trying to light it on fire. "Her address is in this." She held up the envelope. "What would you do?"

I pinched the bridge of my nose. "I don't know how much you know about me except my brothers and me were in a gang and Grace disappeared, but I'm not the best person to ask." I scratched my head. "My mother took off when I was a kid. But she left because my old man is a drunk and a bastard. It might be good for you to settle your curiosity about why she did what she did." As much as I was angry with my mom, I wouldn't mind seeing her and hearing her side of the story. Granted, I was ninety-nine percent sure she had left because of my father, but I'd never actually heard her say that. I would also like to understand how a mom could leave her children with a man who was abusive. That was the huge question on my mind.

Maggie sat down beside me. Then she covered her face with her hands.

My fingers were primed and ready to dance down her back and rub her troubles away. But I was afraid she would get the wrong idea and tense up, and that would pain me.

"Is your mom the reason you sounded upset on the phone after you left Ted's precinct?" I asked.

She shuddered as she nodded.

"If it helps, I had to leave you the other night because my father was in the hospital for alcohol poisoning. I didn't want to go, but given the news from Syd about Grace, she might have gone home to find me or one of my brothers. It turns out my dad saw Grace about four months ago in her room, packing some clothes. Or at least he thinks it was four months. Since he's constantly drunk, who knows?"

She whipped around. "For real?"

"Crazy, right? Look, Maggie, you don't need to make a decision on whether to see your mother or not at this moment. My advice? Take some more time. I can see you're not ready."

She gave me a warm smile as the tension left her.

As for me, I was ready to release some tension too, but not the emotional kind.

18

———

MAGGIE

I sat crossed-legged next to Dillon, wanting nothing more than to curl up in his lap. The game room, as he called it, was cozy, and with him in it, it was even more relaxing. I'd debated whether to come over or not. After the exchange we'd had in his kitchen, I didn't know if our friendship would go anywhere because maybe he'd been cold or hurt. I couldn't tell. I was finding that Dillon didn't wear his emotions on his sleeve, although when he'd brought up Kelton, I knew he was jealous.

Despite Dillon's feelings, his place was a one-hundred-eighty-degree difference from my apartment. The couch my butt was planted on was covered in a suede fabric, and the springs weren't poking my bum like the one I owned. Not only that, the large-screen TV gave me the sense I was living like a queen. Foster homes barely had a TV the size of a small cardboard box, and I didn't own a television.

Dillon tucked one leg underneath him, while the other dangled over the edge of the cushion. I was learning that Dillon liked to be barefoot, or so it seemed.

I relaxed back, cocked my elbow against the couch, and rested my head in my hands. "I wanted to ask you something else."

He flicked hair from his forehead. His hair was always so disheveled, and that made him more appealing to me.

I gripped my braid with my free hand, mainly to prevent me from touching him. "I'm working on a story about Nadine. Her funeral is tomorrow up in Charlestown at eight a.m. Do you want to go with me?"

He scratched his beard. "I'm supposed to see Denim. If I can get on the road no later than eleven, then sure. Want to tag along?"

Denim was doing some investigative work for me, and Ted hadn't given me anything to print, even though I knew who the leader of the Black Knights was now. What I didn't know was if Cory was part of that gang. Regardless, Denim might have found out something interesting, and even if he hadn't, I would get to hang out with Dillon, and that excited me.

I nodded.

He reached out and tugged on the end of my braid. "Do you always wear your hair in a braid?" His hand lingered close to my breast.

When I glanced down, he removed his hand quickly, as though he'd done something wrong.

I wouldn't say it was wrong. It wasn't a chaste gesture, but at that moment, friendly signs or motions went out the window, especially when the tip of his tongue touched his lip ring. I wanted his tongue to touch places that were hidden and private and throbbing with need.

I leaned in to touch his hair, only to pull back. We'd agreed to keep things nonsexual. *Stupid me.* We should've agreed to be friends with benefits.

A predatory grin lit up his face as his eyes became hooded, dark, and sultry.

My pulse quickened. I reached out again, and this time I laced my fingers through his unkempt hair. It was silky, thick, and shiny. He closed his eyes and let me play. I scooted the tiny distance closer to him, my knee grazing his denim-clad thigh.

"Aren't we doing the friend thing?" he asked on a sigh.

"I want to play." Boy, did I ever. I knew he would ruin me for any other guy from there on out. I knew he would break the lock on my heart.

I also knew I had to release the pressure that was mounting between my legs. I'd used my vibrator the night before, thinking of Dillon as I played with myself. My climax had been great, but the real living being, who was allowing me to play much like he had when he'd had me pinned against his kitchen counter, was icing on the cake. I wanted to scream his name while I was going over that edge to the best orgasm in the world, and I was so darn sure he could give me one to remember.

He didn't move as my fingers danced along his scalp. I was breathing heavy, but he was calm, reserved, and studying me intently. The gold flecks in his brown eyes looked like fire spitting out of a pit. He reminded me of a lion stalking its prey, wild, noiseless, and deadly, waiting for the right moment to pounce.

I abandoned his hair, working my way south, stopping to feel every hill and valley of his chest.

Desire swirled in my belly, a cyclone of heat, warming every nerve ending. As I played, I sank my teeth into my lower lip, my pulse soaring like an eagle over the treetops.

I dared not lower my gaze to his crotch. I was afraid that if he had an erection like the one I'd felt the other day, then I would have my clothes off in a second. That wouldn't be a bad thing, but he wasn't giving me any indication he would reciprocate, and I wanted to savor the anticipation of what I prayed would happen next.

Nevertheless, successful people in the world never reached their goals without taking risks. So I rubbed my way down his abdomen then back up then down a little farther than before. I brought up the image of him shirtless, remembering how that happy trail of his disappeared below his waistline.

I locked eyes with him when my fingers rested on his belt. His eyelids were hooded, almost sleepy with lust. But something else resided in the depths between the brown and gold specks of his irises that I couldn't pinpoint until my fingers slipped in the waistband of his jeans. Then a dragon emerged, breathing fire out of his eyes, and he flipped me onto my back before I could protest.

I squealed and huffed at the same time.

He straddled me, his knees on either side of me, but didn't put his weight on me. "Once we go down this road, Maggie, there's no going back."

"I know." He'd been on my mind when I woke up yesterday and today, during a down moment at work, and while playing with myself.

His hair fell forward, curtaining our faces. "Then we need to get something straight." His tone was raspy and somewhat pained. "We leave our feelings at the door. Like you, I don't want anything serious. My life is too fucked up for a long-term relationship. Deal?"

"No feelings." I was hornier than a dog in heat, so I would have said about anything at that moment. But I also knew he would change me in ways I'd never felt or experienced before. "Oh, and Dillon? Since we're being open about things, I like my men raw and rough. So don't be gentle."

I couldn't help but giggle at how his face lit up as if it were Christmas morning and the biggest box under the tree had his name on it.

In one fluid movement, he hauled me to my feet and over to the pinball machine that I'd barely noticed when I came in. He twirled me around then anchored himself against the monstrous toy. "Strip for me."

My belly did a loopty-loop at his command and another one when I eyed the massive bulge in his jeans.

Stepping away from him, I watched him watch me. His expression was blank, but I knew something primal lived beneath his surface. His biceps flexed as he shoved his hands in his pockets as though he was going to play with himself.

I was soaked to my core and getting wetter if that were possible as I took off my scarf. I'd never stripped for any man, but with Dillon, my inhibitions were gone, left at the door.

I grabbed the hem of my shirt and lifted the fabric slowly, my eyes glued to Dillon as his tongue toyed with his lip ring. I lifted my shirt over my head, lingering for one second and pushing out my breasts before I discarded the fabric.

Where it went, I didn't care. I cupped my breasts then shaped my waist before teasingly dipping my fingers into my capris.

He removed one hand from his pocket and gripped his cock through his jeans. An intimate thread weaved between us, defying the roughness I'd asked for. My pulse sped up at the carnal knowledge of how the hunger, raw, strong, and powerful, oozed off him.

The expression on his face said, "you're beautiful, stunning, and sexy," and for that, I shimmied out of my capris.

His chest was moving up and down while he gnawed his lip. I wanted to be that lip.

When I was standing in nothing but my thong and bra, he groaned, squeezing his erection.

I licked my lip, debating whether I should make the first move or let him. I decided it would be more fun to watch the beautiful disaster that was etched on his face. I got the impression he wanted to pounce and feast on me. I certainly wanted him to rub his hands, his tongue, his lips, and his body all over me. I wanted him to claim me as his own. Why hadn't he thrown me to the floor or bent me over the pinball machine? He was leading me to believe he was all about the foreplay, the anticipation. I couldn't blame him.

Foreplay was the prelude to a dance that was brightened with stars, soaked in sweat, and blanketed in kisses. I wasn't a romantic, but I would be for him.

I reached behind me and unclasped my bra. I slipped one strap off then the other before the fabric floated to the carpet. I wasn't modest. I loved my body, as every woman should, flaws and all. I wasn't rail thin or model skinny. I was pillowy in all the right places, and I was proud to say I wore a size twelve.

Dillon groaned as he unbuckled his jeans.

At that moment, if he didn't do something to me, I was going to start playing with myself. I wanted to approach him, undress him, and do things to him that I'd envisioned doing while using my vibrator. But again, if he wanted me, then I wanted him to show me. I didn't want to guess by witnessing the size of his erection.

He raked his gaze over my breasts, unzipping his jeans. His hand disappeared into his briefs. He closed his eyes briefly before those hooded peepers opened.

I took one step then another toward him with my hand inside my thong, and my breasts on display to admire, touch, and nibble.

He shook his head. "Take your hand out. Play with your breasts."

I did as I was told only because he asked in a tone that said he would die if I didn't.

He shucked his jeans and briefs, watching me play with and pinch my nipples. Soon, he was full-on naked, and his cock was standing erect. And boy, it was a cock that I could write a full-page story about. It was thick, long, and big, and every ounce of willpower I had was about to combust into an orgasm without anyone touching my sex.

He reached out and grabbed hold of my thong. I went to him on wobbly knees. The need to fuck him was beyond painful. I was beginning to understand what men meant by blue balls.

"Please, Dillon," I whined. I sounded pathetic but didn't give a crap. I needed his cock inside me, and I needed to feel the stretch and the friction. I needed my breasts to bounce and for him to play, suck, lick, and slap if that was his thing. It certainly was mine.

I got my wish when he spun me around and guided me to bend over the pinball machine. My vision colored with greens, browns, blues, and reds from the scenery below the glass. My heated skin cooled as my stomach touched the metal of the machine. The mere idea of him taking me from behind sent erratic pulses to my swollen clit.

I swore one touch from him would make me scream to the high heavens.

He ripped off my thong, and I giggled.

Then his cock grazed my butt as he rubbed his hands up and down my back. I pushed back against him, wanting to feel him inside me. I tossed a look over my shoulder, my cheeks as hot as a bonfire on a cold night.

One of his hands pressed into my back, while the other careened down in between my ass checks. I moaned as his fingers found my center.

His expression was more painful than before. "Holy fuck. You're soaked, baby," he said, deep and husky, as he began to rub circles around my clit. Then his other hand disappeared from my back, and before I knew what was happening, two of his fingers were inside me.

I opened wider for him as I rocked my hips back and forth as though I were humping the pinball machine. The irony of my position was that I was plastered against the machine, looking down at the KISS theme and Gene Simmons's enormous tongue.

As if on cue, Dillon kneeled behind me and replaced his fingers with his tongue. His beard was scratchy, sending tingles of electricity down my legs to my toes.

I needed release and badly.

His tongue was hot and wet. One last flick would have done the job, but then he disappeared.

Whimpering, I plastered my cheek to the glass, breathing heavily and holding on since my legs were shaky.

I heard the clink of his belt buckle. For a minute, I thought he was going to whip me, and I whimpered.

He chuckled. "You want to be spanked?"

"Only if you have that ping-pong paddle."

Silence ticked.

I pushed off the machine and found him thinking. His head was angled to one side, his inked and muscled body perfect in every way.

I lowered my hand and clutched his massive erection. "You can use the paddle another time." I assumed he was thinking of where he could find a paddle in his house since the ping-pong table was at the shelter.

He unleashed a menacing grin.

"Now where were we," I said more than asked, only using the question to connect us again.

He tore open the wrapper of a condom that I imagined he'd gotten from his wallet, which lay open on the floor. Then he covered his smooth, silky cock and guided me around once again to bend over the pinball machine.

I slid my hand down to my clit, but he caught my arm. "Oh no, you don't. I promise that what you're about to experience will be well worth the wait."

It already was, and I hadn't even climaxed yet.

One large hand grasped my hip and pulled me toward him, while the other hand guided his cock into my center. "Spread your legs."

As soon as I did, he maneuvered inside me as if he'd done it a million times. I stuck out my hips toward him as much as I could, and instead of plastering my body to the machine, only my hands held on to the edge as I let my breasts hang down.

He jammed into me, hard and fast, and oh my word, he felt like heaven. Stars, bright and sparkly, glimmered behind my eyelids. I lost all sense of where I was.

I twisted my neck to watch him pound into me, and if I thought his earlier expression was a beautiful disaster, I was wrong. He looked like a man who had found the drug he needed to take away all the pain he'd endured in his past.

He pulled out and brought me over to the chaise lounge. "I need to taste you again." He pushed me on my back.

My body was singing, tingling, and on fire.

I let my legs fall open as though he had willed them to. Then he dragged his scratchy beard along the inside of my thigh. Goose bumps shot free and sang *hell yeah.*

"Dillon, now!"

He chuckled before he captured my clit in between his teeth and bit down lightly. "You like it rough, right?"

"Stop talking and do something." I wasn't nice in my deliverance. I was the one in severe pain now.

He went to work, sucking and licking. I could feel a tinge of cold from his lip ring every time he licked, and the mixture of hot and cold added to the blissful feeling taking over my body, even more so when he drove his fingers into me.

I pinched my nipples while my belly tickled, as though Dillon had dipped a million feathers inside me. I writhed, rocking my hips, needing friction. I latched on to his hair as those feathers morphed into a tornado, swirling, spinning, twisting, and turning until I screamed at the top of my lungs. "Dillon Hart!"

He continued to suck on my clit as my vision blurred, and I rode out the orgasm, not wanting it to end.

Then he lifted his head, crawled up my body, and thrust into me, growling, sounding husky and in desperate need of release. "So fucking tight."

My breasts bounced as that lingering orgasm hung in the balance. I rocked my hips with him until he slipped one hand behind me, grabbed my butt, and held on while he rammed into me harder and faster. Then he slowed, sweat sliding down his face.

I pouted.

"I want this to last." Despite his husky tone, he sounded melancholy as though this was our one and only time together.

I squeezed around him to let him know we would tango in the future.

"Mmm. Do that again."

So I did.

His head dipped, his hair grazing my skin, heightening my nerve endings.

He kissed his way up to my scar, my chin, and my ear, but never my lips. He'd wanted to leave our feelings at the door, and kissing was intimate. The act of two people's mouths fusing together, tongues touching, sent a different message, one laced with feelings, closeness, and togetherness.

I was tempted to pull his mouth to mine but decided not to test the waters unless he made the first move. Even then, I wasn't sure if I would concede or not. But I didn't have to make a choice. He nibbled on my chin before he started thrusting into me again.

"Hike your leg over my shoulder," he commanded.

Poof. I was right back under his spell. His voice melted me to the fabric beneath me as I did as he commanded.

He rammed into me deeper and harder, rougher and more ragged, until every muscle in him bunched. He grunted as he locked eyes with me. For a second, I wanted to look away from the desperation saturating every pore on his face. He looked as though he were afraid I would leave him.

Damn heart.

Damn feelings.

Damn him.

He groaned loudly, his face toward the ceiling, and his body shuddered as he pulsed inside me. The way his face contorted and his eyes rolled back in his head as he rode out his orgasm was bewitching.

I knew then that I wanted more of Dillon. The problem was that I'd agreed to leave my feelings at the door, and that was my mistake.

19

MAGGIE

Several of Nadine's family members were sniffling as the priest read a passage from the Bible. I couldn't see Nadine's mom and dad since I was behind them, but I knew who they were since the priest had addressed them before he'd gotten started.

Tears clouded my vision, and I hated that I hadn't been able to help Nadine more. I should've insisted that she speak to Ted. More than anything, I regretted that I hadn't brought Ted in right from the beginning. If I had, she might still be alive. But I understood her apprehension about running to the cops. After Cory had raped me, I'd been scared out of my wits of going to the cops.

The gray-haired priest had a soft voice as he continued to speak.

I dove into my own thoughts as I tuned him out, recalling Lou's funeral, which was the only funeral I'd been to aside from Nadine's. I remembered thinking that I didn't want to end up dead. It had taken me about a year after his death and a few stints in jail for petty crimes to wake up.

As I stood there, next to the man who had given me the best orgasms to date, I realized that I only got one chance to live my life, and I didn't want to miss out on the finer things like a steady boyfriend or, dare I say, marriage. Before Dillon, I had begun to think I couldn't feel that intimate connection with someone. But after the last week, I was slowly changing my tune. Maybe love wasn't overrated. Maybe Dillon was cracking through my cement wall, bit by bit.

I was surely getting ahead of myself, though. I'd all but forced us to be nothing more than friends. If I hadn't gotten all weird about how he was making me feel, then our relationship would've taken a natural course. Maybe we would've kissed, or maybe Dillon wouldn't be closed off. He'd changed from the way he'd acted before that day in his kitchen. Even during sex, I could tell he was holding back from showing me more of his emotions.

On the drive up to Charlestown, we'd talked about everything and anything but us and the night before.

The rustling and louder voices drew me out of my funk.

Dillon cupped my elbow. "Do you want to pay your respects?"

Nadine's parents, Mr. and Mrs. Glover, were standing over the coffin. Mrs. Glover, who wore a simple black dress and her dark-auburn hair pulled back into a tight chignon, had her hand on the casket. Mr. Glover stayed close to his wife, tucking his hands into his pants pockets. I could see where Nadine had gotten her red hair. Both her parents had red hair, although Mr. Glover's was a brighter shade than his wife's.

"I'll wait until she's done," I said in a low voice. I hated to disturb her while she was saying her final goodbyes.

Most of the other guests had departed. Some were talking to each other in the parking lot, which wasn't far from the gravesite.

"Thanks for coming," I said to Dillon.

His whiskey-colored eyes sparkled in the morning sun. "Anytime."

I was learning that my belly was always giddy when I was around him. He looked like a man on the pages of GQ, with the sleeves of his crisp white shirt folded neatly up his forearms and his tattoos peeking out. His nose ring was glimmering. His beard was trimmed and hugged his angular jaw. His cologne was drifting on the light wind, and his wild hair was tamed with a small amount of gel.

Mrs. Glover broke my concentration as she sniffled, walking by me.

My nerves started to sing as I cleared my throat. On the way here, I'd wrestled over whether or not to put on my reporter hat or just pay my respects. Today wasn't the day to probe her parents for information for my story. However, if I only paid my respects, then her parents might ask me how I knew Nadine, and I couldn't tell them without spilling information that Ted didn't want the public to know.

"Mrs. Glover? Mr. Glover?" I interlaced my hands in front of me. "I'm Maggie Marx, a reporter for the *Boston Eagle,* and this is my friend, Dillon Hart. We're very sorry for your loss." I figured if I told them I was a reporter, then they wouldn't ask me how I knew Nadine. In turn, I wouldn't have to lie.

Mr. Glover appraised Dillon and me. "We're in mourning, Ms. Marx. Your questions can wait."

I wasn't surprised. "Honestly, Mr. Glover, I would like to learn more about Nadine. Is there a good time when I can meet with you and Mrs. Glover?" Tears surfaced as I thought about Nadine.

Mrs. Glover handed me a tissue. "I get the feeling you knew Nadine."

Dillon placed his hand on my lower back. "Nadine's body was found not far from where we live. We feel awful about what happened to her."

I'd filled Dillon in on the way there that Ted hadn't divulged anything about Nadine running from that house since he was still working on the case.

Mrs. Glover shuddered, while Mr. Glover relaxed a little bit.

I wanted to kiss Dillon for breaking the ice, especially since I was on the verge of crying along with Mrs. Glover.

Then Mrs. Glover started in. "We never thought our little girl would be swallowed up by the big city. She had such high hopes when she packed her bags and moved to Boston. She wanted to be on her own, and we felt we needed to let her explore her life."

"We gave her enough money to get on her feet," Mr. Glover said.

"She called us frequently, and the last time we spoke to her, about six weeks ago, she informed us she'd found a job working in retail sales. That was the last we heard from her."

Maybe that was how she'd met Miguel. But Ted had said Miguel found runaway girls, homeless girls, and girls prostituting themselves, not girls who worked in retail. It sounded as though Nadine had lied to her parents.

As if Dillon could feel their heartache, he said, "My sister did something similar. Sadly, though, my family and I haven't heard from her in four years."

Mrs. Glover took Dillon's hand. "I'm so sorry."

Dillon sandwiched her hand with both of his. "Thank you. I hope to get closure one day."

I prayed that day would come soon for him.

Mr. Glover cleared his throat. "Ms. Marx, we can't tell you much more than that except we loved our daughter dearly. She was a bright light on a gloomy day. She had high hopes of studying journalism. But as we said, she wanted to take a couple of years and find herself."

Wow! Now I was more intrigued about Nadine. But I would never know more about her. I had enough info to use if the Glovers would let me.

"Do I have your permission to print that, Mr. Marx?" I asked.

He nodded.

Mrs. Glover let go of Dillon. "We appreciate you coming."

That was our cue to go. I wanted to ask more questions, but I couldn't without breaking down, and I had enough to use for an article.

I hooked my arm in Dillon's. "Again, we're so sorry for your loss."

Silence followed us to Dillon's car.

Once we were on the road, I finally sighed. "Thank you for stepping in. I seriously was close to bawling."

He grasped my hand. "I got you."

I liked that. I liked that a ton.

20

DILLON

I sat in my office, taking care of a few administrative items. Since Nadine's funeral, frustration had ridden me hard for so many reasons. No matter how much I lifted weights or exercised to the point of exhaustion, I couldn't relax or sleep.

Waiting for anything had never been my strong suit. I was waiting for Denim to call me. When Maggie and I had gotten to the prison last Friday, we'd learned that Denim was in solitary. He'd gotten into a brutal fight with an inmate, and they had both needed stitches. The guard hadn't told us much more than that. I could only assume Denim had asked the wrong questions, which had rattled the cage of a Black Knight member. I was relieved that Denim hadn't gotten himself killed.

The progress on finding Grace had come to a standstill. Maggie and I were on a friendship ride. My brother Duke was due back in town sometime today, and I couldn't get Maggie out of my head.

I hadn't seen her since we returned from the prison five days ago. She'd been busy at work, and I'd picked up some shifts at the shelter to give Rafe and Hunt a break. Sure, I could've asked her to meet me at my house after work, but I wouldn't have been able to keep my hands off her.

The door to my office flew open. Norma panted, seemingly excited.

My heart did a little dance. "What's wrong?"

"Angel is on the porch, talking to Norton." She caught her breath. "You're not going to believe it, but… he's…"

I went to grab my gun in the top drawer as she held up her hand.

"No need to shoot anyone today." She emphasized the last word as though I would need to use my gun at some point in the shelter's existence.

I stormed out before she could say another word. Even if the man appeared calm and sweet, alcoholics didn't change overnight.

The sun was high in the sky, and the air was still, as though Mother Nature had shut off the air vents. Angel sat in the swinging loveseat that Rafe had installed only days ago, while Norton rested against the porch rail, looking at his wife.

I wanted to scream at her since I'd warned her to be careful.

Her blue eyes shimmered. "It's okay, Dillon. Norton isn't drunk."

From where I stood, which was as close as I'd been to him the night he'd stumbled toward me with a gun in his hand, I could see she was right. I'd checked with Manny every few days, not necessarily to see how Norton was doing, but more to find out if my old man had shown up or even called Manny. To my chagrin, that was a negative. A son could hope, though.

Norton held out his steady hand. "Dillon, I can't thank you enough."

I helped women in need, but never a man. The feeling, though, was the same—warmth, elation, and a sense of relief, knowing that I could affect someone's life in a positive way.

I sized him up and down, mainly in awe of how he didn't stink of booze. His hair wasn't oily, his face was shaven, and he wore pressed clothes that appeared brand-new. He wasn't out of the woods yet. Alcoholics had a steep hill to climb. But he had to start somewhere.

His handshake was firm, which was another good sign.

Angel sidled up to him. "I'm not going anywhere, Dillon."

She must've been reading my mind. My nerves quieted, knowing she wasn't jumping back into the fire.

"I'm staying at Manny's for another two months," Norton added. "I have a ways to go before I can say with certainty that I won't touch alcohol again."

I didn't want to burst his bubble that being a recovering alcoholic was a lifetime commitment and that it would take more than two months.

"As long as you stick to the program, man," I said. "You're well on your way. But please do me a favor. Before you show up, call first. We have an eight hundred number. I can't have you scaring my other guests. Angel, I'm not going to put demands on you, but if Norton shows up unannounced, I need you to get me or one of the staff members." Norton could relapse and bring a gun with him next time like he had before. I couldn't risk that, not only for Angel's sake, but for anyone here or in the neighborhood.

"Agreed," they both said.

They resumed their conversation while I went back inside. As soon as I crossed the threshold between the entryway and the common room, Maggie's voice floated toward me.

My stomach got this weird feeling that I couldn't describe, remembering our wild night of sex when we'd made all kinds of music together.

A hand grasped my arm. "Dillon," Norma said. "Does your tummy feel like it's spinning and flipping?" She tapped on my hand, which was resting on my abs.

I jolted out of my stupor. "No. Why would you ask me that?"

Women were so darn intuitive.

She giggled. "Because you're holding your stomach, and your face is rather pink. It's good to see that Maggie brings out a side of you I haven't seen."

I didn't want to know what side she saw. "When did Maggie get here?" I didn't see her VW Bug outside either. "Who is she talking to?" Rafe wasn't due in to work for four hours, and Hunt had the late-night shift.

Norma went back to her desk. "Kelton. He showed up about ten minutes ago. They're both here to see you. I told them you were busy, but they wanted to wait."

My office was down a hall, away from the main area of the house. So I wouldn't have seen or even heard them come in. "I was doing paperwork." I wouldn't call that busy. Now if I were locked in my office with Maggie, then I would classify that as busy.

My groin tightened. I was losing my battle to leave my feelings at the door with her. Norma was right. Maggie had an effect on me that scared the hell out of me and made me want to shout to the world that I might have found a woman who met all my needs, and fuck if she didn't meet my needs in the bedroom. Her stripping had to be the sexiest darn scene I'd ever laid eyes on, and I'd watched some good porn over the years.

I padded through the common room, my hand whisking through my hair. My hands were always in my hair, and suddenly I wanted Maggie's hands pulling on my hair like she'd done several times that night at my house.

Stop torturing yourself.

My self-torture turned into jealousy. I shouldn't have been jealous of Kelton. After all, he had a girlfriend. *Yeah, the same girl you kissed and the last woman you kissed. You didn't even kiss Maggie.*

I couldn't fuse my lips to Maggie's. I couldn't allow myself to feel that intimate connection, no matter how fucking hard I'd been dying to capture her tongue in my mouth and kiss her lights out while I pumped inside her. That would make me feel something other than the off-the-chart orgasms I'd had with her. I couldn't test those waters, afraid she would leave me the way my mother left my old man.

All thought left me when I laid eyes on Maggie and Kelton. The Maxwell god leaned over, resting his elbows on the island. Maggie stood across from him, mimicking his position. They chatted like two lovers who had finished having sex moments ago. I clenched my fists, wanting to throw the man through the sliding glass door.

Kelton's a flirt, and you know that. No matter how much I knew he would never cheat on Lizzie, I didn't want him touching Maggie.

Suddenly, my head cleared. I was jealous, like extremely mad jealous. I'd never been one to resent another. I'd never had low self-esteem. But that swirly feeling in my stomach soured.

I was beginning to understand why Kade Maxwell sneered anytime a man other than his brothers dared to get near his girl, Lacey. I was beginning to understand why Kelton had wanted to ram his fists into me when I'd sheltered Lizzie from him. I was beginning to understand that maybe I had more than lust for the braided blond woman who had an ass that was mine. She was fucking mine.

I cleared my throat because they hadn't heard me. I didn't expect them to since I was barefoot.

Maggie's head swiveled, and Kelton snapped up as if he'd been caught doing something he wasn't supposed to.

"Hey, man," Kelton said casually, wearing one of his infamous arrogant grins that I wanted to wipe off his face.

My girl's eyes filled with concern. "What's wrong?" One thing I'd noticed when I was balls deep inside her was that her irises shifted from light to dark green, giving me the feeling that I was diving into the deep waters off some tropical shore.

"Are you sure it was just drinking and dancing between you two?" I directed my question more at Maggie.

Kelton rolled those dark-blue eyes that women loved. "Seriously?" He lost that flirty air about him as a snarl formed.

Maggie stuck her hands on her hips and pushed out those breasts I wanted to play with. "You're jealous?" Her full cupid lips curled. "Remember, no feelings." Her tone was light and devoid of any taunts or rudeness, even though she was throwing my words back in my face.

A growl was stuck in my throat.

Kelton tucked a hand in his pocket. "Whatever is going on between you two is none of my business. What is, though, is your brother

Denim. Are you opposed to Maggie hearing any of what I have to say?"

Denim's case wasn't in the least bit private. Yet I appreciated Kelton's professionalism.

"Shoot, man." My gaze never wavered from Maggie's.

Kelton snapped his fingers. "Dude, I need your full attention. I'm on the clock here."

That statement got me out of my funk, even though I wasn't paying him for his advice.

My hands stuck to my hair.

Maggie approached me like a cat slinking down the sidewalk, watching a dog come toward her—hesitant, but ready to use those claws—or maybe she was going to get the paddles from the table behind me.

"I need to talk to Norma," Maggie said. "So you two have the floor." She stopped at my side, placed a hand on my abs, and batted those long eyelashes. "I'm not going anywhere."

She left me dripping with the need to fuck her, and my balls were yelling for me to do just that.

When she was out of the room, I didn't lose an ounce of tension.

Kelton let out a loud laugh. "I've seen that look before, man, on each of my brothers when they found 'the one.'" He made air quotes around the last two words. "I can't say I saw it on myself, but I sure felt it. Right here." He tapped on his chest over his heart. "Give in to the feeling. Because love is one hell of a ride and one you don't want to miss."

I pushed air out of my nostrils. "Says the guy who flirts any chance he gets." I walked deeper into the kitchen until I was standing on the other side of the island, across from Kelton.

"Maggie and I were talking. She was asking me about you, if you really want to know."

The way they'd been whispering had led me to believe they'd been reminiscing about their night at the club. On second thought, I believed him since Maggie had been laughing. "That can't be good."

"Chill. She wanted to know how you and I met. I told her how you helped Lizzie and how you almost cut off my balls when I showed up at your house to talk to Lizzie."

"I was protecting Lizzie from you. Did you tell Maggie that?" Jealousy hadn't played a role when Kelton had shown up that day, although I had been a little envious of how Lizzie had looked at him.

"I told your girl that you're a great man who has a heart of gold." His serious tone matched his expression.

Inwardly, I let out a sigh. "Sounds to me like you want to date me," I teased.

He plastered on his grin. "I don't do men with long hair."

I stuck out my middle finger.

We both laughed.

"Back to Denim," Kelton said. "I looked at his case file. I discovered something odd in it that might bode well for him. But before I go into detail, one of the senior partners will weigh in."

"You're not going to tell me what it is?"

He grabbed his keys off the island. "Sorry, man. Until I can prove I'm right, I don't want to get anyone's hopes up. So Maggie said something about going to a bar to follow up on a lead? Do you need some help?"

I rubbed my chin. It was always good to have any of the Maxwell brothers protecting my ass, but I didn't think the Crow would be dangerous. I also didn't think I would find Grace there.

"I'm good."

"I got to run," Kelton said.

"Thank you." I had enough on my plate, so I didn't push him for answers on Denim's case.

Kelton and I exchanged a manly hug before he left. I found Maggie and Norma whispering at Norma's desk. I wondered where Debbie and the two new guests were. The house seemed quiet. Then again, the shelter wasn't a prison.

Maggie and Norma stopped talking. Then Norma got out of her chair. "I'm going to see how the girls are doing out back."

I guess I had my answer on where they were.

When Norma was out of the room, I crossed my arms over my chest.

Maggie rose from the chair near Norma's desk and swung her hips over to me. "Still jealous?"

I suddenly hated that word. I snatched her hand and guided her into my office. She giggled like a schoolgirl the entire way. Once we were locked in, I pushed her up against the door and planted my hands above her head.

"We never talked about the night we had," she said on a breathy sigh.

I scanned her pretty face. "Do you want to talk?"

She glanced at my couch then back up at me.

I moved a strand of her hair that had escaped her braid off her ear.

Out of nowhere, she cupped my dick. "Wow. Are you always hard?"

"Only around you."

Instantly, her cheeks darkened to red. "Should we do something about him?"

I traced a lazy path along her forehead, eyes, nose, and mouth, as if I were reading braille. She purred like a kitty cat wanting to be petted more. So I obliged, continuing my assault on her. Her tits were sticking out, and I would have bet her nipples were hard and ready. Unfortunately, I couldn't tell because she was wearing a bra.

I slipped a hand up her shirt and under her bra. When I pinched her nipple, she let out a soft squeal.

I leaned in, my crotch never touching her body, although she was rubbing my erection as though she were trying to get me off. I stifled any sounds or moans that wanted to break free. I didn't want anyone to hear me, although Norma had said the ladies were out in the backyard.

My lust was wiped out when my phone rang.

Maggie jumped a little.

I growled before I answered.

"Will you accept a collect call from Denim Hart?" the operator asked.

"Yes. Hey, bro. Are you all right? That must've been one hell of a fight if you're just getting out of solitary."

Maggie perched herself on the arm of the couch and lifted an eyebrow.

"Sorry," Denim said. "I'm good, though. I asked the wrong question to the wrong guy. I only have five minutes to talk."

"I don't want to get your hopes up, but I found out that Grace could be alive."

Denim sucked in air. "For real?"

"I'm working a lead tonight. I'll give you more details later. So did you find out anything on the Black Knights?" I tapped the speaker button. "Bro, I got Maggie Marx in the room with me, and you're on speaker." After all, Denim was hunting for information for her, not me.

"Maggie Marx," Denim said. "Look, girl, stay away from the Black Knights. Only death can come from someone snooping around."

Maggie rolled her eyes. "Did you get any info?"

I had a feeling I might have to tie Maggie up so she wouldn't end up like Nadine.

That isn't happening, dude. The woman is on a narrow and tight road of revenge. It's best if you keep her close.

Denim chuckled. "I see you're still a badass. Anyway, one of the rival gangs here slipped me a name. Does Dallas ring a bell? Apparently, he's one of the pimps for the Black Knights."

Maggie's pretty face twisted. "Not at all. Where can we find him?"

"That's all I got," Denim said. "I have to go. Be careful. Both of you."

"Watch your back, man," I said before the call disconnected.

"Dallas," Maggie mumbled. "That name isn't a whole lot to go on. I could float it by Ted."

I thought about suggesting we finish what we'd started before the phone call, but her mind was on the Black Knights, and mine was on Grace. The Crow opened tonight anyway.

Excitement stirred deep in my stomach at the notion that I could actually run into Grace tonight, despite the possibility that my sister didn't want anything to do with me.

I reached out to take Maggie's hand. "Let's do some detective work."

21

MAGGIE

Darkness crawled through the parking lot as Dillon and I wheeled in slowly behind the bikers rumbling in on their Harleys. One by one, each of the bikers parked in front of the stone facade that displayed a grand reopening sign above the entrance.

The ride over had mostly been in silence. We didn't talk about the flirtatious moment in Dillon's office or our steamy night of sex, or what Denim had shared with us. I didn't know anyone named Dallas. Honestly, I'd been silently swearing like a sailor that Denim hadn't dropped Cory's name.

Dillon found a spot along a fence that backed up to a cluster of industrial buildings and cut the engine, keeping his attention straight ahead.

With the dashboard lights on, I could see his hardened jaw and pinched features. Whatever was on his mind couldn't have been good.

He'd come close to a nervous breakdown at Skins and Needles the other day when he'd found out Grace had been alive six months ago. Even his father had seen Grace recently. Part of me believed that Grace might be into drugs and didn't want her family to know she was an addict. Another part of me thought that she might be selling her body like Nadine had. Or she could have been afraid to contact Dillon for some reason, much like Nadine hadn't wanted to go to the cops. Or worse, Grace could have been sold through sex trafficking.

I reached over the console and grasped his hand. "I got your back."

He jerked his head at me and gave me a panty-dropping grin. "Good to know." The diamond-studded nose ring sparkled when he twitched. "I've been thinking about what Denim said, and you need to watch your back. He's right. If you go snooping around the Black Knights, you're going to end up like Nadine. I know you can take care of yourself, but look what happened to Denim. That has to say something."

Letting go of his hand, I lifted a shoulder. In my experience, all gangs were scary, some more than others. I didn't want to follow in Nadine's footsteps. But I also had a job to do. "I appreciate your concern. I'll be careful."

He drilled his eyes into me. "You're already in harm's way, baby. Remember where they found Nadine's body."

My tummy did a flip over how he called me baby, while acid settled in my throat. "She might've been in the wrong place at the wrong time." The shelter wasn't exactly in an upscale neighborhood.

"Please don't get cocky or let your guard down," he said.

I gave him a two-finger salute. "Yes, sir."

He cringed as he climbed out, mumbling the word stubborn.

I wouldn't disagree. I grew up on my own. None of my foster parents had ever cared if I came home or not. So someone worrying about me was nice, but foreign. I still hadn't gotten used to how Ted worried over me. Not only that, I didn't listen to Ted most of the time. While I would do anything for Dillon in the bedroom, I wasn't going to change who I was as a reporter.

With my messenger bag strapped to my body, I hurried out into the sticky night air. I couldn't wait for the cool fall weather to arrive.

When I ponied up to Dillon, he immediately took hold of my hand. "Stay close."

I scanned the area, wondering what he saw that gave him a reason to warn me or feel protective. Then again, a crowd full of rowdy bikers might be a problem waiting to happen.

Music pumped out as Dillon and I waltzed into a packed house. Men wearing short-sleeve T-shirts and leather vests chatted at tables and booths scattered about. Some sat at the bar, watching a baseball game on the large-screen TV, while others hung out around the pool table, which was located in the large alcove on the other side of the bar. Everyone was so absorbed in what they were doing that they didn't give us a passing glance.

I didn't know if it was the music that was loud or the voices that were trying to talk above the music. It didn't help that the ceilings were high with fans hanging down from the beams every few feet or so.

I detected the light scent of fresh paint as we settled not far from the bar. If a fire had shut the bar down, I didn't see any evidence of it.

I scrutinized the women, in particular their necks, to see if any of them had a hummingbird tattoo.

About six women lounged next to their men in the bar area. None of them were Grace unless she'd bleached her hair blond, and I would have guessed the age of these women to be about twenty-five, not twenty. Two other women sat on high stools in the poolroom, and like the women in the bar area, they didn't appear younger than twenty.

Dillon's hand stiffened in mine. I followed his line of sight to an average-sized girl with short brown hair. She had her back to us as she perused songs on the jukebox. Dillon darted toward the girl, when a biker with a huge gut stalked toward me, sizing me up as if I were his next meal.

Ew!

I suddenly realized my attire was completely out of place in a sea of black vests, chains, piercings, and longhaired men. The women weren't any different in the wardrobe department. Even Dillon fit right in, sans the vest. Me, not so much. I stuck out like a red herring, but I didn't really care. I liked my denim capris, Chucks, and my signature cotton T-shirt with a scarf. I thought for a minute about removing the scarf and showing off my scar, because in this club, I was right at home.

The biker, who had a scar on the side of his face, grinned, showing off his gold tooth. "Hey, darlin', what brings you here?"

I giggled. "Is that your pick-up line?"

He puckered his lips then moved them back and forth as though he were sucking on a lemon. "You sure are a pretty one." He reached for my scarf, but I swatted his hand away.

Dillon was back at my side. "Are you trying to pick up my girlfriend, big guy?" He snarled at Gold Tooth, who matched Dillon in height but nothing else. If I had to wager which of them would win in a fight, I would've liked to have bet on Dillon, but Gold Tooth had the girth and the linebacker arms that could put a hurt on Dillon.

The voices around us died. All eyes in the immediate area waited for a brawl. Some men pressed their hands on the table, ready to attack.

Gold Tooth lifted his meaty hands, which were encrusted with oil or black crud. "Not my gig." After he walked away, the voices hummed again.

I plastered on a gooey grin. "So I'm your girlfriend now?"

Dillon glanced down at me, his snarl ebbing. "I want to check out that girl at the jukebox."

I peered around him. "She's not there."

He whipped his head around then frantically searched the room.

I started to scan the heads. "Was that Grace?"

A petite waitress with her dark hair up in a ponytail bounced up to us. "There's a free table near the pool hall."

"We're looking for someone," I said.

Dillon's eyes darted in all directions. "A brown-haired girl with a hummingbird tattoo on her neck."

The tray of beer bottles she was holding shook slightly. She tossed a look over her shoulder toward the pool hall. "Check with Dominic. He's the guy bending over the pool table right now."

Shock and awe leaked from Dillon's expression like it had at the tattoo shop. "Is the girl here?" he asked in a high-pitched voice.

My heart did a few extra laps around the track. I tried to put myself in Dillon's shoes and wondered how I would react if I found someone after they'd been missing for a couple of years. My mom didn't count since I didn't even know her. If I were in Dillon's situation, I would probably freak out too.

"You'll need to talk to Dom." She dashed away as though she knew a secret and would get beaten if she told us.

Dillon and I skirted around tables and chairs as the other patrons' eyes bore holes into us. I could almost feel the heat of their stares.

The tall and slender guy who had a military haircut, long sideburns, and diamond earrings in both ears lifted his hazel eyes from the cue ball and focused on us. Then he straightened before a short guy with a pool stick flanked him on his left, and a beefy biker with a low ponytail took up a position on his right.

The two twenty-something women, one with a row of piercings up her right ear, and the other with stark gray eyes that had a storm brewing in them, didn't move an inch.

"Are you Dom?" Dillon asked.

Dom gripped the pool stick, his angular jaw as hard as the cue ball. "Who's asking?"

Dillon's shoulders lifted. "Does it matter?" His tone bordered on angry. "I'm looking for a girl with a hummingbird inked on her neck."

The expressions on the faces of everyone in the poolroom were blank. No one winced or shuddered or reared back like the waitress had. No one said a word. The women didn't even react.

"We have a lot of ink in this bar, but I don't know anyone with a tattoo like that." Dom's nostrils moved rapidly.

The man was lying.

Dillon clenched his fists. "Let's try this again. Do you know a girl by the name of Emily?"

The girl with stark gray eyes jerked as if she had Tourette's syndrome.

Dom studied Dillon, not giving his hand away.

Dillon lunged at Dom, and all hell broke loose.

22

DILLON

My hand went around Dom's thick neck, while his compadres pulled guns on me. I'd left mine in my desk once again. I didn't need to kill anyone. What I needed was to squeeze Dom for information because the fucker was lying. Body language was a beautiful giveaway, and rarely could one hide the truth from me unless I was naive, and I was far from being blinded. Gang life had taught me several things. One, always know my surroundings. I'd counted two exits and roughly fifty bikers of all shapes and sizes, not including the two waitresses and two bartenders. And I was one hundred percent certain that all the bikers had some type of weapon on them.

The girl who had piercings up and down her ears, and long-ass legs that disappeared underneath her frayed shorts flew off the stool and started to head toward the bar.

"Oh, no. You're not going anywhere," Maggie growled behind me.

"Your girl is badass, man," Dom squeaked out as his face reddened.

Another thing I'd learned in a gang was to trust that my brethren had my back. I trusted that Maggie could take care of herself like she'd been boasting about, and I had complete confidence in her that she did have my back.

"Craig, Bert," Dom choked out. "Put your guns down."

The short guy and the big guy had death glares on their scraggly faces, not acquiescing.

So I dug my fingers into Dom's neck harder. "Guns don't scare me. I don't give a fuck if the entire bar has guns trained on me. I came here to find my sister, and I'm not leaving until I get answers."

He knitted his eyebrows. "Why didn't you say so?" he barely got out.

Craig and Bert lowered their guns.

The women let out a collective sigh.

I slowly released him.

Dom rubbed his neck as he coughed. "Man, you got one hell of a grip."

I stole a look over my shoulder at Maggie, who was lowering the knife in her hand. When she met my gaze, she gave me one of her ball-busting smiles. I breathed a little easier, knowing she could fend off attackers, although I should have known that anyway since she'd been in a gang, one that had a staunch and deadly leader who had taught her and his underlings how to fight and protect themselves. I was sure Ted had as well.

"So, Emily is your sister," Dom said as more of a confirmation than a question.

My attention swiveled back to him. The girl who reminded me of Lizzie, with her black hair and gray eyes, threw her arms around Dom.

"It's okay, sweetheart," he cooed as he kissed her forehead. Then he tipped his head at the archway. "Everyone out." His statement was directed at everyone but Maggie and me.

I found a stool and patted the one next to me as I eyed Maggie. She tucked her knife into her messenger bag as she sat next to me.

When his friends were gone, Dom pressed the palms of his hands against the edge of the pool table.

"Where is she?" I asked

"You do look like Emily," Dom said. "It's the eyes."

"Spare me the small talk. And my sister's name is Grace." My voice was gruff, and my tone was rude. The shock that had ripped through my body when Syd told me about Grace, and then again when my old man said he'd seen her, was gone. In its place was pure rage that ate at the lining of my stomach like a parasite that was hungry and multiplying by the second. It was directed more at Grace than anyone.

Dom crossed his dirty denim-clad legs at the ankles. "I haven't heard from Emily in two weeks."

I vaulted off the stool. "Say that again."

Dom hunched his shoulders. "I'm sorry. I meant Grace."

I pinned him with what I knew was a scowl that would win a spot in the *Guinness Book of World Records*. "No, asshole, you said two weeks. You saw my sister two weeks ago?" I'd heard him clearly. I just had to torture myself again and again until those parasites chomped on every organ in me.

"Dillon." Maggie said my name as though she were my mother, scolding me for being rude, much like my mom had done when I'd smarted off to my old man.

"So you're the one she looked up to, the one she trusted." Dom delivered the words in an even tone.

His words were nothing short of a dagger piercing my heart over and over again. I began pacing, moving away from Dom before my fist connected with his large nose. I circled the pool table, snagged the eight ball, and rolled it in my hands.

Maggie rushed to my side. "You need to breathe."

I was trying to make sense of what I was hearing.

I haven't heard from Emily in two weeks.

You're the one she looked up to.

The one she trusted.

He was only regurgitating what he knew and what Grace had told him. I'd failed her.

The pool table separated Dom and me, and if it hadn't weighed a ton, I would have flipped the fucker over.

Dom's words were on repeat in my head.

Maggie's small hand rested on my back, rubbing lazy circles, hoping to soothe the raging lion inside me.

I tossed the ball on the table, and it landed with a loud *thwack*. Then I shoved my hands through my hair and paced again. Maggie gave me a pitying look. I wanted to tell her I didn't need her pity. I was the one at fault. I was the one who had left Grace. I was the one who'd forced her onto the streets of Boston. The only thing that made me not lose my shit even more was that she was alive.

I came to an abrupt halt at the archway and looked into the club, scanning for that girl I'd seen at the jukebox. My old man had described Grace as having hair shorter than mine. That girl at the jukebox had had short brown hair, almost cut into a style that mirrored Dom's. But from where I'd been standing, I couldn't tell if that girl had had a hummingbird tat.

Not looking at Dom, I said, "Describe Grace to me."

"Aside from the tat on her neck, she has others on her arms, much like you do. Her hair is short, cut over her ears, long on top, and she's beautiful, if you ask me." He sounded sad, as though he were remembering a lost love.

The girl at the jukebox hadn't had tats on her arms. "Are you in love with my sister?" I returned to Maggie's side. I was doing the math in my head. Grace was twenty. Dom appeared to be in his twenties, around my age, I would guess. "When did you meet my sister?" I shouldn't be trying to play big brother and beat Dom's head in for liking my sister. I had no business deciding who Grace dated. I'd lost that right the day I left for the merchant marines.

"Grace is alive, Dillon," Maggie muttered. I got the impression she was trying to convince herself more than me.

Dom rubbed his chin. "I met Emily about nine months ago. Actually, I found her stealing food from a grocery store. She was filthy, bruised, and her hair was caked in blood."

I hated to think what had happened to Grace. The way he was describing her reminded me of Nadine.

Dom pressed his lips tightly together. "I gave her a room, a warm bed, and food."

Maggie and I rounded the pool table, then Maggie hopped up while I stood.

"I tried to ask her where she'd been," Dom continued, sitting on the edge of the stool along the wall. "Who messed her up? But she wouldn't talk. I tried to get my sister"—he pointed a finger at the entrance—"Fi, the girl with black hair, to talk to her. But Fi struck out too. I've never touched your sister. I've never slept with her either." He touched his chest. "I swear, man."

While I believed him, Dom and Grace sleeping together wasn't why I was boring holes into him. "Continue."

He lowered his shoulders. "All I did was give her a bed to crash. She came and went. After about a month, she started leaving money on the kitchen table before she left in the morning. On a few occasions, she would hang out with Fi and me here before the fire gutted the joint. She was always quiet. Kept to herself. As long as I knew she was safe, I didn't question her. Where she went during the day, I couldn't say. How she got money, I don't know." Dom sighed heavily. "I'm worried about her."

I folded my arms over my chest. "So if she hardly spoke, then how do you know about me, and how do you know she trusted me?" Something wasn't adding up. He sounded as though he knew her but didn't know her. He was leaving something out.

He gnawed on his lip. "I overheard a phone conversation. She mentioned your name and another name." His forehead creased. "Duke, if I remember correctly."

Motherfucker.

"So you're saying she was talking to Duke?" My gut coiled like a rattlesnake ready to sink its fangs into someone.

He shrugged his wide shoulders. "Don't know. Why? Is he related to you?"

Maggie listened intently.

"My brother," I said with venom laced in those two words. I would fuck up Duke so badly if he knew where Grace was. "So you said you overheard her on the phone. Do you have her cell phone number? Or any idea of how to get a hold of her?"

"To my knowledge, she doesn't have a cell phone," Dom said. "She used the phone at my place. And no. I have no clue where to find her."

I could try to choke more info out of him, but I got the impression he wasn't about to tell me anything else.

"Do you know or have you heard of the Black Knights?" Maggie asked. The woman was relentless, both in and out of bed.

Dom snarled. "Who hasn't? Do you think Grace is tied up with them?" He sounded as though he'd asked a question he knew the answer to.

Then again, my mind was a jumbled junkyard of this and that, and I was beginning to wonder if I would ever think clearly again.

Maggie shrugged. "Don't know. I'm doing a story on the gang. I work for the *Boston Eagle,* by the way," she said proudly.

Dom twirled a ring on his pinky finger. "Word on the street is Miguel Rivera is their leader. He has a team of men who meet women, promise them a red-carpet welcome, douse them in glitz, clothes, and money, then *wham!* They're being pimped out or sold."

Maggie's foot dangled and moved furiously. "Mmm. I had to pull teeth to get that info."

I stretched my neck to look at her. "Come again?"

"Ted told me in confidence. I guess it's not a secret anymore." She regarded Dom. "It sounds like you know Miguel's ways firsthand."

He shuddered. "Fi's friend escaped from one of his soldiers."

I shook out of my shock for the moment over the news that Maggie knew the name of the leader of the Black Knights but hadn't bothered to tell me or bring it up when Denim had been on the phone. I could've warned him to back off. Maybe then he wouldn't have gotten hurt. But that discussion was for later.

I stabbed a thumb in the direction of the bar area. "The girl with your sister?"

"No," Dom said. "Hannah is Craig's girl. Fi's friend doesn't live in the state anymore. She went back to her parents."

"Do you know where I can find Miguel?" Maggie asked.

I jerked my head at her again. "Where *you* can find him?" The woman was going to give me an ulcer. "You're not going anywhere near him." Steam was coming out of my nostrils.

"Listen to your boyfriend," Dom said. "Nothing good can come out of you snooping into Miguel's business."

Maggie pulled out a small notebook. "You got a name of any of his pimps?"

My mouth was slightly ajar. Here I was, wrestling with everything Dom had said about Grace, and now I was going to have to tie Maggie up so she wouldn't walk right into the mouth of a dragon.

He sized Maggie up, puffing out his cheeks. "I've heard of reporters getting killed for information. But you won't find any of them. The Black Knights are like ghosts, and you only know they're there when it's too late."

Maggie narrowed her eyes.

I swiped my hand over her leg. "Easy, baby."

Her knuckles whitened as she gripped her pen. "Do you know the name Dallas?"

Dom flinched. "Please tell me you don't know him."

Now we were getting somewhere. "We only heard the name earlier tonight. What do you know about him?"

"On the streets, he's known as Dallas," Dom said. "But Fi's friend mentioned the man who had been breaking her in, so to speak, wanted her to call him Cory."

Maggie's jaw hit the floor.

Suddenly, the web Maggie and I were untangling just got stickier, and whether the Black Knights, Cory, and Grace intersected somehow, one thing was certain. It was time I paid my brother Duke a visit.

23

MAGGIE

I gaped at the ceiling fan in a guest bedroom at Dillon's house, watching it spin around and around and around. It felt as if my brain were on that fan as it too spun around and around and around. When Dom had said Cory's name, I'd literally almost peed in my thong. Misty had mentioned Cory's name, but she hadn't been one hundred percent sure of his involvement with the gang. Dom seemed sure.

I wondered if Ted knew the name Dallas. I would bet that was the reason Ted couldn't connect Cory to anything.

I'd tried to force Dom to give me more information on Fi's friend so I could question her. He wouldn't budge, though. His sister, Fi, wouldn't either. I respected them for maintaining the woman's privacy. Yet I wanted to blast the hell out of the Black Knights. The more I uncovered about the gang, the more my revenge wasn't only about Cory anymore. I wanted all men like Cory to pay for what they'd done to women.

From the bar to Dillon's house, I'd been a zombie. Even when we walked in, I'd had no words. We were both dumbfounded for different reasons.

I climbed out of bed. I'd asked him if I could stay in his guest room. He hadn't tried to coax me into his bed, and he hadn't come onto me. Instead, he'd been a gentleman. After showing me where the bathroom and towels were located, he'd walked me to my room. A part of me had wanted him to ask me to stay with him.

But the main reason I'd wanted to stay at his house was the quiet. I wanted to think without the distraction of the engines, horns, and voices that filled the city streets outside my apartment window. I was failing in that department. I couldn't quiet my mind.

I tiptoed out of my room, trying not to wake Dillon, who was sleeping one door down from the bathroom. Once inside, I splashed water on my face. The nightlight provided ample light for me to see that I was beginning to develop bags under my eyes. I really needed to stop working eighteen-hour days.

I patted my face with a towel, combed my fingers through my long blond hair, and rifled through how to prove Cory Calderon was the scum I knew he was.

I stared at myself in the mirror. "Mirror, mirror, on the wall, how do I get hardcore facts on Cory once and for all?" I whispered.

The first idea that came to mind was to share the news with Ted. He might've heard of the name Dallas and had evidence on Cory's alias. I could also get Dom on record to confirm that Cory was involved with the Black Knights. But Dom wasn't the actual witness. He only knew the name, and it wasn't a strong enough fact that would stick, especially since Cory's father had money to sue the paper if I didn't have concrete facts like a description of Cory.

The other option swimming around in my head was to put myself out there as a prostitute. That would get me concrete evidence. Otherwise, I would be searching for years, and I didn't want to wait forever. The problem I had, though, was that girls no longer walked a city corner, waiting for a john. The pimps now did all the bidding for the girls. They chose the customer. They chose the hotel. All a girl had to do was dress up pretty and wait in some sleazy hotel room or...

The proverbial light bulb came on. Nadine had been at a house, not a hotel room. I should start there. Maybe the gang was stupid enough to return to the house on Bleven and Third. Maybe I could find some clue as to where Miguel lived. Or maybe I could find out who owned the house and follow the money trail. I mentally slapped myself for not thinking about this long before now.

I ironed a hand down my wrinkled shirt. I hadn't even undressed when I flopped on the bed an hour ago. Dillon and I had gotten back to his house around two a.m. No sooner had he shown me to my room than he disappeared in his.

I imagined he had his own war to fight after discovering that Grace was alive two weeks ago, according to Dom. I was beginning to believe that she didn't want her family to know she was alive, which irked me if that were true. She had a brother who loved her, a family. Granted, the Hart clan was a dysfunctional bunch, but nonetheless, she had a family. The contents of the envelope Ted had given me with my mom's address inside were beginning to weigh heavily on me. Everywhere I went seemed to remind me of family.

I quietly went back to the guest room and snatched my messenger bag. Then I pulled out a pen and paper and scribbled down a note for Dillon.

I'm sorry, but I have to find facts. I'll call you later. XO, Maggie.

I folded the note as I slinked down the hallway then slipped it underneath his door. I was tempted to peek inside, but I didn't trust myself not to crawl into bed with him.

My first stop was the house on Bleven and Third. At three in the morning, no one would see me.

I prowled down the stairs like a cat burglar, stopping on each one, praying it didn't creak. When I reached the front door, I let out a soft sigh.

As soon as I pulled open the door, a screeching siren blared.

Wincing, I shouted all kinds of expletives in my head.

Damn alarm.

Dillon flew down the stairs in nothing but his underwear, with a gun drawn on me.

Out of habit, I lifted my hands, an act I'd been used to when the cops would break up a gang fight and bring me down to the police station.

"What the fuck, Maggie?" He lowered his gun, slammed the door, and ran down the hall to punch in the alarm code.

At that moment, I realized I hadn't thought my plan through because my car was at the shelter and not at Dillon's house.

Stupid me.

I dropped my bag on the floor and ambled into the kitchen, holding my ears.

The blaring suddenly ceased at the same time Dillon flicked on the overhead lights.

I didn't know what was worse, the siren or the lights. I blinked a couple of times to adjust my vision. When the kitchen became crystal clear, so did Dillon.

I couldn't help but drag my gaze over his scrumptious body. *Holy cannoli.* That hair of his was wild and crazy. His cheeks were red. His eyes were sleepy, and he stood in his boxer briefs holding a gun at his side. If the looks of him weren't enough to get me soaked, then the semi-erection he was sporting sure was.

He pointed the gun at the table. "Sit." His voice was anything but sleepy.

I stood my ground at the arched doorway, folding my arms over my chest.

"Maggie, you're not going anywhere until we talk."

Or maybe have sex on the kitchen table.

He scratched his head before massaging his fingers through his hair. Then he deposited the gun on top of the fridge. "I'll make some coffee."

Now he was talking my language. I waltzed over to the table, parked my butt in a chair, and continued to admire the man while he made quick work of getting the coffeepot ready. "I can't sleep." As soon as I said that, I yawned, and it happened to be right when he glanced over his shoulder.

"Try again," he said.

"I need to go into the paper. I have work to do." I wasn't lying exactly.

"Why don't I believe you?"

To lie or not to lie. You like him. You probably like him more than you think. You're an upfront kind of gal. Tell him the truth. Plus, if you want to go anywhere, you'll need him to drive you.

When the coffeepot started gurgling, Dillon didn't move from the counter. He seemed so comfortable in his own skin. He didn't care that his hair was sticking up in all directions. He didn't care that his penis was growing by the second, the longer he looked at me. He probably didn't know that he could win the annual *People Magazine* award for the sexiest man alive.

Regardless, the longer he ogled and the longer I didn't answer him, the more the butterflies came alive. He was someone I could date. He was someone I could love. In that moment, the word love didn't scare me.

"I'm waiting," he said, breaking my trance.

The coffeemaker continued to drip, and the aroma filled the room.

"What are we doing?" I asked.

He cocked his head.

I waggled a finger between us. "You and me."

We liked each other. We were attracted to each other.

"We're helping each other," he said.

"We're also having sex," I added.

He grinned as though he was remembering our night together. "And?"

And you're worming your way into my heart.

The coffeemaker murmured one last time before it beeped.

He filled two cups then brought them to the table. "Not sure if you take yours black or not."

Black and strong was perfect.

He dragged a chair out and folded his muscular body into it. "What's really going on, Maggie?"

I took a sip of coffee. "I feel like I haven't accomplished shit in my life." That was the truth. "I feel like I'm pissed off at the world. I want revenge so bad, I can taste it. Yet when I see all the great things you do for the shelter and how big your heart is for those girls, I hate myself." Another truth. Whether it was the coffee, the time of night, or the realization that Cory was working for the Black Knights, I didn't care. It felt amazing to get that off my chest.

"I'm not a saint," he said.

I wanted to say, *You act like a saint and look like a god.* But I refrained from spewing those words only because I wanted to hear more of what he had to say. So I drank more coffee.

He kicked out his bare legs and sat back with no evidence of an erection. "I don't see myself with a big heart. I opened that shelter hoping Grace would walk through the door. As angry as you are at Cory, I'm a little furious with Grace if she is alive, and if I'm being honest, I'm hurt that she hasn't bothered to reach out to me. I'm pissed off at my old man for being drunk and driving away my mom when I was a kid. I have a love-hate relationship with my older brother, Duke. I blame him for Grace, but I blame myself more. We all have problems, Maggie, that will test our resolve. There's nothing wrong with you feeling the way you do. But instead of freaking out about things, especially about you and me, let nature take its course."

"Says the pot calling the kettle black," I added. "You're the one who wanted to leave feelings at the door."

He pursed his lips. "Mmm. And you're the one who said, 'I'm not into relationships, short or long. I hook up with a man, and then I walk away. No strings.' Right?"

He had me there.

He dragged his chair closer to me, then his hands were on my legs. "We're both dealing with some serious stuff. So let's take one day at a time."

I frowned.

He pinched my chin as he guided me to look at him. "Hey, where's that strong, confident, and beautiful woman I know?"

I laughed and blushed at the same time. Actually, I almost shed some tears. I gave myself a mental shake. I'd never gotten emotional over a man before. I felt as though Dillon was rejecting me, when I was the one who'd pushed him away.

Sleep. That was what I needed. I also needed to change the subject. We were walking into deep waters, and he was spot-on. Whatever was happening between us, we needed to let nature take its course.

"So I want to go over to that house where I found Nadine."

He leaned back. "That's why you were sneaking out? And are you mad? The cops probably have that place under surveillance."

All that tension, lust, and emotional conversation vaporized.

"Dillon, my way of helping women is to tell their stories and not just stick it to Cory, but to end the Black Knights once and for all." I knew other sex-trafficking groups existed out there. I knew that girls would still be vulnerable to the charms of bad men. I knew that runaway girls usually pimped themselves out for food and a warm bed. Still, as a reporter, I had the opportunity to warn them.

He batted his sleepy eyes at me. "Baby, I admire you for that. But you heard Dom. Nothing good can come of you snooping. And let's not forget Denim. By the way, I'm a little perturbed that you didn't tell me you knew who the leader of the Black Knights was. I could've warned Denim."

"I'm so sorry," I said. "I never meant for Denim to get hurt." If I had the chance to talk to Denim again, I would apologize.

"I'm not upset so much about Denim. He and I knew he was walking into dangerous territory. What irks me is that we're supposed to be working together. You should've told me you knew about Miguel."

My stomach pitched, not only because Denim had gotten hurt, but more because I'd upset Dillon. He was worried about me. I'd repeatedly bragged about how I could take care of myself. Maybe it was time I let someone take care of me. I liked when Dillon had said, "I got you." He cared. He really cared.

I wasn't going to argue with him. He was right. We'd agreed to work together, and I had put his brother in harm's way. "I should've. I didn't want to break Ted's trust. So do you have something in mind if you don't want me snooping at that house?" Which I couldn't promise I wouldn't do.

He rose, his muscles bunching as he held out his hand. "Come on."

"I'm not going back to bed." *Maybe I would if it was your bed.*

"It's time we pay Duke a visit. I think he's back in town now."

I let him help me to my feet. "We? What does he have to do with the Black Knights?"

"He might know something about the Black Knights, given his reputation with criminals. And Dom said something earlier tonight that makes me believe Duke knows more about Grace's situation than he cares to tell me. We can kill two birds with one stone."

"Seriously? At three in the morning?" I remembered Duke, the oldest of the Hart brothers, and the asshole in the bunch. He'd broken Lou's nose in one of our encounters. Despite that, Dillon wasn't getting any arguments out of me.

"The timing is perfect. If we can catch him off guard, he might reveal more. Who knows? Maybe he'll fix us breakfast."

"You're crazy."

He laughed. "You haven't seen crazy yet."

24

DILLON

The front door of the skyscraper was locked, and a security guard was dozing just inside the entrance, his double chin hitting his chest. He wasn't the same bellman who had been working the day I'd shown up to visit Duke.

"Duke lives here?" Maggie asked in awe.

I knocked on the glass to get the chubby guard's attention. "Crime pays." I banged again. "He started out as a loan shark and bookie. I think he's into money laundering, although I can't confirm that, and the only legitimate business that probably helps him afford this ritzy abode is his nightclub." Duke didn't talk to me at all about his businesses or how much he made. Frankly, I didn't want to know. The less I knew, the less I could throw him under the bus with the cops if it ever came to that.

"Huh," she mumbled.

The tired guard strutted toward us with a scowl. He was mad at us for waking him, when he should have been protecting the lavish building.

"Let me handle him," Maggie said. "Try to look distraught. I hate to say this, but act like Grace died."

Hearing that was more of a blow than I would have expected as my gut cinched. The reality was she *could be* dead.

The elder man had *Daniels* embroidered on his uniform shirt. "Is this an emergency?"

I schooled my features, hoping I came across as upset over Grace's death. Actually, it wasn't hard to do since I sometimes had those morbid thoughts.

Maggie tucked her long and very curly hair behind her ear. I was digging how she'd worn her hair loose around her shoulders instead of in a braid.

"I'm so sorry, Officer Daniels." Maggie sounded downcast. "Mr. Hart here has to see his brother. We found out an hour ago that their sister is in the hospital."

Daniels eyeballed me. "Grace is in the hospital?" He sounded as though he'd seen her only four hours ago.

My whole body wobbled. The fucking security guard knew my sister.

I applauded Maggie for not reacting.

Daniels opened the door wider. "Come in. I'll call up to Mr. Hart's penthouse."

He'd said "Mr. Hart" as if Duke were some earl, prim and proper. I wanted to puke on the shiny waxed floor.

Daniels locked us in then hurried over to the phone on the desk he'd been sleeping behind.

Maggie took in the lobby as if she were in an art gallery. The walls were littered in ugly geometric art. At least it wasn't my taste. I liked pictures and paintings of landscapes. They gave me the sense of faraway escapes that I could dream about.

I ground my back teeth together. The night was turning out to be epic. Grace was living at Dom's. He'd seen her only two weeks ago. He'd then confirmed Maggie's suspicion that Cory Calderon was one of the Black Knights, and now grandpa with the receiver to his ear knew my sister. Not to mention, Maggie wanted a relationship. She wouldn't admit that, but I could tell she was changing her tune about having a steady man in her life.

I was on the verge of a temper tantrum. I shoved a hand in the pocket of my jeans as a savage laugh broke out in my head. Maggie thought I was a saint. Saints didn't lose their shit and destroy things, and I was so fucking primed to shatter all the glass in the lobby. More than that, I was ready to rip Duke to shreds.

Maggie latched on to my hand. "I think this tops the night."

I squeezed her hand, silently thanking her for being with me. If she weren't, no doubt I would be a lunatic.

"Mr. Hart," Daniels said into the phone. "I'm sorry to wake you, but your brother is here with news that Grace is in the hospital. I see. Yes. Yes. Sure will." He lowered the receiver, regret coloring his mocha complexion.

I marched over to Daniels. "Get my brother on the phone."

"I haven't told you what he said yet." Daniels's tired eyes held fear.

I wouldn't hurt the man, or maybe I would if he didn't get Duke back on the phone. "You don't have to. Your face says it all." I bared my teeth. "Now get him on the phone."

"But sir, he says Grace isn't in the hospital."

"Yeah? Then where is she?" *If he so much as says she's upstairs or some crap like that, Maggie will have to pry me off him.*

Daniels shrugged. "All he said was if Grace was in the hospital, then he would know."

Maggie glided up to my side. "Please get Duke on the phone. We don't want trouble." Her melodic voice tempered my rage for the moment.

Grandpa considered us. Well, he considered Maggie. Then he lifted the receiver, pressed four digits, and handed me the phone.

"I told you. I don't want to see my brother." Duke's voice was rough.

"Is that any way to welcome me?" I returned in a cocky tone.

"It's three thirty in the morning," Duke almost yelled. "Grace isn't in the hospital."

"I would suggest you let me come up, or I might have to tell the *Boston Eagle* that you're into money laundering and maybe sex trafficking."

Maggie beamed. Daniels didn't.

Duke growled. "Put the guard on."

I handed the phone to Daniels.

Within seconds, Daniels was escorting Maggie and me to the elevators, where he swiped a keycard over the panel below the numbers. Then he went back to his post.

As soon as the doors closed, I growled so loudly that I probably woke up everyone on the eighth floor.

Maggie hit the stop button, the bell ringing as the car halted. "Maybe this wasn't a good idea."

I pushed the button, and the car moved again. "This needs to be done." I'd waited too long to talk to Duke. Grace was alive, and he was going to tell me where she was.

"Then don't get yourself killed, because I like you a lot, Dillon Hart." For the first time since Maggie had shown up at the shelter, I didn't see her bubbly personality or that badass woman I knew her to be. I saw what she'd been trying to hide in my kitchen earlier—she cared for me. She was revealing herself to me, one layer at a time.

I didn't have time to ponder, question, or analyze Maggie's feelings or what was going on between her and me. The elevator dinged.

We arrived right into Duke's penthouse. The cityscape twinkled in the wall of windows behind my brother.

He stood bare-chested and barefoot in the aisle that separated his kitchen from his massive living room, with the scowl of the century ruining his good looks.

I dove at him, fists first. "Where is she?"

He darted out of the way. Duke had always had quick reflexes. "Grace isn't here."

I tried to punch him again, when Maggie stepped in between us, holding up her hands. Her narrowed green gaze focused on me. "Fighting isn't going to get you answers."

No, but I would feel so much better.

She eased out of the way then addressed Duke. "I suggest you start speaking."

His forehead wrinkled. "Who the fuck are you?"

I lunged this time. "Don't speak to my girl like she's one of your whores." We both fell to the white-carpeted floor, punching each other, grunting, and swearing left and right.

"Are you fucked up, Dillon?" he shouted. "Get off me. I'm your brother for Christ sakes."

He blocked every one of my punches like he'd done many times when we had wrestled as kids in our bedroom. He'd been bigger than me then, but now we matched each other in height and muscle. Still, he was proving to be the victor until I straddled him and jammed my knees into his sides.

"Where's Grace?" I yelled, my knuckles connecting with his jaw.

"Dillon," Maggie protested. "He's your brother."

He could be my savior. I wasn't letting up until he talked. Four solid years of grief, fear, rage, depression, and hopelessness was bottled inside me. Damn Duke to hell if he didn't start spilling his guts, or I would spill them for him.

He had his arms crisscrossed, blocking his face. "Listen to your girl."

Maggie grasped my arm, which was ready to deliver another blow. "Baby," she said in a soft voice.

A stream of goose bumps shot down my arms at her pet name for me, and it seemed to be all I needed to climb off Duke.

When he was upright, he rubbed his jaw then licked the blood off his lip. "Why do you insist that I know where Grace is?"

I walked down the aisle to admire the view of Boston. "The fucking guard downstairs knows Grace. When was she here last? And if you tell me you don't know, I'm sending you through this window. It's a mighty drop down from the eighteenth floor."

He shoved his middle finger in the air before he padded over to the bar tucked between the fireplace and the window.

Maggie whistled. "Nice digs you have here, Duke." I suspected she was trying to change the subject, even for a minute, to give me time to calm down.

Glasses clinked. "Do I know you?"

Maggie made herself at home by sitting on the plush couch facing the marble fireplace. The penthouse belonged in some home magazine. Expensive art hung on the walls, the furniture was in pristine condition, and the red-and-black kitchen had high-end appliances that I would have loved to have in the shelter. I could steal the restaurant-size fridge right now.

I smoothed a hand over my hair. "Duke, meet Maggie Marx, the reporter from the *Boston Eagle.*" I didn't know if Duke would remember Maggie from our teenage years. "Maggie was the girl in the Bloodhounds. Remember?"

He whipped around, a glass of whiskey in hand and horror in his chestnut-brown eyes, making him appear older than his twenty-seven years. Crime did fuck up a person in more ways than one.

I couldn't tell if he was surprised that Maggie was a reporter or a blast from the past.

Nevertheless, Maggie removed her scarf. "Lou was the leader, and I was the girl others whispered about." She pulled down the collar of her shirt, exposing her scar.

Duke combed his fingers through his short brown hair. "Yeah, it's all coming back. So you're really a reporter?"

Maggie got out a pad and pen. "Seems to me, Duke Hart, you've done well for yourself. Tell me how you've managed to amass such a fortune that you could afford to live in a penthouse in the Back Bay. What does this place go for on the open market? Two mil?"

He knocked back the whiskey, grimacing at Maggie. "Get out."

"You were an asshole when you broke Lou's nose, but now you're a dick. How can you not tell your own family your sister is alive?"

Man, my dick got hard. Maggie was on a roll, and I loved every minute of watching my brother flip through every furious expression he could muster.

I sauntered over to the couch and plopped down next to my girl. *My girl* had a nice ring to it. I was beginning to warm to the idea of Maggie and me as boyfriend and girlfriend. But I would deal with that later. Right now, Duke was going to talk.

"Have a seat, brother," I said.

His eyes became pinheads. He poured himself another glass of booze, not even offering us any. It didn't matter. I wasn't about to touch the stuff.

I hung my arms over the back of the couch. "Pop was in the hospital for alcohol poisoning recently."

"So the fuck what? Are you trying to tell me I'm an alcoholic?" With his glass filled to the brim, he sat down on a lone chair across from Maggie and me.

If he was or wasn't, I didn't know, but if he kept drinking, the possibility existed that he could take after our old man.

Maggie positioned her pen over her notepad. I had a feeling she was messing with his head, although I couldn't be sure since she was a reporter.

"Let's cut to the chase. Grace is alive, and I want to know where she is." I pursed my lips. "Don't deny it. I met someone who Grace has been living with. He brought up your name."

Duke downed half the glass of amber liquid, not showing his cards. He'd always been good at poker.

Duke stuck out his chin. "You still owe me money, brother."

True fact. I'd borrowed some money from him when Lizzie wanted to get in on an illegal, underground poker game. I'd never paid him back because he had never asked and I needed my money for the shelter. "Seems to me you don't need it. Now tell me about Grace."

Maggie was writing something down.

Duke finished off the whiskey. "Grace is alive. The last time I saw her was three weeks ago." He scratched his unshaven jaw.

I growled. Hearing him say the words "Grace is alive" felt like a bullet penetrating my skin. I knew what one felt like too—burning and searing pain that gripped me so hard I couldn't breathe. All thanks to a gang fight gone wrong.

"I promise, Dillon, I searched for Grace when she first took off. I know you don't believe me."

I motioned to stand, but Maggie stopped me with a *give him a chance* look. So I pushed my elbows into my thighs.

"About eight months ago, she found me," Duke said. "She walked into my club and asked me for money. I was shocked as hell. Pissed like a motherfucker too. I all but forced her to tell me where she'd been all these years, but she wouldn't talk. She didn't look like she was on drugs. She was well-groomed. She appeared to be healthy. So I gave her the money. My only requirement was she had to check in with me on a monthly basis. If she did and showed me she was alive and well and not doing drugs, then I would continue to give her money."

I was calculating the timeline in my head. Dom had said he found Grace nine months ago. Duke mentioned eight. When Dom had found her, she was bruised and bloody, but a month had passed before she showed up at Duke's club. So the bruises would've been mostly healed. "No signs of bruises on her, then?"

He shook his head. "Not that I could see."

"Do you know what she does during the day? Does she work?" Maggie asked. "Is she a prostitute?"

Duke and I muttered curses at the same time.

Dom had said Grace would leave early and not return until later in the evening.

Duke sucked on his lip. "Don't know."

"Why didn't you tell me any of this?" I asked.

"She came to me a week after you and I talked. Plus, I promised Grace. She asked me not to say anything to you."

I slid to the edge of the cushion, ready to dive at him again. The only thing that stopped me was his last statement, which felt as if a blade was slicing me over and over again. "I've been searching high and low and in every alley, abandoned building, and crevice in this fucking city for years, and you're telling me she doesn't want me to know? Why?"

Duke's features softened. "She has her reasons. What they are, she wouldn't tell me. Brother, she only came to me because I have money."

That didn't make me feel any better. "What about Denim?" I would feel less hurt if she didn't want Denim to know either.

"His name didn't come up. Probably because he's in the slammer."

I had the urge to ask why he hadn't been down to see Denim, but the conversation was about Grace.

"So she checks in with you monthly," I said. "When is she due to check in?"

"If she sticks to her monthly visits like she has been, then I don't expect to see her for another week."

What made me shiver, though, was that Grace had been showing up every night at Dom's up until two weeks ago. "I think she's in trouble. The brother-and-sister duo Grace is staying with hasn't seen her in a couple of weeks."

Duke unfolded his body. "I give her money, so I don't believe she's selling her body. I can have my men scour all the hot spots where the prostitutes hang out, though." He seemed a tad worried now.

The important question was, where was she?

"Maybe Grace got her own place," Maggie said. "Maybe she decided to move out of Dom's."

While that was plausible, my gut was telling me differently. Dom seemed to have a good relationship with Grace.

I believed Duke had told me everything he knew, so I wasn't going to get much more out of him.

Duke escorted us to the elevator.

Maggie tucked her pad and pen into her bag. "Do you know the Black Knights, Miguel Rivera, Dan Silva, Cory Calderon, or a Dallas?"

I wanted to laugh at how persistent she was, but I didn't want my action to come off as trivial, because one, sex trafficking was far from trivial; and two, considering Duke's status in the world of crime, he might know something about the Black Knights.

Duke's features darkened to match the sky outside his window. "My gang days are over. But anyone tied to the streets knows of the Black Knights and how their main operation is sex trafficking. Is that why you're really here?" He was talking directly to Maggie. "Do you think I could be involved in sex trafficking?"

Maggie stood up pin straight.

I placed my hand on Maggie's lower back. "It's a simple question, man."

He groaned. "Do you really think, Dillon, that I could prey on women?"

Raking my gaze over his face, I could see the boy in the man. The boy I knew had protected me from our father. That boy was the brother who had ripped our father off our mother a time or two when she'd been cowering in a corner, taking blows from her husband. I didn't want to believe Duke could hurt a woman, let alone sell her on the open market. As I stood in the quietness of his penthouse, the city lights dimming to the waning night sky, I saw the boy more than the man Duke had become. I saw my brother, the one I loved, the one I blamed for Grace's disappearance.

I left Maggie and went over to Duke, who was holding on to the back of the couch not far from the elevator. He jerked back as though I were going to punch him again.

I stopped when we were eye to eye. "We've been through hell as kids, brother. We've endured so fucking much. I do blame you for Grace taking off, but not as much as I blame myself. But let's be real, Duke. You're into some illegal shit. I mean, look at your expensive digs." I waved my hand around. "Maggie is only asking you about the Black Knights because you have ties to the underworld. She's not insinuating anything. But I get the feeling you're avoiding her question for some reason. Are you involved in sex trafficking?" I wanted to believe he wasn't, but he was not giving me a warm and fuzzy.

A muscle in his jaw acted like a jumping bean as he flared his nostrils. "Get out. You of all people should know that I hated when Dad beat Mom. I hated when Dad laid a hand on Grace. I love our sister more than you know."

I got in his face. "Then fucking show it. You didn't bother to call me when you knew Grace was alive. You knew I put my heart and soul into finding her. Who the fuck does that in a family? Don't answer that." I knew who. He did. My old man did. "Father dearest saw Grace too, you know."

His jaw came unhinged.

"Yeah. Shocking, huh? He didn't bother to call me either. He only calls when his ass is in jail." At least my father had the excuse that he could've been drunk when he saw Grace in her room. I started for Maggie, who was wearing a pity mask and some other emotion I couldn't quite make out. "You have one week. I expect a call from you when Grace shows up. If not, I'll make sure the cops know that you're using your club for money laundering." I didn't know that he was. I was pulling very short straws.

Fear blinked from him like a neon sign in the dark of night. "You wouldn't."

I silently shouted *Bingo!*

Nevertheless, I stabbed the elevator button, and the doors slid open. I walked inside, not waiting for Maggie nor responding to Duke.

Maggie finally got in as the doors were closing. She had even more pity dripping from her. When the car started to move, I did punch the wall.

"Dillon." Maggie said my name in a tender and sad tone. "You're lucky you have a family. You're lucky you can argue with your brother and worry over your sister and hurt for a brother in jail and even spit at your alcoholic father." She gulped in air. "I wish I had one tenth of what you have, no matter how dysfunctional your family is. Cherish what you have."

In that moment, I was the biggest self-absorbed asshole in the world.

25

MAGGIE

The muted noises of the newsroom played in the background while I typed away. Almost a week had gone by since the night Dillon and I had paid Duke a visit. That night had shaken the cobwebs loose for me.

I decided that the revenge I'd been so hung up on wasn't burning inside me as much. I did want Cory to pay for what he'd done to me. But I wanted him along with Miguel and any others to suffer more for what they were doing to other girls out there.

But Cory and the Black Knights weren't the subject of the words that were flying from my fingers. I was a crime reporter. I reported on the ugliness of the streets and people and all the twisted things that happened outside the newsroom, outside of my little bubble.

However, I couldn't get over the exchange between Duke and Dillon. Two brothers who loved each other yet hated one another was the great dichotomy between blood and family.

My heart had broken as they'd punched and yelled and spit venom at each other. Under all that, I'd seen the love in Dillon's eyes for Duke. I'd seen the regret in Duke's eyes for keeping such a huge secret from Dillon. More than that, as crazy as it might sound, their exchange had made me want to talk to my mom. I hadn't opened the envelope. But I would when I put the ending on my story. I'd been glued to my desk for the last week, furiously trying to get the bundle of sentences, thoughts, and words down.

I definitely wouldn't print the story without consulting Dillon, nor would I add Duke or Dillon's name to the story. I wasn't sure if Bruce would print any of what I was writing anyway since it had nothing to do with crime, although in a roundabout way, it did. Crime had taken hold of Duke. The streets had sucked up Grace. Nadine's life had been taken. And I believed that my parents had committed the biggest crime of all by leaving me at a firehouse.

Tap. Tap. Tap. Tap.

My cell rang, halting my fingers over the keyboard.

My body did a little dance. "Hey, Dillon."

"Are you at work?" he asked, his voice raspy and dampening all the right spots.

We hadn't seen each other since Duke's, but we had traded a few texts of the normal "how are you doing" or "what are you up to" variety. I'd thought about stopping by his house or the shelter, but after the encounter at Duke's, I believed he needed space. I was tied to my desk anyway.

"I am. I'm typing away. How about you? Have you talked to Duke since that night at his penthouse?" My fingers were crossed that they had worked out their differences and more importantly, that Grace had shown up.

"No. And he hasn't called. His deadline is in two days."

I prayed that Duke would come through for Dillon's sake. "Are you really going to rat him out if he doesn't call you if Grace shows up?" I couldn't see Dillon sending his brother to jail. That type of behavior wasn't in him as far as I could see.

"I don't know what I'm going to do," he said with no animosity in his voice.

I was so absorbed in talking to Dillon that I didn't hear Bruce until he waved a hand in front of me. Then he perched himself on the edge of my cubicle, waiting.

"I have to go." Normally, Bruce wouldn't interrupt me unless it was important. "Can I call you later?" *Please say yes.*

"Of course. Talk soon."

As soon as I hung up, Bruce asked, "Did you finally prove that Calderon is a soldier for the Black Knights?"

I swiveled my chair. "Not yet. I will, though." My gut gave me a little punch, and my pulse amped up at the thought that Calderon would suffer for his sins. In between writing, I'd been researching who owned that house on Bleven and Third.

Bruce glanced at my screen.

I franticly closed the Word document. I wasn't ready for him to read anything.

He folded his arms over his royal-blue polo shirt. The color brought out his gray eyes more. "Care to tell me what you're working on, then?"

"What if I told you that I have something that would sell more papers on Sunday than we've sold in the last four months?"

He deadpanned, not giving me a read on his thoughts like he usually did when I bragged about a topic. "I'm listening."

I interlocked my fingers to keep any nerves from showing. "Crime is a knife, sharp, jagged, and bloody, immoral in its actions, tearing families apart." I had the first line memorized and had rewritten it several times.

"Go on," Bruce said.

I swallowed the rock in my throat. I shouldn't be timid about sharing. I'd done it so many times in a roundtable discussion when Bruce and all the reporters brainstormed on story ideas. But I was about to get personal, not only about myself, but about two brothers who had shown me that the atrocity in the world was the hatred that took root inside a family. That hatred festered and bled and leaked with poison.

And despite the animosity and mountain of problems that had driven a wedge between them, love for each other and their sister still existed. Sure, I'd seen fights and hate in the foster families I'd stayed with, but I'd never seen love in the mix like I had with Dillon and Duke.

"As evil as crime might be, there's nothing more sinful than the bond of a family being ripped apart, whether the bond is severed from a death or from a loved one who left their child on the doorstep of a firehouse."

His eyebrow lifted. "You want to tell your story."

Nodding, I plucked the envelope that was now crumpled on the edges out of my bag. "In here is my biological mother's address. Ted found her against my wishes. But I think I'm ready to write the ending to my story." Well, maybe not the ending. I had a future ahead of me, and part of that future was to unravel how I felt about Dillon. I'd told him that I liked him a lot, and that was the truth. He made my stomach queasy in a good way. He made my palms sweat and my heart race. I didn't know what to make of all the weird feelings he gave me, but I knew I wanted more with him.

"How do you feel about knowing who your mother is?" Bruce asked evenly. He had his reporter hat on.

I shrugged. "At first, I was dead set on not contacting her. The more I think about it, the more I'm warming to the idea. I am curious, and I do have questions."

"You should know who your mom is. If not, you'll look back and regret that you didn't follow through." He seemed as though he had a regret or two of his own. "So, does Calderon fit into your story?" Bruce asked.

"You mean will I write about the part where he left me for dead? Absolutely." Until I met Dillon, I wouldn't tell anyone the details of what Cory had done to me. Dillon had said in so many words not to hide who I was because of some scar. I couldn't see past the revenge that had dug its nails into me so deep, so hard, and so clear. And while I hated that I was forever marked, or more like disfigured, I had an opportunity to ruin Cory's reputation and warn women of men like Cory.

He gripped my shoulder. "You're healing, and that's good. I'm proud of you, but what you're writing sounds more like a memoir and not for the paper."

I pouted. "What about the editorial section?"

"Mags, your job is to report on the actions of criminals. So stick to the Black Knights story. Find the facts."

His rejection stung like an angry bee. I could argue all day long. It wouldn't get me anywhere. Bruce was super sweet but tough as nails when it came to running a newspaper. He'd also been around the industry long enough to know what would sell papers. After all, the company was in the business to make money, not listen or read my dark history. "Got it, boss." He was right. I had to stick with the Black Knights for now. After all, I had a job to do, but at some point in the near future, I would write about my life. The small amount of words I'd written had seemed cathartic, as though I'd shed years of emotional distress.

"What did you find on the house?" Bruce asked.

I pointed to my notepad on my desk. "Marco Holdings owns the house. Weird that the owner is a holdings company and not an individual or couple. I couldn't find who owns Marco Holdings, though." The house Nadine had been in was in an upscale neighborhood, but a holdings company?

He tucked his hands in the pocket of his khakis. "It might be odd, but not unheard of. Does Ted know what you found?"

"I haven't talked to him," I said. The last time I had was when he'd scolded me about Nadine. I was avoiding him somewhat anyway. He would probably ask if I'd contacted my mother, and when he found out I hadn't, he would launch into a speech about family again.

"Let's not clue him in to what we have," Bruce said. "I don't want him to call my boss like he did when we were working on the bank heist last year."

I'd completely forgotten about that. Then again, I hadn't been the reporter on record. My former colleague who had retired had been working on that story. Regardless, I knew that once Ted had caught wind of what the paper was about to print on identifying the mastermind behind the bank robbery, he had taken the sails out of the entire article. Bruce had been livid. Needless to say, he wasn't all that thrilled when he found out Ted and I were tight.

I gnawed on my lip. "You won't get an argument out of me." I was tired of hearing "Go home, Maggie, or you're going to get yourself hurt." I liked that Ted worried, but damn it. I had a job to do as well.

"Good. So whatever you find and have solid proof on with the Black Knights, then you come to me. Our goal is to sell papers, not kiss the ass of the police force." His tone was as sharp as the scissors next to my notepad.

I hadn't given up on snooping around the house that Marco Holdings owned. I knew the house could be under surveillance as Dillon had mentioned, but I didn't see any harm in driving by it at least. Maybe I would get lucky and find Cory walking in or out. I was about to tell Bruce my plan, when I heard my name.

"Maggie is over there," Fran said.

Bruce glanced out at the newsroom. "I think you have a visitor."

I popped up and peered over the array of cubicles. My mouth opened, and my belly went haywire as butterflies flapped their wings.

Dillon's hair was tamed like it had been at Nadine's funeral, and while he would look good no matter what hairstyle he wore, I preferred the tousled, out-of-control vibe he usually wore—the one that shouted rugged, rough, raw, and red-hot. Despite his hair, the crooked grin he was giving me heated my cheeks.

Bruce leaned in. "You're blushing, Mags. That's a first, and it suits you."

Dillon came around the cubicle wall with a bouquet of colorful carnations. "I hope I'm not interrupting."

He was a sight for sore eyes, literally and figuratively. My eyes needed a break, and I'd missed Dillon.

Bruce extended his hand. "I'm Bruce, Maggie's editor and boss."

"Dillon Hart." He oozed all kinds of sex appeal from the way his fresh-ocean-scented cologne drifted off him, to his wardrobe—tattered jeans, biker boots, and a starched red button-up shirt with the sleeves pushed up to his elbows.

After the two exchanged pleasantries, Bruce scurried into his office. I glanced around to find that most of the women in the office were riveted on my cubicle.

I pulled him in. "You're going to give the women a meltdown."

His rugged features crumpled as he sat on the edge of my desk in the exact spot where Bruce had been. His gaze scanned the contents of my messy desk.

I lowered myself into my rolling chair. "Don't be so coy. Hot guy walks into the newsroom with flowers. It's every girl's dream."

He let out a deep laugh. "Is that your dream, Maggie?"

I thought my dream would be round two with him in bed or having him spank me with a ping-pong paddle, but that wasn't enough anymore. In between writing, I'd had a chance to seriously think about things I wanted. One was a family. I had no one in my life other than Ted, and it was time to do something about that. I wanted a steady relationship with someone, that person being the delicious specimen next to me. I longed for him to kiss me, to touch me as if I were porcelain and breakable, and to tell me I was the only woman he wanted. I'd never wanted any of those things from a man. I was content with who I was and what I had. I was confident and bold and aggressive. If I wanted something, I went for it.

With Dillon, though, I didn't want to be bold. I believed I had forced him into keeping his distance, hence, leaving our feelings at the door. So I'd come to the conclusion that I had to let him make the next move. I was super stoked his move involved flowers.

I was crushing hard. "What are the flowers for?"

The orchestra of the newsroom restarted, and the pounding of computer keys, the phones ringing, and the voices droning tittered around us.

He handed the bouquet to me. "They're for a beautiful woman that I want to take to dinner."

I liked the romantic side of Dillon. "Are we leaving our feelings at the door?"

"It wouldn't be a date if we did," he said.

I wondered what had changed on his part while the blood raced through my system at breakneck speeds.

I wagged my finger between us. "This is us letting nature take its course?"

He nodded. "Something like that."

I'd never been out on a real date with dinner and flowers and wine and conversation. I'd never had a first crush either—one where girls got all giddy and gaga over a boy. Dillon might be my crush, my first love.

He licked his lip ring. "If dating isn't your thing, then I'm cool."

I was beginning to realize that him playing with his lip ring was a nervous tick.

"I'm not sure how to date." But if the date meant a first kiss, then hell yeah. I was on board. He'd licked and kissed parts of me, but he had never touched my lips.

He chuckled. "Neither do I."

I could hear my neighbor, Rosemary, choke.

"What changed?"

He shoved his hands into his jeans pockets. "Time. A week. You. Me. Grace. Life. I realized after leaving Duke's that I've been living in the past. I've been helping others and not putting myself first. It's time I start, and I would like to start by taking you on a date."

Rosemary peeked over her cubicle, her blue eyes wide and shifting. "What are you waiting for, Maggie? Say yes to the hunk."

I puckered my lips. Dillon and I were so much alike. We both had a dark past. We both had demons that drove our actions. I for sure was living in the past, but that was about to change. "So boyfriend and girlfriend. Dillon and Maggie. I do like the sound of that."

Rosemary clapped.

Dillon gave me one of his heart-pounding grins.

I believed all that had happened in our pasts had prepared us for that moment. Whether it was one date or more with Dillon Hart, I was ready for him. I was ready for feelings and, dare I say, love.

26

DILLON

Norma lingered in the doorway of my office with a proud smile. In a small way, she reminded me of Grace, who had done something similar when I combed my hair in the bathroom mirror. Right now, I was threading my fingers through my hair without a mirror.

Norma popped off the doorjamb. "You look good. You're nervous, aren't you?"

I pocketed my phone and keys. "I've never been on a date." I wouldn't call the night Maggie and I had had sex a date.

Norma moved deeper inside. "Not even in high school?"

"Nope." My high school days were a blur, and girls back then hadn't belonged with a guy who was in a gang. I'd had enough worries with making sure my enemies didn't come after my family.

Heavy footsteps clobbered down the hall. Then Hunt's big body filled the doorway. His blond hair was as unruly as mine. I'd thought about styling my mane much like I had when I'd gone to see Maggie at the newspaper the day before. But the GQ look wasn't me. I couldn't be somebody I wasn't. Plus, Maggie kept looking at my hair for some reason. I'd concluded when I left her building that she didn't like my hairstyle.

"Dillon, you have a guest," Hunt announced. "He says he's your brother. Kind of looks like you."

I didn't know how to react. Duke's deadline to produce Grace was tomorrow. Maybe she'd shown up early. Or maybe I had my days wrong. Maybe he was there to tell me Grace hadn't shown up, and he wanted to plead with me not to rat him out to the cops. But I hadn't had time to worry about him or Grace. The time between Duke's penthouse and now had been an eye-opener in many ways.

I'd had time to think about Maggie, Grace, my family, the shelter, and me. Rafe had been so right when he'd said, "Put yourself first." I needed to take his advice. He'd been concerned about my health, and with my chest burning constantly, I had to agree with him. The rage, the worry, and the sleepless nights were mounting into an ulcer or a breakdown. My turning point had been what Maggie had said in the elevator. "Cherish what you have." What I had was the shelter and her, and I wanted to explore what I was feeling for her.

I couldn't keep on my quest to find Grace. It was evident she didn't want me to know she was alive. I would have been fooling myself if I said that didn't hurt like hell.

I did want to put my mission to find Grace behind me. I did want to see her. I did want to understand what had happened to her. But if she was alive, then I had to let her come to me.

"Anyone with him?" I asked, my pulse staccato.

Hunt shook his head. "Sorry, man. Do you want me to send him away?"

The large knotted ball in the pit of my stomach tightened, and that pain in my chest resurfaced.

"Yes," Norma blurted out. "You're going to be late for your date. Duke has been a dick to you, so screw him."

I'd given Duke an ultimatum. I wasn't backing out of it, and since he was there, I had to at least hear what he had to say. "I have over an hour before I meet Maggie. This won't take long."

Anger darkened Norma's pretty face.

I kissed Norma on the forehead. "You're right about Duke. But I need to end this once and for all. Close the proverbial door." That way, I could relax and enjoy Maggie in every way. I had big plans after dinner that involved her and me and slow, tantalizing lovemaking. No rough sex, at least not tonight. I wanted her to feel every touch and every kiss I gave her and her body.

I walked out with Hunt and Norma on my heels.

I didn't doubt that they would want to watch and protect me, and while I didn't mind Norma and Hunt eavesdropping, I didn't want the women in the shelter to hear. My personal life wasn't for their ears. They had enough problems in their own lives.

I stalked down the hall as though I were getting into a boxing ring. But when I reached the common room, Duke wasn't around. The room was empty and so was the kitchen.

"Where is he?" I asked Hunt.

Norma stayed at my side as if she were my bodyguard. Hunt hurried to the computer on Norma's desk and brought up the security cameras.

"Why don't you check on the women?" I said to Norma more than asked. We had a total of seven women residing in the shelter, and I couldn't be happier about that. What I wasn't happy about was Duke showing up there. If things got out of control between us, I wanted to make sure our guests didn't witness the argument.

Norma took off upstairs. Angel, Debbie, and the other ladies had been in the kitchen earlier. Most of them liked to relax in their rooms, and a couple of them had bonded as friends.

Hunt tapped on a key. "He's on the porch. I'll be right here in case you need me."

I found Duke leaning against the support beam on the top step with his back to me. "You shouldn't have shown up here. This is my place of business."

Dusk was setting in. The days were growing shorter as we approached fall. I was ready for cold weather. I loved the cold, the snow, and at times the rain. I could do without the heat and humidity.

"The neighborhood sucks," Duke said, not bothering to turn around.

I could also do without his insults and his pissy attitude. "Where's Grace?" I leaned against the opposite column of the porch.

His expensive blue Navigator with dark-tinted windows didn't fit against the backdrop of low-income homes.

He swiveled his head toward me. "You shouldn't care so fucking much."

My eyebrows cinched. "Who gave you the black eye?" I'd punched him but not in the nose or the eyes.

"None of your business." He was talking to me as if I were one of his thugs.

"Why don't you care, Duke?" I regulated my breathing to keep my anger under wraps.

He set his jaw. "The minute I care for anyone or anything is the minute they'll find a way to screw me from here to hell."

I didn't know who *they* were, and honestly, I didn't want to know unless he meant Grace. The less I knew about Duke's personal or professional life, the better it was for him more than me. With all his illegal shit, I didn't want to be the one to throw him in jail. My ultimatum had only been a scare tactic.

He walked down the steps and kept going until he got to his car.

Steam came out of my nose.

I was beginning to see my old man in Duke—the drinking and the rudeness.

Duke opened the back door of his Navigator, his attention far away, as though he were a robot doing what he'd been told.

I saw army boots first then skinny-jean-covered legs. When the girl was upright and in full view, I gripped the railing to prevent me from collapsing.

My pulse shot out of my body and straight to the moon like a rocket taking off at Cape Canaveral. I swore my heart would burst mid-flight and drizzle down into tiny pieces over the earth.

The girl tossed her bangs out of her eyes with a quick jerk of her head, reminding me of a celebrity walking the red carpet.

Duke said something to her that I couldn't make out. Then again, the only thing I could hear was a pounding sound, as if someone were banging a hammer on a nail that wouldn't cooperate.

Boom. Boom. Boom.

Breathe, man.

Smiling at Duke, she angled her head slightly, and I spied her hummingbird tattoo. It wasn't hard to see with her short hair.

Grace Hart, sister to Denim, Duke, and Dillon Hart, born to Jerome and Emily Hart, found after four years.

I always thought I would run to her if I ever saw her again, or that I would break down and cry like a baby who was hungry and needed his diaper changed. All the anger I'd built up over knowing she didn't want me to know she was alive wasn't even there. I was numb from head to toe. I pinched myself for good measure.

She glided toward me, almost as if she were skating on ice, something she'd loved to do as a kid. Her legs were long, her brown eyes wide and slightly slanted, her curves defined, and her black T-shirt stretched across her breasts. My baby sister was a woman. Gone was the innocence I remembered. Gone were the chubby cheeks and baby fat.

I was looking at a woman who had been through some kind of hell —hell worse than my father could dish out. I only knew that because that bright spark she'd always had had been snuffed out.

I open and closed my fists, not at Grace but at whoever had had the fucking nerve to touch her and change her. The anger I'd held toward Grace was now directed at someone else, stronger, meaner, and fiercer, jolting my adrenaline.

I descended the steps and met her halfway.

We sized each other up, not saying a word. Up close, she was out-of-this-world beautiful. Her eyelashes were long and her heart-shaped lips were still pink like they had been when she was a little girl. Even though I remembered her with long hair, the Halle Berry hairstyle suited her even better and brought out her round face.

A tear escaped down her cheek.

I wasn't a crier. I couldn't remember the last time I'd shed any tears. But there I was ready to wail.

I wanted to touch her, throw my arms around her, hold her tight, and not let go, but I wasn't sure if I should. We were blood yet strangers to one another. I reached out with my hand, and as if that were all she needed, she flew into my arms.

My hands went around her tiny waist, and suddenly I was at peace. Every sleepless night, every minute of scouring the streets of Boston, every fucking day since she'd left, and every emotion I'd endured all vanished.

"I'm so sorry, Grace. I'm sorry for leaving you. I'm sorry I didn't protect you. I'm sorry that I didn't come home sooner."

She bawled in my arms. "I'm the one who's sorry."

I had so many questions, but I didn't want to ruin the moment.

Duke's deep and rude voice severed my bliss. "We're both here now, Grace. So you need to tell us where you've been for four years."

She tensed in my arms before she broke away from me, wiping her eyes. Fear gripped her through the sadness.

All I could think about at the moment was my old man slapping her around because she'd had that same look on her face before he unleashed his wrath on her.

Duke shoved his hands into the pockets of his black slacks. My brother was dressed as though he were going out on a date.

Shit! Maggie! I had a small window of time.

Red splotches dotted Grace's snow-white skin. "You know, don't you?"

I did a double take as I glanced at my brother then back at Grace. "What are you talking about?"

Duke pushed out his shoulders. "I'm clueless."

I recalled Duke saying he didn't know where Grace had run off to.

"Look, I need to make a phone call." I had to tell Maggie I might be late. "Then I need answers, Grace."

"Fuck yeah," Duke added.

Wow! My brother and I agreed on something.

Grace hung her head. "I'll tell you everything."

Damn straight she would.

I strode in the direction of the porch, tapping on Maggie's name in the favorites on my phone. The line rang until her voice mail picked up. "Maggie, call me as soon as you get this."

Maybe she was working up until we were supposed to meet. The woman worked nonstop. I knew she was trying to crack the big story. I knew she wanted the dirt on the Black Knights.

The line to her desk rang five times before a male voice answered.

"*Boston Eagle*, Bruce speaking."

"Bruce, this is Dillon Hart. We met yesterday. Is Maggie still working? I've tried her cell phone, but she's not answering."

"No. She left early to follow up on a quick lead before her date with you, and she forgot her cell phone. It's sitting in the charger on her desk. Is everything okay?"

"Fine. Thanks, man." I hung up.

I could call the restaurant, or I had a better idea because I wasn't leaving Grace until I got answers, even if Grace had to chaperone my date.

I returned to my siblings, who were not speaking to one another, which was odd. Grace had run to Duke when she needed money. "I'm supposed to meet my girl for dinner in the city, but I can't get ahold of her. She forgot her cell at work. So we're going on a little trip." I directed the last line at Grace. I wasn't giving her a chance to skip out.

From the regret written all over her face, I knew she wouldn't run.

"As much as I loathe family shit, I'll drive," Duke said. "I want answers too."

We probably needed more time than the twenty- to thirty-minute car ride, but at least it was a start.

27

MAGGIE

I parked in between two cars across the street from the house on Bleven and Third that belonged to Marco Holdings. I'd skipped out of work early so I could check out the house before I had to meet Dillon. My goal was to snoop around the home, but when I arrived, a car sat in the driveway.

The upscale neighborhood looked different in the light. Pear trees lined the sidewalks. The lawns were pristine green with shrubs pruned to round and oblong shapes. A handful of leaves fluttered to the ground in the light summer breeze.

The two-story brick home sat up on a slight incline. Its cement steps that led up to the high-columned porch were embedded in the earth, with colorful perennials lining the edges.

Any evidence of a raid or shootout didn't exist. The windows were intact. The front door was solid with no signs of anyone having broken it down.

The souped-up black Jeep in the driveway told me someone was inside. I debated whether to go up and ring the bell. I could always use the excuse that I had the wrong house just to see who would answer the door.

Marco Holdings was a mystery. The more I peeled the onion, the more I couldn't find who was behind the company. The only piece of information I had found was an address in Brazil, which was odd for a home. But it wasn't odd if the Black Knights were the real owners. Another definition for a shell company was a *person or entity that wants to hide their business from the law.*

I suspected the gang owned the home. After all, Dan Silva, the guy Ted's unit had arrested, was a Black Knight.

I scanned the area once again, not finding any unmarked cars or vans that Ted and his team used, and I didn't see any police cruisers either.

The longer I sat there, watching and waiting for someone to walk out that door, the more I prayed Cory Calderon was inside.

If he is, then what?

I had no clue. It was idiotic to attempt to poke my nose or poke the bear. Nothing good would come from me investigating the very place Nadine ran from. Yeah, I didn't want to end up like her. Yet I wanted to put the Black Knights story to bed once and for all.

I checked the time on my watch. I had thirty minutes before my smoking-hot date. While the restaurant wasn't far, I should get going.

So I lowered my gaze and turned the key in the ignition, when someone banged on the passenger's window. I squealed as I whipped my head around to see a man I didn't recognize peering inside my car. He had evil beady blue eyes, a hooknose, and a flat chin. His black hair was thick, with long sideburns that melded into the thin beard hugging his jaw.

My VW Bug was old and didn't have power windows, so I couldn't exactly roll down the passenger's window. I didn't want to either. For all I knew, the man probably snuck out of the house I was watching. *Note to self: Keep your guard up.*

"What do you want?" I asked in a raised voice so he could hear me.

"Are you a cop?" Hooknose asked. "You seem to be watching that house pretty intently."

Gang members had a cocksure attitude dripping off them that said *fuck with me, and I'll kill you.* This man had that MO.

The engine idled, and I sped off, adrenaline pumping through me as if someone had shot me up with a high dose of crack. I glanced in the rearview mirror to find the man with his phone to his ear as he watched me drive away.

Great job, Mags. Now he'll call the cops. An alert will go out for my car, and then Ted will be all over my ass.

Bruce didn't want me to clue Ted in if I found anything out about the Black Knights. And no law said I had to either. I considered Ted family, but I had a job to do just like he did.

I blew out a breath as I sailed through the city streets, zipping in and around cars and checking the rearview mirror every second.

Dillon and I agreed to meet at Tapas, a bar in the city where they served my favorite Spanish cuisine. Lou had cooked the best paella in all of Boston. I missed him. We were never an item, but he'd been a big brother to me. He'd been in his twenties when he found me at age fourteen, beaten and a second away from dying.

Fifteen minutes or so later, I found a spot on the street outside the restaurant. I was five minutes early. Maybe Dillon was too. As soon as I walked in, the spicy aromas found their way to my nose, making my stomach growl. I hadn't had a decent meal in quite some time. Subs from Hank's and Chinese food didn't count as decent since I practically ate that all the time.

A line of people waited for the hostess to take down their names. Others sat on benches along both walls near the entrance. Glasses clinked. Voices droned. The double doors straight ahead squeaked as waiters and waitresses shuffled in and out of the kitchen, with trays of food and empty dishes.

I scanned the bar and the eating area for Dillon but didn't see him. I even asked the hostess with heavy makeup if Dillon Hart had checked in. Once she gave me the headshake that he hadn't, I gave her my name then found an empty section of wall in the somewhat large waiting area and leaned against it.

Out of habit, I dug out my phone from my messenger bag… or tried. I tore the inside of my bag apart but didn't find my phone. I hurried out to my car only to find it wasn't there either. In my head, I retraced my steps before I'd left the newspaper. I'd hung up from talking to Ted. He'd called me to ask if I had contacted my mom, which hadn't surprised me.

"I will soon," I had said.

He seemed happy with my answer. Then I asked him questions about his case on the Black Knights. He was still hush-hush about it.

I then reread what I'd written over the last week on what I was tentatively calling my memoir. Afterward, I talked to Bruce, who was working late. He asked me how I felt about Dillon.

"I have some strong feelings for him, but I'm not sure what they mean," I said.

"Mmm," Bruce returned. "You'll know if you get this tickling feeling in your stomach anytime you see him or hear his voice, or when you're not with him, you'll itch like a drug addict needing that fix for him."

I laughed at Bruce's description of how he'd felt when he met his wife.

I certainly had all those feelings when it came to Dillon. But I wasn't going down that road yet to love.

One day at a time. Date first.

Once I'd finished my conversation with Bruce, I grabbed my bag and left. I had Dillon and Marco Holdings on the brain and had forgotten to snag my phone from the charger.

Argh!

I didn't have time to go back to the news building. It was clear on the other side of the city. So I ambled back toward the entrance, when I spotted a black Jeep that looked exactly like the one I'd seen parked at the house on Bleven and Third. Surely, it couldn't be the same one. Nevertheless, I stood at a parking meter with horror hurtling through me at the notion that Hooknose had followed me.

The Jeep stopped at a red light about a quarter of a block from me.

The street sign up ahead read No Right Turn On Red. When the light changed to green, the Jeep banked right.

Curiosity was a bitch. I jogged up to the corner past the restaurant. When I rounded the edge of the building, I bumped into a wall of muscle, almost knocking the breath out of me.

I would've kneed the man in the groin if it weren't for him saying my name. "Maggie?"

I glanced up, losing sight of the Jeep. "Dom?"

Sirens were going off in my head, blaring, *caution, caution, caution*, more because of the Jeep than Dom.

"It looks like you've seen a ghost," Dom said.

I knew the Jeep was long gone, and my pulse slowed a smidge, but the bad feeling was seeping into my bones.

"Funny running into you," I said.

He swept his gaze over me, his diamond earrings twinkling in the headlights of an oncoming car. "Fi works at Tapas."

I hadn't seen her. Then again, I'd only been in the restaurant for a second before I dashed out. "Oh."

He offered me his elbow. "Come on. I can get us a great table."

I took his arm as though I were dating him and not Dillon. Dom had an aura about him that pulled me in. He was handsome with a powerful badass quality. I wasn't afraid of much except dark alleys, and Dom didn't push any of my fear buttons. But the untrusting side of me was waving a red flag.

"You're awful presumptuous." I scanned the streets up and down, looking as far as I could for the Jeep.

Dom let out a deep chuckle. "And you're mighty pretty."

A normal girl would get sucked into his biker charm and blush all kinds of reds and pinks. I was Maggie Marx, former gang member, albeit my gang had been a group of kids who'd protected each other and their neighborhoods, not a gang involved in drugs, guns, and possibly sex trafficking. The city had changed drastically over the years. At one time, the mafia had had a hold on the city, and I would guess they still did. But gangs were multiplying. The commonality between gangs and mafia was bad shit. The difference between the organizations was that the mafia had an old-school mentality about family and didn't prey on women. I only knew that from Ted's time on the streets. On the other hand, the new era of gangs had a moral code of doing whatever it took to make money.

I should thank Dom for his compliment. I had an important question for him, though. "Any signs of Grace?"

He placed his rugged and calloused hand over mine. "Nothing. Fi hasn't seen her either. I hope she's okay." He gazed out into the somewhat busy street as though he were remembering a lost love.

"You like Grace." It was more of a statement than a question.

We reached the entrance to Tapas. A lady in a sharp business suit hurried in.

He unhooked my arm from his. Those bottomless eyes had a filing cabinet full of secrets. "I do like Grace."

"Dom, if you know where she is, tell me."

His phone rang.

We were locked in a stare-down.

His phone continued to ring. He blinked as he fished it out of the back pocket of his black jeans.

I wondered if it was Grace calling him.

He lifted the phone and strutted down the street in the opposite direction we'd come from.

I wasn't sure what was happening, but that bad feeling I'd had earlier was slowly rearing its ugly head. Dillon would be furious if Dom knew where Grace was and didn't tell him when he'd had the chance. I'd seen the rage in Dillon when we'd gone to Duke's penthouse. I had also seen how he'd held back from seriously hurting his own brother. With Dom being a stranger, Dillon wouldn't think twice about smashing his skull through the wall, an action I was sure Dillon had held back at the Crow.

I wished I had my phone. For some odd reason, I felt safe with the stupid piece of technology, and I wanted to call Dillon. I was getting worried since he wasn't there yet.

I clutched my messenger bag and lingered near the entrance of Tapas. It was probably best if I waited for Dillon out front anyway. It was rather stuffy inside, and the aromas would only make me hungrier.

Dom was talking animatedly, waving his free hand around as though he were arguing with someone. I didn't have time to guess who was on the other end of his phone.

Headlights drew my attention away from Dom. At first, the car was rolling slowly as though the driver were looking at the addresses of the buildings lining both sides of the street. Then the car accelerated as though he'd found the address he was looking for. It took me a second to realize the car was the black Jeep.

Two gorilla-looking men—strong, huge, and with mean expressions—jumped out, darted in between a truck and a Mercedes, and hopped the curb as if they were firefighters there to put out a fire. For a brief second, I thought they were running inside to get someone until they scooped me up. I barely had time to scream before something stung me in the arm.

Then the city went black.

28
─────

DILLON

The inside of Duke's SUV was filled with nothing. No one was talking. Duke was driving, and from where I sat, which was behind him, I could see the pain on his face. My brother seemed to be in agony. Whether it was me, Grace biting her nails beside me, or all three of us together, it didn't matter. Whatever Grace had to say or whatever family feud we were about to get into, it needed to be done.

I reached over and placed a gentle hand on Grace's leg.

She stiffened before turning from looking out the window to setting her tear-filled eyes on me.

"Why didn't you want me to know you were alive?" I asked.

Duke's gaze was more in the rearview mirror than on the road. He was moving slowly through the side streets. "Tell us already, Grace. I've been patient with you."

My sister looked to me for help like she had when she was a kid and our father was scolding her for some stupid reason.

"You're an adult, Grace. Whatever you have to say, Duke and I won't judge." I was trying to be calm, cool, and collected, but my insides were knotted and mangled.

She slumped, the fight leaving her. "When you guys left me to fend for myself with Dad, I hated both you and Denim." She lowered her gaze to her lap.

Nausea crept inside me like a slow-moving train.

"I decided that I was better off living somewhere else. Where Dad couldn't beat me, tell me I was nothing but a whore, and make my life miserable. Anywhere in this city had to be better than living in that house with an alcoholic. But I had blinders on. At first, I crashed with friends. I had a little bit of money I'd stolen from Dad's wallet. It didn't get me far. I couldn't keep scrounging off my friends, so I decided to find a job, or I should say the person found me. All you have to do, he said, was go to dinner with a rich client of ours. All you have to do is dress pretty, act nice, and keep them company. You don't have to do anything you don't want to." Grace shuddered.

Duke eyed me, breathing fire.

I was gritting my teeth so hard, it hurt. I knew where she was going. I knew what she was about to tell us, and if she gave me a name, then I was about to go hunting. I had no doubt that Duke would accompany me.

"At first, everything was cool," she said softly. "I ate well. He put me up in a nice apartment. I had a bed, pretty clothes, and true to his word, I didn't have to have sex with anyone unless I wanted to. The men I went out with were polite and didn't make me do things I didn't want to. Until one day when things took a drastic turn. I was plucked from my bed in the middle of the night, drugged, and thrown into a cage."

Duke took a sharp left into a boarded-up gas station then came to a screeching halt. He swiveled in his seat. "Who? Who threw you into a cage?" The fury pouring off my brother was far greater than any madness he'd shown to our old man.

Grace let out a throaty noise. "Why do you care now? Huh? You didn't come home to check on me. You didn't bother to find out if I was okay."

Duke's knuckles were snow-white as he gripped the back of the passenger's seat. "You could've called me."

She released a laugh that sent shivers down my spine. My baby sister, the little girl I knew, was in that moment someone I didn't know at all. I hated to even think about it, but she'd been raped and held against her will.

"The only way I knew how to protect myself was to run from Dad." She swiveled her head to face me. "That was your advice before you left home."

My heart stopped. I always knew I'd said the wrong thing. It had gutted me every minute of every day and still did. Even as my heart broke for her, even though she was sitting next to me, I couldn't erase the past or what had happened to her. I wished like a motherfucker I could. I wished I'd never walked out that door and left her behind.

"I didn't mean away from home."

Her nose wrinkled. "What would you have done? I'm not a guy. I didn't have the strength at twelve years old or even at sixteen to fight off Dad."

"Did Dad rape you, Grace?" Duke asked, holding back every ounce of fury he had in him. I could see the restraint in the way he was clutching the top of the passenger's seat. "Tell me now. I swear that man is dead."

Her jaw tightened. "What Dad did to me was a walk in the park compared to what I've been through."

My old man was a lot of things, but I didn't think he was a rapist. "Answer his question," I ordered, not sure if I was right in my assumption. I was done feeling sorry for myself, even though my heart was not done shattering into a gazillion pieces.

"I don't have to do squat." She grabbed the door handle and pulled.

Duke plastered on a cold smile only reserved for someone he was about to unleash his wrath on. "Child locks, sister. I've given you time to heal. I've given you lots of money. I've bitten my tongue so many times in the last few months that I have cuts on it that haven't healed. I even let you give me the black eye. So continue."

She spit in his face. "Go fuck yourself."

While I didn't disagree with Duke that she needed to tell us where she'd been, I knew Grace needed help. She was dealing with a ton of shit that I couldn't even imagine. "She gave you the shiner?" I asked Duke.

"It was an accident," Grace added.

I flicked off my seat belt that was squeezing the breath out of my lungs. "How did you get away from the person who promised you the world? Where did you go during the day when you were staying with Dom and Fi? Why did you go to Dad's house? Why were you using Mom's name? Why haven't you contacted me? Why are you afraid of me? What in the hell is going on, Grace?" I started the first question in a low voice, and from there, my voice ramped up, much like a song reaching its crescendo. I inhaled the air filled with fury, helplessness, shock, pain, and so much more.

Her chin quivered while she looked at her legs. "Dad never touched me like that. He might be a lot of things, but he isn't a rapist."

Duke's hard features loosened.

I didn't know how I felt yet. Our father still hurt her. Dad was still responsible for Grace's fate. He'd forced her out of the house. He'd forced her to make decisions she shouldn't have had to make at sixteen.

"Let's start again," I said after taking a deep breath. "When you say he gave you nice things, who is he?"

"Miguel Rivera," she said with disgust.

I scrubbed my hand down my face. "Come again? The man running the Black Knights?"

Duke sucked in his bottom lip. "Where did he keep you? Did he sell you to someone? How did you get away?" Duke was practically foaming at the mouth.

I couldn't blame him. My mind was a bit overwhelmed as I slowly processed what was happening in the confines of the car.

Darkness was setting in, and so was the nausea in my stomach. The only reason I didn't open the door to puke was Maggie. Regardless if I was running late, she was safe. She was in a restaurant full of people. But then something Bruce had said hit me. Maggie was chasing a lead.

She'd wanted to go back to that house where Nadine had run from. Then acidic bile rose, quick and hot. If something did happen to Maggie, she didn't have her phone.

Nothing happened to your girl. She's fine. She's waiting for you. The clock on the dashboard blinked 8:10. I wasn't that late.

"Answer the question," Duke prodded Grace in a toxic tone.

"I killed my owner," she said without any remorse, sitting up straighter. "Where Miguel kept me doesn't matter because he changes places like he changes his underwear. Every day he's looking at real estate. Every day he's buying some new house or some new abandoned building. He needs both. He keeps his drugged-up women in a warehouse and then uses the home to have lavish parties or quiet dinners, where he introduces his clients to the girls. I didn't run to you, Dillon, because I wasn't ready to face you. And I wasn't ready for you to look at me the way you're looking at me now, with revulsion written all over your face." A tear slid down her cheek.

"Grace." My voice broke, and my heart hurt. I could tell her how angry, worried, and everything else I'd been feeling for the last four years, but she was there now. She was alive. "I don't know what you see on my face, but I'm so sorry for what you've been through. And you probably see a bit of shock. I'm still processing that you killed someone." I didn't know what I would do if I'd been in her shoes.

She dashed away a tear. "So am I." This time, there was a small amount of regret in her voice. "During the day, I searched for Duke. It took me a month to find him. When I did, he told me about your shelter. He told me to stay with you."

Duke's eyes were glossy. "I'm not a complete dick," he said to me.

Grace laid her hand on my leg. "I couldn't risk Miguel finding me and putting your shelter in jeopardy. Duke's businesses are different. Still, I was cautious with Duke."

"And the money I gave you?" Duke asked.

"I used the money to pay Dom for letting me stay. I used it to buy some essentials for living. And I gave some of the money to girls on the streets who need it."

"Dom said he hadn't seen you in two weeks. Where have you been?" I asked.

She gave Duke and me a weak smile. "I've been hiding. One of Miguel's men found me, and that's when I dropped off the radar. I couldn't lead them to Dom."

Her hand was still on my leg as though she didn't want to remove it. So I covered her hand with mine. Four years of tension slowly left my body. "How do you know you weren't followed to Duke's tonight, or even the shelter?" I held my breath. I couldn't let anything happen to the girls at the shelter.

"Because the man Miguel had on my tail got hit by a car, chasing me. He's not dead if that's your next question. He was hurt, though."

I let out a sigh, relieved she hadn't killed him.

Duke rubbed his temples. "Why not go to the cops?"

Grace removed her hand from my leg. "No way. I would be dead before I even opened my mouth. Miguel has some cops in his back pocket."

I couldn't disagree with her. Nadine had been frightened to go to the police. Hell, she hadn't even talked to the cops, and they'd killed her. But Grace couldn't keep hiding and running scared.

"And Mom's name?" I asked.

She picked at something on her jeans. "When I got away, I had to disguise myself. So I cut my hair, changed my name, then used some of the money Duke gave me to get tattoos."

My phone rang. I fumbled it out of my pocket in hopes it was Maggie calling me from the restaurant. "Yeah."

"Dillon, it's Dom." His voice was panicked and loud enough for Duke and Grace to hear.

I put him on speaker. "My brother Duke is in the car, and Grace is sitting with me.

"Dom, I'm fine," Grace said.

A whoosh of breath came out of his mouth. "Dillon, I'm calling with bad news. The Black Knights took Maggie."

My vision blurred before rage cleared it.

Duke spun around and got on the road.

"Tell me where you are," I said.

"Tapas. But don't come here."

What the fuck is he doing at Tapas?

"Don't call the cops either," Dom continued. "I know Maggie is friends with Detective Hughes. Grace, honey, bring your brother to the factory." Then the line went dead.

And so did my heart.

29

———

MAGGIE

My head lolled, or maybe my whole body was rocking like a ship on high seas. I was having an out-of-body experience. I felt light, as if I were walking on air, almost like I was drunk. I lifted my hand but found I couldn't move it. I tried the other one with the same result.

Wherever I was, the room was warm and had a faint odor of dead earth.

I struggled to straighten in the chair I sat in as I oriented my vision, searching, scanning, and trying to make out what was around me. I saw two figures, but I wasn't sure if they were short or tall. I swiveled my head from right to left. Dizziness, strong and sharp, almost made me throw up.

Voices buzzed in the distance.

I blinked my heavy lids several times then opened my peepers as wide as I could. I licked my bone-dry lips. Water, I needed water.

"Water." I sounded as if I had downed a bottle of hard liquor and smoked two packs of Ted's Pall Mall cigarettes. "I need water." I thought I'd seen two figures, but maybe I was hallucinating.

As my head hung freely, I took a road trip back in time to see if I could remember what had happened. I had nothing. My brain was empty.

Think.

I did what I usually did when trying to locate something. I retraced my steps. My body continued to sway as I tried to get the neurons in my brain to come to life.

Think hard.

My name was Maggie Marx. I was a reporter. I was also on a date, or maybe not. *Date. Yeah. Dillon Hart.* I squeezed my eyes tightly shut as if that would help me remember. Tall, physically fit, broad shoulders, tatted arms, shoulder-length hair. I smiled as I continued to bring up images of my hot and virile man. *Is that the reason I'm here? Where is here? The restaurant. That's it.* I was waiting for Dillon when two big gorillas grabbed me.

My eyes flew open. My heart rammed against my ribs. I began to perspire.

Heavy footfalls approached.

I shook my head, hoping to clear the fog from my vision as well as my brain.

The stench of cigarettes invaded my nostrils as the person drew closer.

I narrowed my focus to see who was before me. "Ted?"

"No, sweetheart. Ted isn't here."

The word *sweetheart* jolted me as if the male voice had shot me. I knew that voice. The man sounded vaguely familiar, but it wasn't Ted. And it wasn't Dillon.

Slap. My head swung to one side. *Slap.* Then my head swung to the other side. "Wake up, little one."

I was awake. I was lethargic, but my eyes were open. The problem was my vision.

Blink. Blink. Blink. Then I shook my head once again.

Slap. Slap. I barely registered the pain when he hit me again. If his hand touched me one more time, I would... A hysterical laugh broke out, loud and echoing. I couldn't move, let alone try to fight back.

"They gave her too much of that drug when they knocked her out, boss." A new voice, brittle and more grating than the one who had hit me, trickled in from somewhere in the room.

I blinked one more time, and a man's face started to come into focus. Icy claws crawled down my spine, and I shivered.

Hooknose examined me intently. I'd seen Hooknose before. My head flopped back like a rag doll. Cobwebs hung from the rafters, giving me the feeling that they were reaching down to save me.

The man's hands gripped my ears and righted my head. Then he blew his vile breath in my face. It was exactly what the doctor had ordered to clear my vision and sharpen my senses.

His hooknose stood out like a beacon in the night. Only this beacon wasn't going to guide me to safety. I dragged my gaze slowly down and found his flat chin.

He had ice-blue eyes, a hooknose, and a flat chin.

Quick and sharp, a pain gripped my chest. He was the man who'd tapped on my window while I was watching that gang house.

I wrinkled my nose and squirmed, pulling up on my hands that I found zip-tied to a chair.

Hooknose angled his head one way then the other. "You sure are a pretty thing with those big greens." His thorny voice felt as if he were sticking thousands of pins in me all at once.

Horror, dark, twisted, and eerie, swirled in my gut. Any numbness I had was history. Maybe if I went back to sleep and woke up again, I would find myself in a cozy room, curled up next to Dillon with his arms around me, protecting me. Or we would be sitting at a table at Tapas, eating, talking, and laughing. Then maybe he would kiss me.

Instead, I sat chained to a chair in an open and vast warehouse. I took inventory from all sides that I could. Windows high above told me it was dark outside. A door was carved in the corner on my right, and when my gaze darted to my left, my jaw fell into my lap. Six cages lined the side wall. They were filled with women who were watching what was about to happen to me. They'd probably been in my shoes not that long ago. I gripped the arms of the wooden chair so hard, a splinter dug into my palm.

I welcomed the pain. It reminded me I was alive, at least for now.

"Boss," the other man who I couldn't quite see said. "Do you want me to throw her in the cage until she's ready?"

Ready?

Hooknose produced a large hunting knife from somewhere behind him.

On instinct, I thrashed around, even though it was pointless.

The man came at me, holding the tip of the blade eerily close to my face. I tried to kick, but my legs were tied to the chair too.

He dragged the blade down my face until he reached the scar on my neck. "Who gave you this horrible scar?" He sounded as if he cared.

I spit in his face, or tried. My spittle only dribbled down my chin.

Hooknose guffawed loudly, grating on my nerves.

"Boss?" the other man said, his feet clicking on the cracked cement floor. When he drew up alongside his boss, my blood pooled at my feet.

I slid my gaze to Hooknose. "Who gave me this scar?" I bared my teeth and flicked my chin at his soldier. "He did."

The flashback was swift, and I couldn't stop it.

"Shut the fuck up," Cory had shouted as he rammed his dick into me over and over again.

I had shut up only because I'd munched on his ear.

I smiled at the memory before zeroing in on his right earlobe. A small piece of his skin was missing, and that earlobe was shorter than the other.

Studying me as if he were an animal trying to figure out his prey, Cory Calderon loomed over me once again. Only this time, he wasn't holding a knife or raping me. He wasn't tearing my body apart like he had when I was fourteen. Nausea rose like a fast-moving hurricane. I had wanted this moment since that horrific day. I'd wanted to catch him doing something illegal so I could give Ted the evidence he needed to put Cory away. But as I sat there, shrugging out of a drug-induced state, more than anything else, I wanted to kill Cory with my bare hands.

I wanted to erase that smugness he was wearing with pride.

Hooknose gave Cory a sidelong glance. "Are you sure this man gave you that scar?"

Cory bore his dark, evil, and ghostly eyes into me as though he dared me to say yes.

I glowered at Cory while answering Hooknose. "Why do you care?"

"I don't like when my girls are scarred," Cory's boss said. "I lose clients."

Cory swiped a fat hand over his thinning black hair. He seemed to be thinking quite hard. Then a chilling smirk emerged. "I remember you now. You were my first victim." He sounded proud of that. "You fought hard." Then as if the doors opened wide to the memory, he tugged on his ear.

Come closer, I chanted silently. I wanted nothing more than to rip off the rest of his ear. "You deserved that scar," I seethed.

He spat on the floor. "You and me are going to have a good time tonight."

His boss watched as though he were enjoying the show. I could've sworn I saw admiration wash over Hooknose's hardened face.

Sick bastard.

I knew what I was thinking shouldn't be said, but I had to say it anyway. I had to show Cory I wasn't afraid like I'd been that night. I had to show him that ears weren't the only things I could bite off or rip apart.

"You're right about one thing," I said. "*I'm* going to have a good time." I would do everything in my power to make sure Cory felt pain. Up until now, I'd wanted to do the right thing in my revenge to take down Cory. Not anymore. I wanted to kill him once and for all. I wanted to end his life so he wouldn't violate and hurt another woman again. Jail would be easy for him. A slow death would be a far better punishment.

The women in the cages were silent, though I bet they would want the same. I could only imagine how many women Cory had ruined both physically and mentally in the years since he'd attacked me.

First though, I had questions. "Why am I here?" I addressed Cory's boss.

"I need your help," Hooknose said.

I laughed, a hearty one, and in that moment, I realized something. *Caged women. Cory. Black Knights.* I was talking to Miguel Rivera. "You're the leader of the Black Knights. You're Miguel." I'd been so obsessed with Cory that I hadn't connected the dots sooner.

Cory chewed on his thin lip. "Miguel, let's end her now. I'll take care of her body."

I should have been shaking in my flats, and part of me was, but I'd wanted to infiltrate the Black Knights as an undercover prostitute. So there I was. Only I was confused. Miguel wanted my help?

Miguel hauled short, stubby fingers down the length of his jaw, while the lone light from above glinted off the blade he held with his other hand. "I see we have a smarty-pants here. Bravo. You figured out I'm Miguel. Let me share some facts about you."

Cory folded his arms over his white shirt, which I hoped would be saturated in red by the time I was done with him. He opened his stance then cupped his hands in front of him.

I snarled for no other reason than to make me feel as though I were doing something.

"Maggie Marx," Miguel started. "Reporter for the *Boston Eagle.* Grew up in the foster care system. A former gang member for…" He tapped the blade to his lips. "Bloodhounds. Yep, that's right. Friends with Detective Ted Hughes. You live by yourself in a run-down apartment in the south end, drive a beat-up VW Bug. Your boyfriend is Dillon Hart, who runs a shelter for runaway girls. It recently opened if I'm not mistaken. How am I doing so far?"

Most of that information on me was public knowledge. Well,

maybe not foster care or that I was close to Ted. Dillon's shelter, on the other hand, was a business, which meant that was public record. Nevertheless, sex trafficking and runaway girls at a shelter mixed quite well for Miguel. At least the spark in his eyes said so, and that made me grip the arms of the chair tighter.

"You're wrong about one thing." My tone was even. "Dillon Hart isn't my boyfriend."

Miguel bobbed his head. "You don't mind if I kill him, then. You don't mind if I kill his sister either or his brother doing time in the joint?"

My pulse was sprinting around the track. "You can't kill someone who is dead, and the Hart sister is dead." I all but spat poisonous venom at him. I couldn't show I cared. The minute he got any notion that I did, he would use it to his advantage somehow. "Anyway, how does your knowledge of me got anything to do with me helping you?"

Miguel ran a finger over the sharp edge of the blade. "You're going to help me get Hart's sister. The one you claim is dead isn't. The one who has been working for me."

Grace had run away at sixteen. A runaway girl at that age would be vulnerable, would fall into the charms of a man, especially if she was seeing the world for the first time. And she would be the perfect candidate for sex trafficking—young, pretty, and naive. "Say she is alive, I can't see how I could help." I'd never met Grace, and a total stranger wouldn't trade her life for mine.

"Ah," Cory said. "As smart as you are, you're kind of stupid."

I rolled my eyes.

"You see, Maggie," Miguel continued, ignoring his underling. "I'm banking that Dillon Hart has a soft spot for you. After all, you were at his house all night not that long ago."

The bastard had been tailing me. Ted had been right. Dillon had been right. I'd never gotten the sense someone had been following me, though, not until earlier that night.

Cory gave me a smirk of all smirks that said *you're going to be great bait.* "He's going to come for his girl."

Miguel's upper lip lifted as a glimmer of excitement swept across his face. "We're going to make it easy for him. He'll come for you. Grace will show up to save her brother, and boom, I get what I want. You see, Maggie, Grace loves her brothers. She'll do anything for them. That's one of the reasons I haven't killed Denim yet, although my men in prison did a number on him. It's funny what my men can uncover in prison. But I couldn't use Denim for this job. I couldn't even use Duke, not with all his bodyguards. Besides, I eventually want to do business with the older Hart brother."

Duke was an ass, but after his furious exchange with Dillon recently, I didn't get the impression that he would delve into the sex-trafficking business.

Regardless, Miguel was underestimating Dillon. Rafe was a badass that I wouldn't want to be caught on a dark street with. Hunt was equally as scary, and he worked for the Guardian, which was owned by a mob boss if I weren't mistaken. I had tried to do a story on Jeremy Pitt when I'd first started at the *Eagle.* To my inexperienced surprise, my story hadn't gone to print. I suspected Jeremy had paid off the big bosses upstairs. I didn't know that for sure. Still, Hunt had an army of ex-military dudes he could call on if Dillon needed backup.

What am I thinking? All Dillon has to do is contact Ted. I'm not sure if he will given the tense interaction they had.

The gorilla who had grabbed me at the restaurant marched up and whispered something into Miguel's ear.

Miguel waved his hand. "I'll be right there."

Gorilla hustled out.

"Throw her in a cage. I have to see if I can convince her boyfriend to do a swap," Miguel said to Cory.

"He's not coming to save me." I prayed he would. Dillon had a big heart, regardless of whether he had feelings for someone. Case and point being the shelter. He had put his hard-earned money into a project to help women. Yet as big as his heart was, blood trumped everything. He'd even said his sister came first. He wouldn't dare swap me for Grace, especially after finding her again.

I wouldn't complain if he stormed in with guns and an army to save me, but deep down, I wanted him to save me because I meant more to him than a random girl who needed help.

But I couldn't wait for help. I had to find a way out of there. I had to find a way to save me and those six young girls in the cages.

Miguel pocketed his knife. "Oh, and Maggie? Next time you want to snoop around someone's house, you should be more inconspicuous." He started to walk away.

"Was it you who killed Nadine?" I wanted to hear him say yes.

Cory pulled out a switchblade. The clicking sound made the hackles rise on my neck. "No, sweetheart. I hold that honor. She knew too much about our organization."

Sick bastard.

"Daddy will be proud to hear that," I shot back.

Harold Calderon's business would be ruined once my story went to print. Whether the elder Calderon knew of his son's illegal involvement with the Black Knights, it didn't matter. People would scurry to pull out their investments faster than the speed of light, Dillon included.

Cory pressed the tip of the blade underneath my chin, spitting his vile onion breath in my face. "My father will never know what I do in my spare time."

I lifted my chin as Cory pushed the blade a little harder into my skin without breaking through.

Miguel and the other gorilla faded from view, and I heard the door squeak open then closed.

Cory searched my face. "I should end you now."

"Do it, then," I taunted. "But first let's at least have a fair fight. Unless you really are afraid of me." I could handle Cory. Adrenaline was a great weapon to have, and I knew how to fight.

He seemed to be considering my offer.

"No weapons," I added.

He was much taller than me, broad in the shoulders, fat hands, and big arms. None of that mattered. I knew the points on the body to hurt, and I wasn't talking about his balls, although that was a great start. Lou had taught me to subdue my enemy first. I had to get him into a position where I could go for the throat and knock the air out of him. Once I did that, I could help those girls, and we could run like the wind.

I had an advantage over the girls in the cages. I was big-boned. I had hips. I had strong muscles in my arms.

Cory threw his head back and roared with laughter so loud that the girls in the cages cringed as though they'd heard that nail-grating sound before. If it weren't for my legs being tied to the chair, I would've kicked him right in the nuts.

When he was done laughing, he puffed out his chest. "You want to fight me?"

I tilted my head. "Are you afraid?" Men like Cory were all about ego, regardless of sex. Considering Cory preyed on women, I was banking that he would jump at the chance to swing his fists at me.

In two seconds flat, he cut the ties off me. "Let's see what you got." He pocketed his switchblade.

I rose too fast, and the room spun. Whatever drug they'd given me hadn't worn off completely.

Cory waved me on. "This should be fun."

I sized him up and studied his body language. He was loose, not afraid. His arms were at his side, which meant that he was begging me to run at him. He wore a gold hoop earring in his good ear, and his hair had a bottle of gel in it. The grease would make it hard for me to pull out his strands one by one. But I didn't cat fight like other girls. I wasn't going for the hair but rather his throat and then his balls.

He looked down his short nose at me. "Are you going to stare at me all day?"

"Kill him," one of the girls shouted.

"I could break you in two," Cory said.

I opened my arms. "What are you waiting for?"

He rushed at me like a linebacker in a football game. I darted out of the way. He stumbled then caught himself, growling.

His nostrils flared. "I will end you." He took out his switchblade and charged me.

I would have liked to say that my eyes didn't bug out of my head. But I couldn't stop the memory of the sound of the switchblade engaging or the image of him on top of me.

His face was beet red. Mine had to be too. But all I could think about was protecting myself. I would never let him hurt me again.

I sidestepped him. He was onto me, though. He swung around quickly, and the blade scored my face. Hot rage gripped my chest. I reared back my arm and went for my target. My fist connected with his throat.

All he did was laugh.

Well, Lou, that didn't work, not on Cory. That move had worked on one guy I'd tussled with in a gang fight once.

All six girls were making noises of "ah," "oh no," and "watch out."

"You can't hurt me," Cory cooed.

The warmth of blood trickled down my neck then my chest.

Cory stomped closer to me. This time I didn't move.

All I could think about was getting the blade.

He bowed his head, admiring his artwork that he'd carved into me so long ago. My chest heaved rapidly, trying to quell the panic. Before I could do anything, he traced the blade over my scar then ripped off my shirt.

I gulped in air and blew it out. "You like when a girl submits to you?"

"I like when she fights," he whispered, his gaze lingering on my big breasts. "You sure turned out to be a fine-looking woman." He fingered my blond locks that I'd left unbraided for Dillon.

Nausea tumbled deep in the pit of my stomach. I hated Cory, and I hated what I was about to do. But I had to inflict pain on him. I had to feel some satisfaction after what he'd done to me. I lifted up on my toes and kissed Cory on the mouth.

He stiffened. Then as though a light bulb brightened in his head, he positioned the knife against the side of my neck. "Not going to work."

We'll see about that. I continued to use my female charms, tuning out the girls who were telling me not to go there. They knew something I didn't. But I was invested now. So I let my hands roam along his chest as I locked eyes with him, hoping mine weren't showing fear and hoping he was buying my moves, which I was almost certain he wasn't. But a man, especially one that raped women, could be tempted.

He allowed me to feel his chest and abs, which were surprisingly firm. When my hands reached the buckle of his belt, he pressed the tip of the blade into my skin.

I didn't flinch. I feigned a sultry grin. "I like it rough." Okay, I just puked in my mouth. That was true. I did like rough sex, but with someone that turned me on.

As if my statement was the assurance he needed, his body slackened. With one hand on his belt, I dragged the other one down to his crotch and found that he was fully hard.

I squeezed his erection and kissed him on the mouth again. He hadn't lowered the blade. In fact, I could feel the pressure of the tip. But any pain was nonexistent.

I stuck my tongue through his lips, trying not to die from the stench of onions. He opened for me before his free hand went around to my lower back. He yanked me to him, pressing his erection into me.

As soon as his tongue hit mine, I bit down so hard, the knife dropped from his hand.

Cory wailed, his voice bouncing off the rafters.

The girls cheered. "Get the knife."

I dove for the weapon that had fallen far from my feet.

Cory brought his hand to his mouth before spitting out blood. "You bitch." He sounded as though he had a lisp.

"Get the keys," one girl shouted.

I retrieved the blade and stalked closer to him.

I was about to drive the knife into his groin when men stormed back into the building.

Miguel jogged up with a gun pointed at me. "Put the knife down, Maggie."

"Not happening. You'll have to shoot me," I said, not taking my eyes off Cory, who was still spitting out blood.

Then Miguel fired, the sound exploding along with a burning, shooting pain somewhere on my body. The knife fell from my hands, and my body collapsed with it.

30

DILLON

The factory was an abandoned building that once was home to a paint manufacturer. Rusty old drums and paint cans littered the place. The perimeter was outlined with corroded pipes, and plastic pails were stacked two high with a sheet of wood draped over them and a computer on top.

All the way there, I itched to call the cops, but I believed Grace when she'd said Miguel had cops on his payroll. I was afraid if I called them, I might not get anywhere in finding Maggie.

Grace ran up to Dom and practically jumped into his arms before the two locked lips.

Duke hustled up behind me and growled as he laid eyes on Grace and Dom.

I cleared my throat.

"I have no idea what is happening," Duke said at my side.

I had no inkling either. I felt as if someone had pistol-whipped me. Or maybe I was under a spell or in a bad dream that didn't seem to end. My sister was alive, and Maggie had been kidnapped all within a matter of two hours. The latter was freaking me the fuck out as my pulse beat wildly.

I was ready to snag one of the two handguns next to the computer and threaten Dom if he didn't start talking.

Instead, I waved a hand around. "Dom, what the fuck are we doing here? We need to bring in the cops. We're not going to find Maggie with a laptop. And you fucking lied to me about my sister. You know her quite well. Did you lie about not seeing her for two weeks?"

Dom wrapped an arm around Grace, who seemed to be more relaxed now that she was in his presence.

"Bro, who cares if he lied about Grace. She's here. Let's concentrate on finding your girl."

I full-on laughed. "What's with the change in attitude, Duke?" He hadn't wanted anything to do with me when I showed up at his penthouse, and now he was all in to help, although he had a point. But we weren't going to find Maggie in a run-down factory or splitting hairs over why Dom lied. And Dom wasn't a cop unless he was undercover, but a biker dude dressed all in black with a few tats inked on his arm didn't scream cop to me.

However, it did cross my mind that he could be involved with the Black Knights. "Why were you at Tapas anyway?"

He rubbed his arm, which had a tattoo of an anchor with wings. "Fi works there," he said as though I were supposed to know that piece of information. "I'm not with a gang, and I'm not out to hurt anyone. I genuinely care about Grace. I did leave out some info when I talked to you at the Crow, but I had to. Grace didn't want you to know where she was since Miguel has been hunting the city for her."

"I get you don't want to go to the cops," I said to Grace. "But you can't keep running from Miguel."

"That's no way to live," Duke added.

Dom raised his hands. "All we're trying to do is find a location on Miguel. Once we do that, then we can bring in the cops."

"How do you know the Black Knights took Maggie?" I asked.

"Because Miguel drives a black Jeep," Dom said as a matter of fact.

He'd left out a ton during our convo at the Crow.

I snatched my phone from my jeans. "I'm calling Detective Hughes." He was the only one I knew who had the team and firepower and knowledge behind him. Not to mention, Ted would do whatever it took to get Maggie back since they were like father and daughter. "He's been tracking the Black Knights."

Dom started for me. "No cops."

Duke blocked him.

Inside I was cheering like a fan at a football game that my older brother hadn't lost the urge to protect me.

"I told you," Grace said. "Miguel has cops on the payroll."

Stepping back, Dom briefly closed his eyes. "I understand you don't trust me. Just give me time. I might be able to get a location on Miguel."

Maggie didn't have time.

Grace set her soft brown eyes on me, pleading. "Dom is ex-military and has a friend who's good at finding things on the Internet. He's been helping us try and find Miguel's warehouses, where he keeps the girls. I know you want to help Maggie, and I do too. But I also want to rescue all the girls that Miguel has."

It was admirable that she wanted to be the savior, and if they could get a location, then it would be easier for Ted to get his team in and take Miguel down.

"We've found Miguel's bank," Dom said. "My buddy is trying to crack through the firewall to look at all the properties Miguel's purchased recently."

If I called Hughes, and someone inside the police department was working for Miguel, then Miguel would find out, and I might never find or see Maggie again, much like Grace. She'd been gone for four years, and the only way she'd gotten free was by killing her owner. I would die if something happened to Maggie or if she disappeared and I never saw her again. I couldn't live through that.

"How long?" I asked. "Maggie doesn't have time."

Dom slid over to the laptop on the table. "Give me thirty minutes. He was working on things when I called him earlier."

I eyed Duke, who had been quiet the whole time. "It's worth a shot," he said. "And if Miguel does have a cop or two on his payroll, they'll alert Miguel, and we might not find Maggie."

"Thirty minutes," I said before heading outside. I needed air.

Duke was right on my heels. "I need to check in with my guys."

"Dillon." Grace's tone was all doom and gloom. "We'll find Maggie."

She didn't sound so sure, and I checked my watch, marking the time. In exactly thirty minutes, if we didn't have a lead, I was calling Hughes. Hell, I might call him anyway. He adored Maggie. And I wasn't comfortable putting Maggie's life in the hands of two people I hardly knew. I really didn't know my sister anymore, and frankly, Maggie was my concern. She was my girl and the woman my heart was opening up to.

When Duke and I were out in the open night air, I asked. "Do you trust Dom? You think he's legit?" Duke dealt with morons and thugs who lied and the whole gamut of criminals and jerks. I didn't think Dom was a moron. I couldn't say for sure if he was a thug. Just because he was ex-military didn't mean he was trustworthy. Or maybe I was too untrusting.

Duke scratched his nose. "He seems like a good guy. Give him the time to find out something. I also agree with them on the cops. Jeremy Pitt is mafia, and he has most of the cops on his payroll. So Miguel could too. I have to call the club." He walked in the opposite direction toward his SUV.

I ambled toward the water along the side of the building that had rusty metal drums piled high. I inhaled the salty air then called Hunt. He knew Detective Hughes. He also worked for a mafia-run company owned by Jeremy Pitt, and he had access to a team of ex-military folks.

"I've been waiting for your call," Hunt said as soon as the line connected.

"Sorry." I'd called him and Rafe on the way to the factory to check on the shelter and to let them know what I knew at the time. I'd relaxed some when I found out that the girls at the shelter were tucked into their rooms. I filled Hunt in on Dom's plan and what I knew from Grace about Miguel and the cops. "I need my own plan to find Maggie. I'm debating on calling Hughes. You seem to know the detective. Is he good or corrupt?"

"He's one of the good ones," Hunt said. "However, I don't know his gang unit very well. Before you call him, let me check with my brother, Wes. He's Pitt's right-hand man and knows most cops in the city. Give me fifteen minutes." He ended the call.

I dropped my head back, hoping that Hunt would come through with something I could work with in finding Maggie.

A crescent moon brightened the sky.

The night was turning out to be one for the books. My sister had shown up alive and well after four years. Then Maggie had been kidnapped on a busy city street. The question "why?" flitted through my head. Then it dawned on me. Denim had been asking around the prison gangs. He might've mentioned Maggie's name to the wrong person. Or maybe they took her because she helped Nadine.

Grace came running out. "Dom is close. We just found out that Miguel purchased a house on Bleven in the name of Marco Holdings."

Duke rushed over.

My eyebrows dove down.

"What is it?" Duke asked.

"I saw Marco Holdings on a notepad on Maggie's desk when I was at her office yesterday." Maggie hadn't been kidnapped because of Denim or Nadine. She'd been taken because she'd been investigating Miguel, and he wanted to shut her up. I gripped the back of my neck to keep my hands from shaking.

Grace's tone softened. "If we found the house, then we can find his other properties."

I didn't want to get all pissy with Grace. It wasn't her fault that Maggie had been kidnapped. "Maggie's life is on the line."

She stuck her hands on her small hips. "What are you going to do?"

I peered down at my sister, whose expression was swirling with emotional pain. I suspected she wanted revenge on Miguel, much like

Maggie wanted on Cory. "I know you're trying to help. Go back inside and see what else Dom finds. Duke and I will be out here." I couldn't go back into that stuffy building. "I want to talk to Duke anyway." I wanted to know why Duke's attitude had changed from dick to jerk to prickly to the brother I knew as a kid.

She didn't argue as she left Duke and me standing in a deserted parking lot near the water with the city lights twinkling in the distance.

Duke grunted, sounding exasperated and torn.

"I've seen several sides of you recently," I began. "One minute, you're an asshole, and the next, you got my back. Right now you seem to be irritated again."

He let out a laugh that didn't sound all too cheery. "I can't stop thinking how someone bought our sister. Then she killed him. And she's been in hiding from a psycho." For the first time, he was showing me how concerned he was for Grace.

I'd worried about Grace until I was sick to my stomach. Now that I knew she was alive and had fought her way out of Miguel's organization, I didn't think Duke and I should be concerned. Not only that, she had Dom, an ex-military dude. I didn't exactly like him, not after he'd lied, but he seemed to adore Grace. "I can't wrap my head around the fact that Grace was sold to some sick fuck and that she had to kill him to save herself, but as you said, she's alive. She's got Dom, and right now, I need to find Maggie." The image of some guy's hands on her made me more furious than anything. I hadn't been able to save Grace, but I had a chance to save Maggie.

Duke clamped a hand on my shoulder. "Love, brother, will get you killed. Love will only end in bloodshed and tears and heartbreak. You know, I've been keeping tabs on you. Since when do you let a woman into your life? You haven't gotten close to anyone except your buddy, Rafe, and that family you look up to. What's their name? Maxwell. That's it."

I fidgeted with my phone. "It sounds to me like a woman massacred your heart."

He let go of me as his biceps bunched.

My phone trilled. I didn't recognize the number, but I answered it anyway. "Yeah."

Duke slipped his hands into the pockets of his slacks.

"Dillon Hart, I'm Miguel Rivera."

I hit the speaker button. Duke's eyebrows furrowed.

"Where's Maggie?" I gritted my teeth. "If you so much as hurt her, I will kill you."

"That isn't any way to negotiate." Miguel's voice was sharp.

Duke and I swapped a *what the fuck* look.

"I'm listening." My tone was flat, even though I was twitchy.

"Here's how this will go down. You'll bring me your sister. In exchange, I'll give you Maggie."

I scrubbed a hand over my beard. "What? This is all about my sister?" Grace had said Miguel was hunting her. I imagined he wanted her because she'd killed his client.

"Her and I have unfinished business," he said.

Duke shook his head and mouthed "No."

I spied a black cat watching us from on top of one of the rusty barrels. The superstition that black cats were bad luck was proving to be true. "I'm not handing you my sister."

"Too bad. I guess you'll never see your girl again." The line went dead.

I growled, ready to throw my phone, when it rang again. I put Hunt on speaker. "Talk to me."

"Bad news," Hunt said. "That Rick detective you met with Hughes when they showed up at the shelter is a bad seed. He's in bed with the Black Knights. He's been feeding them intel on cop activity and probably on Maggie. So be careful if you go to Hughes on this one."

I clutched a handful of my hair. "Thanks."

"Rafe and I have things locked down at the shelter. Go find your girl." Hunt hung up.

"Bro." Duke sat back. "Don't do what I think you're going to do."

I pressed my lips together as I hit the number that Miguel had called me from.

Miguel answered on the first ring. "You came to your senses."

"I want to talk to Maggie first." I wasn't rolling over like a dog that wanted his belly rubbed.

I heard him snap his fingers. "Talk to your boyfriend."

"Maggie?" My voice pitched, and my stomach rolled.

"Dillon?" She sounded groggy and drunk and maybe in pain. "Don't give him Grace. I'm already dead."

My heart splintered.

Miguel came back on the line. "Do we have a deal?"

I balled my free hand into a fist. "What does she mean by she's already dead?"

Duke's face morphed into the Tasmanian devil.

"Answer me," Miguel said. "Or your girl is right. She's dead."

Taunting him, telling him I would kill him, or any other threats wouldn't speed up the process of getting Maggie back. "Where? When?" Those were the only two questions that were needed. Anything else, then I would be the one killing Maggie, and I wasn't going to let that happen, regardless of how much I loved my sister.

"That's a good boy." Miguel laughed. "I knew you were the brother that would listen."

Duke jerked. I didn't have the call on speaker this time, but Miguel was talking loudly, and Duke was leaning in close to me to hear.

My jaw tightened when Denim came to mind. I couldn't worry about my brother right now. "On second thought, I'll pick the spot. I want to make sure you don't have anything up your sleeve."

"Fair enough," he said rather quickly.

I didn't have to think hard as to why. If Rick were feeding him info, then Miguel would know if we brought Hughes in on the deal.

"Meet Grace and me at Mooney's Paint Factory at sunrise." This was the perfect spot. No one was around. There was no public to worry about. The building was surrounded by water on the backside and a chain-link fence on the other three sides. The only possible place for his goons to hide was the abandoned building across the street.

"Any funny stuff, and your girl dies. Oh, and one more thing—

don't waste your time on Hughes. If you alert him, I'll know." He clicked off.

I marched toward the factory door.

Duke was on my heels. "Seriously, Dillon? You can't think Grace is going to walk into the enemy's arms."

"I do, and she will." I flew into the building.

Dom hopped up from his chair, while Grace whipped her head at me.

"I just got off the phone with Miguel. Grace and I will be meeting him at sunrise right outside here. He wants Grace in exchange for Maggie."

Grace moved her head back and forth repeatedly. "I'm not going back to Miguel."

"Why does Miguel want you?" Duke asked. "He's jumping through hoops for you, Grace."

The four of us stood in a circle of sorts.

Grace tugged on her ear, a habit she'd had as a kid when she didn't want to talk but knew she had to when one of her brothers demanded an answer, especially when it came to an incident between her and our old man. "The man who bought me. The one I killed. His family put a bounty on my head and Miguel's if he didn't return me to the family."

Dom mumbled something under his breath that I couldn't make out.

Duke growled low.

I was numb.

"She's not going back to him," Dom said through clenched teeth. "She's been through hell. Do you know how she was tortured?" He tipped his head at Grace. "Show them."

Her shoulders slumped as tears clouded her eyes. "I can't."

Dom cupped her face. "Baby cakes, they're your brothers. They need to know."

Duke turned multiple shades of red. I was holding my breath.

Dom guided Grace around so her back was to us. Then he lifted up her shirt.

Duke paled. I was on the verge of throwing up.

Grace's back was littered with scars as though someone had whipped her. Then the idea of Maggie going through something similar made my stomach even queasier.

Motherfucker.

Grace fumbled to pull down her shirt. When she pivoted, her cheeks were coated in tears.

Duke had his arms around her before I could blink. "I'm so fucking sorry." He rested his chin on her head.

Her arms went around Duke as she cried.

Sandy grit lined my throat. I couldn't let my feelings get in the way. Duke had just told me love would get me killed. Love would also get Maggie killed if I let my love for Grace get in the way. "I'm not into throwing Grace to the wolves. So we have eight hours to work out a new plan and find where Miguel is keeping Maggie." If we couldn't, then I wasn't sure what our next move would be. "I'm calling in Detective Hughes and only him. Apparently, one of Hughes's underlings is on Miguel's payroll." I blew out all the air in my lungs. "One thing I know for sure is that Detective Hughes cares a great deal about Maggie. That means he'll do what we ask without his unit."

Or so I prayed.

31
____

MAGGIE

ory shoved me into an empty cage. "Bitch."

I fell hard on my knees, barely catching myself with my hands before my head went through the other side of the cage. Loose pebbles sank into the palms of my hands, and excruciating pain gripped my thigh where Miguel had shot me. As hard as it was to suppress any sign that I was in agony, I schooled my features as best I could then raised myself to a sitting position and rested my back against the hard steel of the cage.

Cory slammed the door before wiping the blood that was running down his chin and neck. I should've flinched at being confined to a small space, but with my tan pants absorbing the blood oozing out of my leg, I didn't have the energy to move. Shock was setting in and so was the nausea.

I covered my leg with my hand. I would've used my shirt to forge a makeshift bandage, but Cory had ripped that off me. And I didn't have the oomph to tear off a portion of my pants. So there I was, locked in a steel trap. My only hope of survival was Dillon, and while I knew he would do whatever he could to rescue me, I couldn't see him handing over Grace. Apart from that, sunrise was hours away. Miguel had delivered the meeting time to Cory when he'd hung up from talking with Dillon.

The women in the other cages spat at Cory as he hurried by them. Then Miguel and his men left the building.

"Maggie," the girl next to me said.

Slowly, I turned my head, and even that was a monumental feat.

"Hey, it's Misty. Remember me? I'm your source on the street."

Her petite form came in and out of focus.

"You need to tie your leg with something to stop the blood," she said. "Did you hear me? Maggie, you can't fall asleep. You need to stop the bleeding."

I knew that name, but my efforts to do anything other than keep my eyes open were becoming difficult by the minute.

"Come closer. Can you do that?" she asked, her voice becoming white noise. "Please."

Something hard hit me in the head, and I opened my eyes.

"I'll throw another rock at you if you don't come closer to me," she said as if she were my mother.

Oh no, my mom! I wouldn't get to meet her after all. Tears started to run down my face. I wouldn't get to go out on a date with Dillon. I wouldn't get to feel what it was like to be kissed by him.

"Maggie," Misty shouted at the top of her lungs.

I woke up.

"Get your ass over here," she ordered.

I obeyed for the mere reason that I wanted her to be quiet. I used my hands and butt to navigate the short distance to her side of the cage. Once I made it, I almost passed out.

She tore her tank top off, exposing her pretty pink bra, and I noticed bruises along her arms. "Good girl."

"How did you get here?" *Please don't say because of me or because you talked to me.*

"One of Miguel's men saw me talking to you a few weeks ago."

More tears spilled out. "I'm so sorry." God, I was getting women killed. I groaned more than cried. The pain was to the point that I seriously felt as though I were going to pass out. I felt as if someone had taken a hot fireplace poker and rammed it into my leg.

Shivers racked my body.

Misty flipped her oily auburn hair away from her freckled face. "It's not your fault. Working the streets as a call girl comes with risks." She ripped her tank top before shoving the piece of fabric through the small mesh hole. "Tie this around your leg. It should slow the bleeding."

"She needs to get to a hospital," a girl said from one of the other cages. "She's not going to make it. She's lost a lot of blood."

That girl was right. I was fading fast. In between blinks and some blurriness, I could make out the four-sided steel cage that looked exactly like one that Ted used at the precinct to hold perps who hadn't been processed yet. I knew there was no way out. Cages were tamper-proof from the inside.

Misty rubbed a hand up her bruised arm. "Use the shirt, Maggie. You're losing a lot of blood. The bullet might've damaged your main artery."

Her statement should've scared the lights out of me, but panicking would only send me deeper into shock.

I lifted my arm to pull the thin fabric through the hole, but even that small act was hard. My arm felt like a heavy weight. I took a breath when I finally had the shirt in my lap. In slow movements, I managed to secure it around my leg, groaning and swearing the entire time.

Push past the pain. You need to get out of here. You need to get these girls out. I didn't want to give up, but I was kind of screwed. I couldn't walk. I couldn't get out, and I couldn't save anyone including myself.

When I told Dillon I was already dead, I was serious.

"Miguel!" I screamed as loud as I could. I would continue to scream bloody murder until the man showed his face, if I lasted that long. It took all the energy I had to push air out of my lungs.

"What are you doing?" Misty didn't sound thrilled. "Don't bring attention to yourself. He'll kill you."

I let out a weak laugh. "No, he won't. He needs me." That much, I was certain of.

"I hate to say this, but you'll be lucky if you last the next hour," Misty added.

I heard a faint click of shoes, or I might have imagined it. Then Cory, the ugly bastard, grinned down at me from the other side of the cage. He'd cleaned up his bloody mouth.

"How's your tongue, asshole?"

He narrowed his eyes and threw me the finger.

"Aw, cat bit it off?" I shouldn't have been cocky or sarcastic, but as much pain as I was in, I was enjoying the heck out of the fact that I'd hurt him in some small way.

His nostrils flared, and his cheeks reddened.

"I want to talk to Miguel."

"You can tell me." His speech was off.

I spied Miguel strutting over, his short legs moving fast, or maybe I was imagining things.

"What do you want?" He settled next to Cory, his hooknose protruding more than I remembered.

I was about to answer him until I spotted Rick sauntering over with a grin the size of California. No, it couldn't be him. My mind had to be playing tricks on me.

Miguel followed my line of sight. Then he laughed, the sound making all my hairs stand up. "Everyone can be bought, Maggie."

Rick studied me. "Miguel, you said you weren't going to hurt her. This wasn't supposed to happen."

"Spare me the emotion, Rick. You can't possibly believe someone like these two." I tried to wag my finger between asshole one and asshole two.

"I wasn't planning on it, but she gave me no choice," Miguel said as though it were my fault he'd shot me.

"Who is he?" Misty whispered.

"Ladies," I said, "meet Rick the cop. You can't trust anyone anymore, not even the law."

The girls made noises, but quiet ones just in case Miguel had any inkling to unleash his abuse.

"I see you want to get shot again." He sounded excited to have the opportunity to use his gun on me.

Jerk.

"If I die, you will never get Grace." I glanced at my leg. The blood wasn't coming out as fast. "So get me a doctor. Now." Whatever plan Dillon had up his sleeve, I prayed it would work. I couldn't die. I had a lot to live for, and by golly, if I was going to give my life to the good Lord today, then I wanted to at least try like a bitch to save myself and the girls in this warehouse.

He considered me as Cory harrumphed. Rick had an impassive expression. No surprise there since he was an experienced cop.

"I can help her," Misty chimed in. "Get me some medical supplies and a knife and tweezers. Oh, and I'll need a syringe of that Special K drug you use to knock us out with."

The men eyed Misty as if she had five heads.

"Do you want your prize possession?" Misty asked. "If so, you're wasting time. She's going to die."

I wanted to say "you're not a doctor," but what did I know? The only thing I knew about Misty was that she'd sold her body for a high price on the streets.

Miguel snapped his fingers at Cory. "Get the first-aid supplies and a syringe of the drug." He gave me the impression that he patched people up all the time.

Cory left, and Miguel glowered at me then at Misty. "I'm locking you in the cage with her," he said to Misty. "Any funny stuff, and I'll shoot you in the head."

Misty didn't flinch or make a sound. "Kind of hard to try to escape when you're locked in a cage."

Miguel moved Misty in with me before he walked away. Rick was on his heels.

"Does Ted know?" I shouted at Rick as best I could. But he kept walking.

Traitor.

Misty kneeled at my side.

"Do you know what you're doing?" I guess it really didn't matter if she did or not. If she didn't get the bullet out, I was a dead girl.

"I was studying to be a nurse, but I've never removed a bullet from anyone."

I laughed. "Then why did you volunteer?"

I could hear the girls talking but couldn't make out what they were saying.

"Because if you die, I don't want you to die alone. And maybe we can get out of here if he brings us that Special K drug."

I was a little woozy, so I wasn't following her train of thought too well. "Special K?"

"It's a drug they use that knocks out the girls pretty quickly so they can transport them. The street name is Special K. In some circles, it's known as a date rape drug or valium. Anyway, if we can take one of the men out, we can grab his gun and find a way out of here."

I loved the way she was thinking. "I won't be able to walk. You go and get help. If you can get out of here, contact Detective Ted Hughes."

Cory returned with medical supplies. He quickly unlocked the cage door and threw them in before securing the lock again.

Misty rifled through the medical supplies and pulled out tweezers. "Where's the knife and the Special K? Miguel told you to bring it. She's going to need a sedative." She snarled at Cory.

"Miguel changed his mind," he said. "Bandage her up and make sure she doesn't die. If she does, then you do too." He stalked away.

Her plan was shot to hell.

Her light-blue eyes filled with tears as she pulled out a small bottle of peroxide.

I grasped her hand. "Hey, we'll get out of here. If I know Dillon, he'll find us." He probably wouldn't find us in time, but I was trying to convince myself more than her.

She uncapped the bottle. "This is going to sting." She poured the chemical on my leg.

I screamed holy hell.

"Sorry." She examined the wound then tore open a gauze pad and dabbed more peroxide on it before cleaning the area around the hole. "The blood is clotting. That's good news." She checked my pulse. "Your pulse is extremely slow. That's not good." Then she tightened the makeshift tourniquet a little more.

I closed my eyes, willing the pain to go away.

Misty tapped on my face. "Stay awake." Her voiced reminded me of one of my foster moms, who'd scolded me for breaking a glass.

I fluttered my eyelids, shivering.

"Good girl," Misty said. "Okay, tell me something about yourself."

I inhaled a large breath, knowing she was trying to keep me awake. I said the first thing that came to mind. "I've never had a crush on a boy until now. Or had a mind-blowing kiss." I slurred the last three words.

She giggled. "Have you been hiding under a rock? You're what? Twenty-five or so? No crushes in high school? First loves?"

I didn't go to high school. I'd gotten my GED then applied to college. Living in a gang and on the streets was all about survival and not about learning algebra or any subject other than how to stay alive. "When Cory raped me at fourteen, I didn't go near any men until I was in college, and even then, I only had one-night stands. Sure, men kissed me, but not like they were in love with me or like I meant anything to them other than a girl to have sex with. So when I say I haven't had a mind-blowing kiss, I mean by a man who loves me."

"You mean that asshole." She stabbed her thumb in the direction Cory had rushed off. "Raped you when you were fourteen?"

I nodded.

"Whoa. I say we kill him, then."

I smiled as best I could. "Slowly. We need to torture him." It was freeing to inflict Cory with pain, but I didn't get the satisfaction from it that I thought I would.

Silence hung in the air. Even the girls in the other cages had gone quiet, listening to Misty and me.

"So, kissing isn't all that great. My first time"—Misty fiddled with my tourniquet—"was with a boy named Chase. His lips were hard. His tongue was nasty. I think he ate a clove of garlic before he kissed me."

I giggled.

"So you've never been in love?" she asked.

I frowned "No. Love is overrated. Or maybe it isn't. This guy, Dillon, who I was supposed to be on a date with tonight, gives me all kinds of cozy feelings."

It was her turn to giggle. "I would say you're experiencing your first love."

"Misty," I barely said. "I can't keep my eyes open."

She tapped my cheek. "Stay with me."

Darkness crept in along the edges of my vision. "Tell Dillon that I'm sorry."

"You tell him." Her voice began to fade. "Maggie. Mag—"

My heart beat one last time before the noises, pain, and voices died.

32

DILLON

I sat in a booth in an all-night diner not far from the paint factory, waiting on Detective Hughes. I wanted to feel him out before I brought him over to the factory. My brother didn't want anything to do with cops. So he'd stayed behind to watch over Grace and Dom in the event Dom found where Miguel was holed up and decided to tackle things on his own.

When I'd left, Dom wasn't having any luck on finding more properties owned by Marco Holdings, and neither was his buddy. I believed that Miguel wasn't stupid enough to put all his eggs in one basket. He knew Grace had probably heard too much while she was with him. Not only that, but after the raid on the house, I was sure Miguel had probably locked down his organization any way he could.

The bell on the door dinged, and Hughes sauntered through it, heading directly toward me. He looked tired and a tad pissed off. I imagined he hadn't been too happy to get out of bed in the wee hours of the morning. We only had three hours left before Miguel showed up with Maggie. I'd been trying for hours to get ahold of Hughes. After I'd left several messages and called the precinct, he finally returned my call, and only because I'd mentioned that Maggie was in danger. I hadn't given more detail than that. I was afraid if I had, he would've alerted his team, in particular Rick.

He slid into the booth across from me with a crease in between his bushy eyebrows. He combed his mustache with his fingers. "Start talking."

Since we didn't have a great relationship, his tone was rather brusque.

I played with a napkin as the aroma from my coffee cup wafted up my nose.

The plump waitress came over with a mug in one hand and a pot of coffee in the other. "Coffee?" she asked Ted.

Hughes nodded.

Once she had filled his cup and gone back behind the counter, Hughes said, "Talk."

I raked my gaze over his skin, which was weathered and worn, no doubt from years of fighting crime on the streets of Boston. I gnawed on my bottom lip, debating where to start—with Maggie or the snitch in his ranks. If I began with Maggie, Hughes wouldn't hear anything else. If I came out and told him about Rick, he wouldn't believe me. He would storm out and get Rick on the phone. Rick would deny that he was feeding Miguel information, then Hughes would get his team together to search for Maggie while Rick alerted Miguel.

Maybe bringing Hughes into this wasn't a good idea. Maybe Dom and Grace were right.

He eyed me over the rim of his coffee cup. "Hart, are you going to tell me why you got me out of bed or not?"

"I get the feeling you don't like me. You certainly don't like my brother, Denim. And you have no reason to believe what I'm about to say. But I don't want you to fly out of here without considering the consequences."

He slammed his cup down.

The waitress cocked an eyebrow.

Aside from the waitress, the two of us, and the cook in the back room who had poked his head out earlier, the diner was empty.

Hughes pressed his elbows into the table, pushing his head forward. "Get to the point, Hart." He was a second away from tearing me to shreds.

I sat back. "I have reason to believe that you have a guy on your team that works for Miguel Rivera."

He didn't move. His nicotine breath sprayed with spit. "What are you smoking?"

You're wasting time. Tell him quickly.

I sighed. "Here's the deal. You know Hunt Thompson. You seemed to like him when you saw him at my shelter. He has a source who says Rick is the rat. I need you to believe me, or at least try, because Maggie has been kidnapped."

His angular jaw bounced off the Formica tabletop. "You're bullshitting me."

It was my turn to lean in. "Really? I got you out of bed to tell you lies? Listen, I want your help. But if you bring your team in on this, Maggie will be dead. Miguel told me that I couldn't tell you about him kidnapping Maggie or where I'll be meeting him"—I glanced at my watch—"in two hours and fifty minutes. And if I do, he'll get a call, and then I'll never see Maggie again. You'll never either."

Ever so slowly, his body moved until his back was against the vinyl booth bench, seething either at the situation or at me.

I checked on the waitress, if for no other reason than to give Hughes a minute to process what I'd told him. The middle-aged woman was making another pot of coffee. When I swung my attention back to Detective Hughes, he was giving me a death glare full of disbelief and rage.

"You might not like me. I know I lied to you when you asked me if I'd seen Nadine. I'm sorry about that. I was thinking of Maggie, and she wanted to tell you."

He sighed as though he'd needed my apology.

I gripped my coffee cup. "I don't bullshit. It's one of the things I learned from my father." Not that my old man had actually taught me anything. I'd learned by observing, and he was the type of man to tell it like it was. "I care for Maggie, a lot. I will kill Miguel if he so much as hurts her. That, you can bank on."

He puffed out his chest from taking in a large amount of air and toyed with his mustache. "I refuse to believe one of my men is tainted. What I do believe, though, is you're telling the truth about Maggie. I spoke to her before she left her office. She said she had a date with you, which I wasn't thrilled about. I tried to call her before I hit the sack—several times, actually. I wanted to make sure she got home okay. I'd been more concerned since Nadine was murdered. But I figured she was having a good time and ignoring my messages."

I didn't expect him to jump for joy. He was her protector, and I was glad he was, especially now.

Some of the color returned to his face. "I do respect Hunt. I know he works for Pitt, who knows these streets back and forth. Tell me everything."

I told him how Grace had worked for Miguel. I filled him in on the phone conversation with Miguel, and I told him that Cory Calderon was a Black Knight. When I finished, he didn't say anything.

"When I spoke to Maggie, she sounded off," I said. "I think they drugged her."

Creases lined his forehead. "This Dom guy told you that Cory was involved in the Black Knights?"

I found it odd that he didn't come back with a question about Maggie. After all, he cared for her. "Yeah. But Cory doesn't use his real name. He goes by an alias of Dallas."

Ted reared back. "Fuck. My team and I are familiar with that name, but we've never been able to identify or find anything on a Dallas. Now I know why." He glanced out the window. "Maggie always believed Cory was a Black Knight. She swore by her source." His Adam's apple bobbed. "Up until recently, we didn't know that Miguel was running the show. We only got that info out of one of his men who we arrested at that standoff." He returned his attention back inside, picked up his cup, and took a swig, looking despondent.

"What's wrong?" I'd been waiting for him to run out of there since

I mentioned that Miguel had kidnapped Maggie, unless Hunt had it wrong, and Hughes was the inside informant within the gang unit rather than Rick. Maybe that was the reason Hughes had never confirmed to Maggie that Calderon was a Black Knight. Maybe that was why Hughes had kept Maggie at a distance from the case on the gang and sex trafficking. Hughes would probably handcuff me for asking him my next question or jump over the table and choke me to death. "Are you the one working for Miguel?"

For the first time since I'd met the detective, his features brightened like a street full of Christmas lights. "I take back what I said. I like you, Hart. You got some balls." Then his whole body went rigid. His nostrils flared, and his mustache twitched. "You think I would put Maggie in harm's way? You think I would botch a case I've been working on for over a year?"

My fingers dove into my hair. "I don't know you. I do know you're proud you arrested my brother." Which was odd in my book. I suspected there was more to the story, but this wasn't the time or the place. "I do know Maggie cares for you. So let's not beat around the bush. I have to find my girl, and I need your help. Although if you are working for Miguel—"

"Save the rest of the speech, Hart. I can assure you on my wife's grave I'm not the one working for a thug like Miguel." He spoke with conviction. "Why does Miguel want your sister?"

If I told him, then Grace could be seeing the inside of a prison like Denim. She'd been through enough. Images of Grace's back flashed before me. If her captor wasn't dead, I would kill him. Plus, I had no proof. "My sister was sold to a man she ended up escaping from, and he wants her back. Apparently, if Miguel doesn't return her, then both Grace and Miguel are dead." I tore apart a napkin as I visualized the scarred welts on Grace's soft skin.

"I'm sorry." It was the first time I'd heard sympathy from the man.

"Are you going to help us or not?" I asked.

"Let's get Hunt in on the action. He's good with his gun, and I trust him," Hughes said. "Now I want to see where we're meeting Miguel."

"My sister isn't going to be part of this exchange." I couldn't blame Grace. As desperate as I was to get Maggie back, I couldn't force Grace, nor would I. "Please tell me you have some leads on where you can find Miguel."

He mashed his lips together. "I might, but that would involve my team."

If Dom struck out on locating the warehouse where Miguel was keeping Maggie, then I had a plan C. And that involved either me going to jail for murder, or worse—me dead.

33

DILLON

We had thirty minutes until the sun peeked over the horizon. Thirty minutes until all hell broke loose.

I paced the paint factory, wearing a hole in the floor, while Hunt checked his gun and Hughes talked to his computer analyst about Marco Holdings. Hughes had assured me that the conversation was normal since he was the boss. His guy would only think that Hughes was doing his job.

Duke was on the roof, keeping watch. Dom was pulling his car into the building. Hughes wanted Miguel to think that no one except Grace and me were here, although I didn't think Miguel was that stupid.

Grace sat in the only chair, gnawing on her nails.

I went over to her, rubbing my eyes. All of us had been up all night. Dom had failed to find Miguel's location. Hughes had tried to call Rick to give him a bogus lead on another case his team was working on. He wanted to test Rick. But to Hughes's surprise, Rick didn't answer, which according to Hughes was odd. His team was always ready to go whenever a call came in on gang activity.

I squatted down in front of Grace. "You don't have to do this."

My plan C was to kill Miguel. It wasn't the greatest plan, but it was the only one I could see happening since we hadn't found a location on him. Hughes had shot that idea down, reminding me that a plan like that would put me in a cell next to Denim.

Grace jerked her head, her golden-brown eyes swimming with dread and rage. "It's our only option. I was hoping we would find Miguel before now, but I can't let one more girl suffer or die at his hands, especially one you care about. You've always been my favorite brother. I love you, Dillon. I hope you forgive me for running away and then not contacting you when I could."

I rose and held out my hand. "Let's take a walk."

My nerves subsided for the moment as though she had valium in her palm.

As we walked, I said, "Don't talk like you won't make it out of this. I'll kill Miguel before I'll let him take you."

The sound of Dom's car engine rumbled in the building.

A wide-open aisle stretched from one end of the factory to the other, flanked by machinery on both sides. The machines were disassembled, with rusted parts lying on the ground around them.

When we came to a stop at a cross section that led to offices, my sister blinked, and tears welled in her eyes. "It's a possibility, even though that family wants me alive."

That family would always be a problem for Grace. But my goal was to get Maggie back and make sure Grace walked away with me. Anything else was for another day, although Hughes's mission was to bring in Miguel, Cory, and whoever else was part of his organization and throw them all in a cell for quite some time.

"Hunt and Hughes are very good at what they do," I said. "And you trust Dom?"

She blinked then nodded.

"Then nothing will happen to you." I couldn't ask her to trust me. We hardly knew each other. But I would protect her even if it meant my life for hers. "On another topic, I wanted you to know that I didn't tell Hughes about you taking out the man who bought you." Saying that last part gave me stomach pains and made Grace wince.

"If you want to tell him, that's up to you. But you've been through hell."

"Let's just get through today," she said.

She would get no argument from me.

"Dillon," Hughes called. "Let's go through our plan one more time."

My watch said we had twenty minutes.

Dom strutted up the aisle, his long legs eating up the space until he was draping an arm over Grace. "Hey. Are you doing okay?"

She snuggled into him, smiling as though she needed his touch.

I was beginning to realize Dom adored my sister.

Once all three of us joined Hughes and Hunt, Hughes handed out tiny two-way earbuds that were invisible when worn. "Put these in." He had given a pair to Duke before my brother went up to the roof.

"Duke, do you copy?" Ted asked.

"Loud and clear," Duke said as if he were part of the police force.

Inwardly, I laughed. Duke was fidgety around Hughes. I couldn't blame my brother since he was not exactly an upstanding citizen.

"Still quiet," Duke added. "I don't see anything in the building across the street."

Hughes had suspected that Miguel would have men stationed around the area.

"Recently, my analyst found a money trail that led us to a bank in Brazil for Marco Holdings, but he isn't having any success breaking through the firewall," Hughes said.

Dom had been shocked that his buddy couldn't either.

"I was hoping," Ted added. "If he could, then my team would surround the warehouse until we had Miguel. It's coming down to the wire anyway." He set his eyes on Grace. "Are you still good to go through with this?"

She hadn't left Dom's side. "I'm ready."

I wasn't sure I was. My pulse was pounding as I reached around to my lower back. The gun was still there. I was using one of Dom's guns that had been sitting on the makeshift table.

Hunt crossed one ankle over the other as he leaned against the pump I'd been sitting on earlier. He showed no signs of nerves. It was as though he lived for shit like this.

Hughes pinned each of us with a look. "The only way onto this property is through the gate unless Miguel's men climb fences. So Dom, I need you on the second floor, facing west. And Hunt, you'll be on the east, which is where Miguel and team will come in. I'll be right inside. As soon as Miguel gets out of the car and we have eyes on Maggie, I'll make the call to the precinct. Grace and Dillon, you need to stall Miguel. It will take the cops at least ten minutes to get here."

"No sirens," Hunt said.

I couldn't help but think of how so many things could go wrong in ten minutes. But Ted wanted to make sure we captured Miguel, and he had to follow procedure as much as he could without compromising Maggie's life, or any lives for that matter.

Ted smoothed his fingers over his mustache. "One last thing. No one dies today."

Dom made sure Grace's bulletproof vest was secure. "I killed enough in Iraq. I don't need to be killing anymore."

Hunt straightened. "We need to get in position."

I inhaled the musty air, but it did nothing to calm my out-of-control pulse.

Dom hugged Grace. "You're strong. You've survived worse than this. Remember that." He kissed her on the forehead and took off.

Hunt clapped me on the shoulder. "We got your back. Grace, stay close to Dillon." Then he was gone.

"We've got a black Jeep coming down the road," Duke said.

I grabbed Grace's shaky hand. "Hughes, have you considered what you'll do if Rick shows up to this party?"

Hughes removed his gun from his holster. "Arrest him like all the others." No emotion whatsoever was evident when he delivered those words. Even his features were schooled. "Now get out there."

Do or die.

Grace and I walked out and found our spot behind two of the rusty barrels that we had positioned in the middle of the empty parking lot.

Orange glowed on the horizon as a fine mist of fog hovered over the water behind us.

We had a direct view of the gate and the Jeep turning in. I scanned the area as wide and as far as I could see. No other cars approached. The abandoned building across the street showed no signs of activity that I could see. Duke was the one with the binoculars, though.

Grace's eyes were filled with fear. "This isn't going to go well," she muttered.

I gently touched her arm. "Dom's right. You're strong, and let's not forget Miguel isn't going to kill you. He needs you."

"What if something goes wrong and he takes me? I can't go back to him, Dillon."

"You're not. We're going to take him down today," I said as sure as the sun was rising. But my insides weren't so confident.

The Jeep pulled to a stop about four yards ahead of us and idled.

Grace went ramrod straight. I held my breath. The gun at my back was burning a hole into my skin.

The sun's rays were beginning to brighten.

My heart was punching my ribs as if Kross Maxwell were using me as one of his sparring partners.

The front passenger's door opened as the driver cut the engine.

Grace and I watched and waited, breathing a little heavier than normal. We had our vests on. The drums were shielding parts of our lower bodies, but our heads weren't protected.

The first man to appear was Cory. I only knew what he looked like from a picture in the office of my financial advisor. In the photo, Cory was posing with the elder Calderon on some golf course.

"There's Cory," I whispered.

"Cory is a beast," Grace mumbled. "He should be shot dead like the animal he is."

Maggie would agree.

The next man to exit the Jeep from the driver's seat was none other than Detective Rick Banfield. His balding head shone in the morning light. He lingered at the driver's side door with his hands in front of him, not looking at us.

My heart galloped so hard, I swore I was having a heart attack.

Hughes's voice came through my earpiece. "What the fuck?"

"Easy." I spoke low, more for me than Ted, who seemed to want to burst out of the building and tear off Rick's head. "We don't see Maggie yet."

The Jeep was parked slightly off to my left, and the windows were tinted, so I couldn't see inside.

Cory came around the Jeep and stood next to Rick.

Then the back door on the passenger's side opened. I was beginning to sweat.

A short man came into view, joining his men.

"That's Miguel." Derision coated each of Grace's words.

Miguel said something to Rick before Cory and Miguel ambled over, stopping about three yards from us.

Miguel's posture was as stiff as a board. "Well, Dillon, we're here." He glanced around. "I know you got a couple of guns on us. I wouldn't expect anything less. But we're not here to kill anyone or cause a scene. You hand over Grace." Miguel waved stubby fingers at my sister. "Hi, honey. Did you miss me?"

Grace cringed. "Always the asshole. Aren't you, Miguel?"

"The deal was Maggie for Grace," I said as calmly as I could. "Where is she?"

Miguel snapped his fingers.

Rick opened the back door on the driver's side. When Maggie emerged, I blinked several times to make sure my eyes weren't playing tricks on me.

Her blond hair was a mess as though it had been windblown. Her pants were soaked in blood, and she looked like a rag doll. If it weren't for Rick holding her up, she wouldn't have been upright.

I growled low and deep.

Grace's hand clutched mine. "Miguel needs to die today," she whispered.

I agreed with her. I couldn't tell if Maggie had been shot or stabbed. No matter what had happened to her, the person responsible would pay.

Hughes also growled, then several expletives came out of his mouth before he said, "Dillon, stick with the plan."

A roar of laughter blared in my head. The need to kill jabbed me in the gut and made me tense every muscle in my body.

Maggie was breathing heavily as she locked eyes with me and smiled. My heart soared and plummeted at the same time. The need to kill was stronger than I'd imagined.

Reluctantly, I tore my gaze away from Maggie and pinned it on Miguel, who had a smug grin on his ugly face. "Stay here," I said to Grace.

She wouldn't let go of my hand. "You heard Hughes. Stick to the plan. We need to stall Miguel." Her voice was barely a whisper. "Remember, they want me alive, not you."

Grace was right, but I didn't care. *You better, dude, if you want a life with your girl and your family.* I didn't see any guns on any of them, but that didn't mean they weren't packing.

"Keep him talking," Hughes said. "I called in the cavalry. ETA seven minutes."

Maggie's head bobbed. I wasn't going to last seven minutes, and from the looks of it, Maggie wasn't either.

34

MAGGIE

I couldn't walk to save my life. The pain in my leg was so unbearable that I wanted someone to cut it off immediately. But any pain that had taken hold of my body died when I saw Dillon. He'd come for me. Then I saw Grace, and I wanted to bawl my eyes out. She looked like an angel with a halo around her, or maybe I was seeing things. I saw the resemblance of brother and sister, and I didn't even need to lay eyes on her hummingbird tattoo. Pretty was the first word that surfaced. She had short brown hair and wide brown eyes. She was petite yet somewhat tall, and tats covered both her arms, like Dillon.

My tears were ready to spill. He'd found his sister after four years. Not only that, she was putting her life in jeopardy for me—a woman she didn't even know.

Miguel dug his dirty nails into my arm as he sandwiched me in between him and Cory. "Any funny stuff, and your boyfriend dies right before your eyes."

I was grateful that I was even looking at Dillon. I'd passed out cold in Misty's lap in that cage. Then Cory had shot me up with a high dose of epinephrine before he'd thrown me in the Jeep. The effects were wearing off, though.

If I had the energy to run, I would. But losing a ton of blood then finding out Rick was a traitor had every hair on my body at attention. I wondered if Ted knew. Nah, he couldn't know. If he did, I would know. I couldn't say I saw that one coming because I would've never bet my life that Rick was working for Miguel. Rick had always been kind to me and had always given me information to use for stories until Ted had cut him off.

I tried to laugh, but it hurt. "Like I can run, asshole."

I was lucky I was alive. If the bullet had severed the artery to my heart, then I would be dead, although maybe the higher powers that be had a better plan for me.

I bit my lip as I fixated on Dillon as if he was the drug I needed to take away the unbearable pain in my leg.

His scowl was rather scary. I wanted to yell at him for standing out in the open with Grace at his side and a gun pointed at his head, albeit both were semi-protected behind two steel drums.

Miguel had two gunmen in the building across the street behind us with orders to fire when Rick raised his hand. I'd overheard a ton when I'd been bound and gagged in the back seat. The plan was to kill Dillon and me then snag Grace. In their minds, it was a simple and easy plan, at least according to Rick. He'd bragged about how Dillon had followed Miguel's orders not to contact Ted. Apparently, Rick had gotten a voicemail from Ted detailing a lead on another case that the gang unit had been working on, which had nothing to do with the Black Knights.

Miguel let go of me. "Hold her up." He pushed me into Cory, who inflicted more pain in a bruising grip.

Rick swiveled his head with mechanical precision as he inched closer to the paint factory. "Something's not right."

The bad part of coming to a fight with a cop was his gut telling him that it was too quiet.

Miguel opened his arms. "Grace, it's time to come home." His tone was sickly sweet.

Dillon jutted out his chin as a morning breeze whisked through his hair, which I noticed was tied back in a ponytail. "Nice to see that I was right about you, Rick."

Rick was about to open the door to the building when Dillon asked, "What made you become a traitor, Rick?" Dillon sounded as if he were the cop and not Rick.

Rick spun on his heel. "None of your fucking business."

"Money." My voice was barely audible. I was guessing that was the reason since Rick had refused to talk to me.

Cory whipped out his gun faster than I could blink then pressed the barrel into the cheek he'd scored with his knife in our tussle. "Talk again, and I'll shoot you." His lisp was worse now than when I'd first chomped on his tongue.

Dillon held steady, even though rage was pouring off him.

I didn't move. I was reserving my energy to run if I had to.

"Easy," Miguel said. He was as calm as the water in the distance. "I need Grace."

"Fuck you," Grace said in a tone that was reserved for scum.

Miguel made a growling noise. "Querida, that's no way to talk to the man who supported you and gave you nice things."

Grace narrowed her eyes. "I'm not your sweetheart."

As the sharpness of the pain lessened a tiny bit, I straightened a little.

I liked her spunk, and it seemed as though we had something in common. We both hated to be called sweetheart.

Grace moved around the drums and began heading toward us. "Let my brother and his girl go."

"Don't, Grace." I couldn't live with myself if she traded her life for mine.

Before I knew what was happening, Miguel pushed his fingers into my leg wound.

I opened my mouth as I bent over, but nothing came out.

"Stand up, bitch," Cory ordered as he jammed the gun into my neck.

Dillon threw himself in front of his sister. "Our deal is off." He sounded as sure as I'd been shot.

Rick drew his gun on Dillon and Grace. "What are you both up to?"

Dillon lifted his hands. "Miguel, the new deal goes like this. Take me in exchange for Grace. That family she was sold to can have my head." He wouldn't look at me.

My breathing was labored, and I was a second from passing out. "Are you mad?"

Rick laughed.

"Shut up," I tried to scream at him, but I failed, sounding like a hurt animal. "Ted is so going to make sure you rot in prison."

Rick took one step, his gun not wavering from Dillon. "Ted is an idiot. He'll never figure out I've been working with the Black Knights."

Dillon grinned. It was one of those grins that said, "joke's on you."

The door to the building creaked open, sounding like something out of a horror movie.

Rick whipped around with his gun ready to fire. Instead, he faltered.

I would have shouted for joy if it weren't for my lack of energy or the hot tears pouring out.

Ted had his gun pointed at Rick. "You're the idiot."

"I knew the cops had to be here," Rick said, not backing down. "I could almost feel you. So I'm not the idiot. I drew you out, didn't I?" He tipped his head at Dillon. "I know a stall tactic, and he was stalling. Where's the team?"

Dillon was shielding Grace.

Miguel pulled out a gun and aimed it at Dillon. "I suggest you move because I'm not leaving here without Grace."

I could act as a bowling pin, but I could only knock one of my captors off-kilter. With a gun aimed at Dillon, my decision was easy. The only problem with my plan was the two men Miguel had in the building across the street.

"If you're going to shoot me," Ted said to Rick, "then you better do it now."

Cory jammed the gun farther into me. "Move, and you're dead."

"Rick, give the fucking order now," Miguel said.

I didn't have time to think, only react. I pushed into Miguel then threw myself toward Dillon, or I tried to. I stumbled, the pavement rising up fast, when a gunshot rang out in the morning air. Suddenly, a stinging and stabbing pain erupted in me once again. Only this time, it was in my chest. The sky began to darken. I hated the dark more than anything.

I tried to scramble to my feet, when Dillon said, "Don't, Grace."

Grunts and groans ensued from others around me.

Cars screeched to a halt somewhere close.

I managed to get up on my knees before Dillon's hands were on my arms. He guided me to the drums then lowered me to a sitting position.

He smelled like heaven and freedom and life.

"You're not dying today." The huskiness in his tone warmed every part of me. Or maybe the warmth was a sign of death. I discarded that last thought. Death was shivers and coldness like I'd experienced in the cage. "I'll be right back."

He rushed to Grace and cupped her shaking arm. "Grace, put the gun down."

She had the weapon aimed at Miguel, as did several men on Ted's team, which had surrounded the area. Rick was in handcuffs, hanging his head.

Ted smiled at me with relief evident in his eyes.

"Miguel has to die," Grace cried.

There was so much pain in her voice, and it splintered me in two. Still, I wanted to ask her if she could shoot Cory too. That cocksure grin he'd worn was gone as a cop handcuffed him. In its place was defeat. His rich daddy wasn't going to get him out of this one.

Dillon's fingers went around Grace's wrist. "He'll get what's coming to him in prison."

If I was reading in between lines, then he meant Denim would make sure of it.

Dom eased out of the building. "Grace, please don't do this."

As though she'd needed to hear his voice, she collapsed in Dillon's arms. Dillon grabbed the gun and handed it to Ted, who was close by, as were others from the gang unit, waiting to arrest Miguel.

I swayed, ready to puke as I pressed my hand to my shoulder to stop the blood from leaking out.

Dom wrapped Grace in his arms.

Then Dillon dropped to his knees at my side. He ripped off his shirt and covered my shoulder wound with it. "Hold this to the wound. The ambulance is almost here."

A siren blared, getting louder by the second.

Ted rushed over to me, his hand smoothing over my head. "I've been so worried about you."

My eyes drooped, and the feeling that I was about to pass out was strong. "Miguel has girls locked in cages in a warehouse." My entire left side burned. "Not sure where. They had me blindfolded until we got here." Miguel had taken off my blindfold before he'd gotten out of the Jeep. "There's also two gunmen in that building across the street."

"We know," Ted said. "I got men over there now. I'll get the location out of one of these assholes about the girls. Dillon, can you go with her to the hospital? I need to clean up things here."

The ambulance pulled up.

Dillon furrowed his brow at Ted. "I'm not leaving her side."

After I was laid out on a stretcher in the back of the ambulance with Dillon on one side of me and the medic on the other, Dillon said, "I was so fucking worried. I couldn't go through losing someone again, especially you, Maggie."

The medic, who looked to be in his thirties, kept checking my vital signs. "Her pulse is dropping."

"ETA is two minutes," the driver said.

My eyelids were extremely heavy. "I'm sorry about our date."

Dillon opened his mouth, but I heard nothing as I passed out.

35

DILLON

I sat in a chair next to Maggie's hospital bed. She was bandaged from head to toe. Her face was cut due to Cory. She'd been shot by Miguel, the fucker. And she'd taken a bullet to save my life. My heart was bursting with so many emotions, including a tinge of anger for putting herself in the line of fire.

The worse part of Maggie's injuries was the bullet in her leg. We'd learned from Misty that Miguel had shot Maggie. The doctor who operated on her had said she was lucky to be alive. The bullet missed her artery by a fraction. Not to mention, she'd lost a lot of blood. Thank God for blood banks because she'd had to have a transfusion.

I adjusted my position in my seat. My ass was becoming numb. Maggie had been out for five days, and during that time, I'd been in hell. I hadn't slept. I'd only showered once, and that was a rush job so I could get back to her. I wanted to be there when she woke up. I'd hardly eaten. Hughes had been in and out with food for me and to check on Maggie.

He'd been as much of a basket case as I was. But he couldn't hang around since he had work to do, like making sure Miguel, Cory, and his man, Rick, didn't make bail.

Ted strutted in, looking as deathly as I probably did. "Damn. She's not awake yet."

The fact that her heart was beating was the only thing keeping me from losing my shit.

Ted settled on the other side of Maggie's bed. "You should go home and get some sleep. I'll take this watch."

I shook my head. "Not happening."

He chuckled. "I take back what I said about you. You're not bad, Hart."

I didn't need his approval when it came to Maggie, but it sure helped, considering Ted and Maggie were close. "I never thanked you for giving Maggie that lead on the tattoo shop. If it weren't for that, I'm not sure I would've uncovered all that I did on Grace or that I would have found her." And I wouldn't have been able to force Duke's hand.

Duke and I had parted ways with a hug and handshake. He was dealing with something heavy, but I knew not to pry. Duke was the type to process information in his own way, and if he needed to talk, then he would. For now, I was happy he and I weren't at each other's throat, and I was thankful and grateful he had helped me out with finding Maggie. It had been the first time since our gang days that I'd spent any time with my brother.

"I was surprised the lead amounted to anything. How's Grace, by the way?"

"She's got a lot to deal with considering the four years of torture she went through. But she's okay. She's staying at the shelter with the girls you rescued from Miguel and the other guests I have."

Considering the family who wanted her returned to them for killing their son was still a threat, I was surprised Grace didn't want to go into hiding. She'd said that she couldn't keep running, and she had Dom, my brother Duke, and me to protect her. As far as the man she'd killed, she hadn't said a word about him to Ted. She might when she was ready.

Maggie stirred. Her eyes flickered open, and she blinked. Then her eyes closed again.

I jumped up from the chair.

Hughes leaned over her bed and grabbed her hand. "Mags?"

She licked her lips then winced.

I commandeered her other hand. "Hey, beautiful."

Her eyes flickered around, landing on Hughes then me. When she smiled, my heart soared high up into the sky.

Then she turned to Hughes. "Did you get the girls?"

"Shh," Hughes said. "All taken care of."

As if the heavens opened up, tears filled her stunning green eyes that were so darn mesmerizing.

Ted's phone rang. He plucked it from his belt and answered. After a pause, he said, "I'll be right there." He lowered the phone. "Good to see that you're back with us. I have to go, but I'll come see you later." He kissed her on the forehead, then his long legs carried him out of the room.

Maggie rubbed her chapped lips together.

I grabbed the cup of water I'd been drinking and brought it up to her mouth. She sipped a little, then a little more until the water was gone.

As I deposited the cup on the bedside table, she said, "Grace. Is she okay?"

I sat on the edge of the bed. "She's fine. She's at the shelter. You scared me. What were you thinking, taking a bullet for me?"

She batted her eyelashes, and a tear fell. "I had to. I couldn't lose you."

"You weren't going to lose me, baby doll. Ted, Hunt, Dom, Duke, Grace, and I had everything under control. Well, Ted's men were too late in getting to Miguel's men before one of them fired his gun."

"How long have I been in here?" she asked.

"Five days."

She frowned. "Where are Misty and the girls?"

"They're at the shelter, and Miguel and company are in a jail cell, even Rick. He was the one to give Ted the location of the girls and everything about Miguel's organization in exchange for a reduced sentence."

Color started to return to her cheeks as she lowered her gaze to her lap.

I leaned in to do something I'd been dying to do.

When my lips were a millimeter away from hers, she planted a hand on my face. "My breath stinks."

I wasn't going to lie. She was in dire need of a toothbrush and toothpaste, but I didn't care. "They say when you love someone, nothing matters or gets in the way, even bad breath."

Her mouth fell open. "You love me?"

I'd had five days of nothing but my own thoughts. I had watched her sleep. I had listened to the medical machine beep every now and then. I'd rubbed her arms, her hands, and even sat on the bed and rested my head on her stomach. Kelton had said to give in to the feeling. Because love was one hell of a ride, and one I didn't want to miss. I was on the ride of a lifetime. No woman had affected my heart, head, and stomach like Maggie did.

"You came out of nowhere, Maggie, and when you did, you scared the hell out of me. And I'm not only talking about when you were kidnapped or shot. When you showed up at the shelter that night with Nadine, I couldn't believe my eyes. I did have a thing for you as a teenager." I took a breath.

She sniffled. "No one in my life has ever told me they loved me. No one."

I kissed the back of her hand. "I've always been afraid any girl I got serious with would walk out on me like my mom did with my old man. I put my life on hold to find Grace, and it wasn't until you told me to cherish what I have that I woke up. I knew in that elevator that you were the one I wanted to cherish. You are the girl I want to be with. So if you call love"—I twirled a finger around my stomach —"this tightening feeling, and how I think about you constantly, and how I want to kiss you until someone calls the paramedics to give us oxygen, then yes, I love you."

She giggled and sniffled. "Why didn't you kiss me when we had sex?"

"Because I knew one taste of your mouth, and I would've professed my undying love for you. I wasn't sure I was ready to do that. Plus you were all about putting up a barrier between us."

"Well, I don't want to anymore," she said. "I always thought love was overrated, and honestly, I've never felt so connected to another man like I am with you. I want us, Dillon Hart. I want you."

I kissed her before she could object about her bad breath. When our tongues collided, she moaned. The kiss was wet, sloppy, and all over the place. She held my head in her hands, and I kissed her with everything I had. She spewed little noises every time I nibbled on her tongue and her lips, making my dick grow hard.

She slowed the kiss. "I don't want you to use a ping-pong paddle on me. I don't want rough sex. I want slow and sensual. I want you to be gentle. I want you to kiss me nonstop. I love you, Dillon Hart. I would take a bullet for you anytime."

While I admired her to no end for wanting to protect me, we wouldn't be in harm's way again. From here on out, our lives would be normal. She had her job, and I had the shelter, and we weren't chasing any more bad guys.

As far as my family, they had to work out their own problems. When they did, including my old man, maybe we could be somewhat of a cohesive family. Until then, Maggie was my family and future. She was the one I would give all my time to, aside from the shelter.

36

MAGGIE

Dillon threaded his fingers through mine as we stood on the grounds of Kensington High School.

The crisp November air gave me a chill. More than two months had passed since I'd gotten out of the hospital. My shoulder and leg were on the mend, although I had a slight limp in my gait, but I barely had a scar on my face. Cory hadn't broken through several layers like he had when I was fourteen.

As for Cory, he'd been sentenced to twenty years in prison, and that made me sleep better at night. Miguel and Rick had received similar sentences, except Rick had cut a deal for early parole.

Dillon's shelter was thriving, and the girls that had been prisoners of Miguel's were now back with their families, except Misty. She'd worked out an agreement with Dillon. She would live at the shelter while she went back to nursing school, and in exchange, she would help Norma with odds and ends and maybe even provide counseling.

The trees swayed as the colorful leaves floated to the ground.

"I can't believe your mom lives in Ashford and teaches at the local high school," Dillon said.

"It's a small world for sure."

The Maxwell family, whom I'd learned a great deal about during my recovery, lived in Ashford. The Maxwell brothers had attended this very high school where my mom worked.

"Are you ready?" Dillon asked. "Do you want me to go in with you?"

I was more than ready. I was healed. I was alive, and I was ready to hear why she'd abandoned me. I would've reached out to her sooner, but between the painkillers and the therapy, it hadn't been a good time.

The school had let out for the day, so only a handful of kids lingered on the grounds.

A car rolled up, and Kross poked out his head. "Hey."

Dillon was going with Kross to check out a building that Kross was thinking of purchasing for his boxing school.

I lifted up on my toes and kissed Dillon on the lips. "Go. I need to do this alone."

His hands cupped my face. "I'm only a phone call away." Then his tongue was in my mouth, dancing and swirling. If he didn't stop, we might have to find a closet in the school.

He and I had been in bed more than anything, when I wasn't writing. I was on medical leave from the paper and had loads of time to think and write. So I was penning my story, not Dillon's or his family's. His story wasn't mine to tell anyway.

After my experience of being shot, caged like an animal, and almost dying, I had a whole new view on life. Every time I recalled the kidnapping, shooting, and how I'd fought for my life, I couldn't believe I was actually kissing Dillon.

The Latin phrase he had inked on his chest, *alis grave, nil,* meant *nothing is heavy to those who have wings.* I'd had wings that day. I also had angels in Misty, Dillon, Ted, Grace, and everyone who had helped save me and take down Miguel, Cory, and Rick.

Dillon broke the kiss. "I'll be back in about an hour." He skirted around Kross's car and got in the passenger's side.

As the car sped away, I walked down the path toward the front door. When I'd called to set up a meeting, I had learned my mom was a guidance counselor at the local high school. I'd wanted to talk somewhere less personal than her house, for the first meeting anyway.

A lady rose from the cement bench that was outside the main doors. Her blond hair fell to her shoulders, and her smile said she was the person I was looking for. "Maggie?"

My pulse sang in my ears, and suddenly I wanted Dillon at my side to hold my hand.

You're an adult. You don't need anyone holding your hand.

Up until Dillon, I hadn't thought so. But I liked having him as a lover and an equal partner. He wasn't overprotective. He wasn't possessive. He was Dillon—he had a big heart, a lot of love to give, and was the one man who only saw me when I entered a room.

My chest rose. "Sophie. Right?"

She eased down onto the bench then patted the spot next to her. "We can chat out here. It's a beautiful fall day."

It didn't matter to me. I didn't plan to be there long anyway. Dillon and I were due to have dinner at Kross's parents' house.

As I sat down, two girls emerged from the school. "Hi, Mrs. Flowers," one of them said as they continued walking.

I examined my mother from top to bottom. She was a head shorter than me. Aside from her blond hair, she had a lighter shade of green eyes than me. Her nose was small like mine, and she was a pretty lady. "Flowers? Is that your married name?"

She fidgeted with her fingers and nodded.

"Why did you abandon me?" I might as well get to the heart of why I was there. "Who and where is my father? Did you marry him?"

She gave me a tentative smile. "I was fifteen when I found out I was pregnant, and I was scared to death. I had no father. My mother was a drug addict, and I couldn't end up like her. She had me at sixteen. She did the best she could, but somewhere along the way, she cracked. She lost her job and fell into a deep depression and started using drugs." She paused and swept her gaze over me.

I felt compelled to say, "I'm listening." I got the impression she thought I would run.

"I kind of followed in her footsteps. I got in with the wrong crowd and the wrong boy. Before I knew it, I was pregnant. I didn't know what to do. The boy I slept with wanted no part of me. I debated whether to have an abortion, but I couldn't bring myself to do that. Then after you were born, life became difficult. I didn't have money for food or clothes or diapers. Every day was a struggle. You deserved better."

The main door opened, and three more students came out, chatting and giggling. Both Sophie and I watched them until they faded from view.

She sighed. "Every state has a safe-haven law, and so I decided that you would have a better life with a family who could take care of you."

I chewed on my bottom lip. She definitely held an enormous amount of regret, which was evident in her tone. But to forgive or not to forgive. The question flittering through my mind was whether to tell her my life story and make her feel even worse.

Her gaze was on my neck. I was wearing a scoop-neck blouse and no scarf. I'd come to the conclusion that I shouldn't be ashamed of what had happened to me because it wasn't my fault. Dillon helped me to come to terms with my scar. It also helped that he thought I was beautiful despite all my scars, and I had a couple more thanks to Miguel and Cory.

I took hold of her hand. "Sophie, I'm not going to sit here and tell you how angry I was with you for abandoning me. That wouldn't change what happened. Honestly, I don't know what I would've done in your shoes." I thought back to how Cory had raped me. I could've gotten pregnant. Then I might've been in the same predicament she had been in with me. "But I'm here, and that means I want to get to know you."

She threw her arms around me and hugged me so darn tight, I couldn't breathe. Then she sobbed. "Thank you."

I couldn't help but cry either, and all those pent-up emotions I'd harbored for so long vanished. I hugged her back.

We stayed in that embrace for several long seconds until she shuddered and let go. "You turned out to be such a strong and beautiful woman."

"Just like you," I said as I dashed away the tears on my cheeks.

"Let's take a walk. I have something for you in my car."

Once we were at her modest SUV, she ducked into the back seat and emerged with a framed photo. "Before I gave you up, I took a picture of you. I never forgot about you." She handed me the picture.

I eyed the photo of the chubby baby with light-blond hair, wrapped in a pink blanket. "Thank you," was all I could say as I choked back more tears. I'd never taken pictures of myself or with friends or even with Ted. But I would make it my mission to make sure Dillon and I had lots of photos of us sprinkled around his house.

He'd asked me to move in with him two weeks ago. Actually, he'd been taking care of me since I'd gotten out of the hospital.

"When you got your life together, why didn't you try and find me?" I asked.

She gripped the edge of the car door. "I did. I started at the firehouse where I left you, but no one there knew of the incident. One fireman steered me to a retired man who had been working there, but when I contacted him, his wife informed me he'd died. I didn't even have a name for you. So it was difficult to find you, especially when social services won't divulge cases."

She had a point, and she wasn't a detective like Ted, who could find details civilians couldn't.

"Do you have a family now?" I wasn't sure how that would sit with me, but as I asked the question, I was cool, especially after hearing her reasons for leaving me at a firehouse.

She closed her car door. "After you, I couldn't have any more children. I have a husband, though. I saw you with your boyfriend when he dropped you off. Are you happy?"

I smiled and got all giddy inside. "He's a great guy, and he loves me, and I couldn't be happier."

As if Dillon knew we were talking about him, he and Kross drove up and stopped behind Sophie's SUV.

Dillon climbed out. His hair was tousled as usual. I'd told him not to ever cut his hair. He rounded the car then waved to Kross as he sped away. Dillon tucked his hands into the pockets of his jeans, keeping his distance and giving me privacy.

"Dillon," I called.

He sauntered over and gave me a chaste kiss on the lips. "The real estate gal had to cancel on Kross."

Sophie extended her hand. "Sophie Flowers."

"Dillon Hart. Nice to meet you, ma'am. Baby doll, we should get going."

"We're having dinner with the Maxwells," I said to Sophie.

Dillon had mentioned that the Maxwells were well-known in Ashford.

"Great family. Maybe we could meet for dinner next week. I can come to Boston."

I hugged her. "I would like that."

We said our goodbyes, and when Dillon and I were on the road, I started crying.

He held my hand. "What's wrong?"

"They're happy tears. I never thought my life would turn out with a man I love to pieces, and me getting to know my mom."

One side of his mouth curled before he kissed the back of my hand. "You are my queen, Maggie. I love you."

I giggled. After he'd brought me home from the hospital, he had made me feel like a queen, and I'd told him so. Since then, not only did he refer to me as his queen, but he treated me like one too. The way he made love to me for hours, the way he played with my hair as we cuddled on the couch, watching some movie, and the way he looked at me and only me were more than I could ask for. And for that, our future was brighter than I'd ever thought possible.

DEAR READER

I hope you enjoyed Dillon's book as much as I enjoyed writing his story. When you have a moment, I would super appreciate a quick review. It doesn't have to be long, but would love for you to share your excitement about Hart of Darkness. You can leave a review on Amazon, Goodreads or Bookbub. Links to these platforms can be found on the next page.

In addition, there's more to come in the Hart Family. Denim and Duke will have their own books. Come join us in Maxwell Mania and stay up-to-date on all book news: Facebook: https://www.facebook.com/groups/maxwellmania/

DON'T MISS OUT

Stay up-to-date on sales and new releases. I post frequent updates in
my reader group on Facebook. You can join here: Maxwell Mania:
https://www.facebook.com/groups/maxwellmania/
Follow me on any of the platforms below or signup for my newsletter
at http://sbalexander.com/newsletter or visit my website at
http://sbalexander.com

facebook.com/sbalexander.authorpage

twitter.com/sbalex_author

instagram.com/sbalexanderauthor

amazon.com/author/sbalexander

bookbub.com/authors/s-b-alexander

goodreads.com/sbalexander

TITLES BY S.B. ALEXANDER

To find out where to purchase all books visit: http://sbalexander.com.

The Maxwell Family Saga:

My Heart to Touch - Book 1

My Heart to Hold – Book 2

My Heart to Give – Book 3

My Heart to Keep - Book 4 (releasing late 2019)

The Maxwell Series:

Dare to Kiss - Book 1

Dare to Dream – Book 2

Dare to Love – Book 3

Dare to Dance - Book 4

Dare to Live - Book 5

Dare to Breathe - Book 6

The Maxwell Series Boxed Set – Books 1-3

The Maxwell Series Boxed Set - Books 4-6

Dare to Kiss Coloring Book Companion

The Vampire SEAL Series:

On the Edge of Humanity – Book 1

On the Edge of Eternity – Book 2

On the Edge of Destiny – Book 3

On the Edge of Misery - Book 4

On the Edge of Infinity - Book 5

The Vampire SEAL Collection - Boxed Set

Stand Alone Books

Breaking Rules

Rescuing Riley

The Hart Series:

Hart of Darkness

Hart of Vengeance - Coming Soon

Hart of Redemption - Coming Soon

ACKNOWLEDGMENTS

Writing and publishing a book takes a village. But I couldn't be more thankful to the one person who gives me the inspiration to do what I love—my husband. He's been such a guiding light as he battles one of the worse diseases with no cure. He fills my heart with so much joy. He always has a smile on his face, he's always laughing, and he's always making sure I'm taken care of. He's my angel. I couldn't do this without him.

I'm also grateful to the team behind me who helps me every step of the way from my editor, RedAdept Editing, my beta readers, my ARC team, my cover designer, Hang Le, my assistant, Alexandra Amor, JKS Communications, and everyone in Maxwell Mania. Thank you, thank you, thank you!

A huge thank you to Christopher John at CJC Photography and his mad photography skills, and to the handsome Brock Grady for making the cover come to life.

A special shoutout to Megan Linski for her help in working out plot ideas with me.

A big hug and mad love for Heather Carver for keeping me focused and motivating me everyday to write, and to Kylie Sharp for always being a phone call away. Love you gals.

Finally, to all the readers and bloggers around the world, thank you for taking a chance on me.